THE DARK ANGEL

Dominique Sylvain

Translated from the French by Nick Caistor

MACLEHOSE PRESS
QUERCUS · LONDON

First published in the French language as *Passage du Désir*
by Éditions Viviane Hamy, Paris, in 2004

First published in Great Britain in 2013 by MacLehose Press

MacLehose Press
an imprint of Quercus
55 Baker Street
7th Floor, South Block
London W1U 8EW

A CIP catalogue reference for this book
is available from the British Library

ISBN (HB) 978 0 85705 213 1
ISBN (TPB) 978 0 85705 214 8
ISBN (Ebook) 978 1 78087 603 0

2 4 6 8 10 9 7 5 3 1

Designed and typeset in 11/16pt Columbus by Patty Rennie
Printed and bound in Great Britain by Clays Ltd, St Ives plc

TO FRANK

WHEN YOU'RE A KID, TO BE SOMEONE, YOU
HAVE TO BE SEVERAL PEOPLE

Émile Ajar

1 NOVEMBER 2002

PARIS IS A BLONDE . . . THAT EVERYONE ADORES . . . well I
don't . . . so shut the fuck up . . . what is this anyway? . . . WITH
HER LITTLE SNUB NOSE . . . AND MOCKING EYES . . . You're
getting on my nerves with your eyes and your hair . . .

THAT PROMISE PARADISE!

Jean-Luc gave himself a few moments to gather his wits, scattered
all over the duvet. That singer's voice is coming from my radio-alarm.
It's four in the morning.

And Jean-Luc remembered it was Sunday. The day he had to smash,
teeth clenched, buttocks ditto, straight into the wall. He switched
the radio-alarm off. Noah and Farid must have come in and played a
trick on him. They'd chosen a station that played nostalgic tunes, and
turned the volume up to the max. If they were trying to help him
conquer his fear, they'd failed. Jean-Luc's stomach was churning.

He got up, went to the bathroom, splashed cold water on his face.
In the mirror he eyeballed a young guy with shaven head and brown
goatee who looked even more unkempt than the night before. He took
an antacid tablet, dressed, and went down to the kitchen.

Noah and Farid were there. Sitting with coffee. Straight-faced. But
he could see they were laughing inside. Noah and Farid, dressed in
black, black-haired, Farid with black eyes, Noah blue, but apart from

that a pair of Siamese twins from the Mediterranean. They were nibbling on *biscottes*.

"YES, THAT'S PARIS!" Farid sang.

"Yeth, thath Paris," Noah said, his mouth full of crumbs. "Sleep well, Jean-Luc?"

Farid had chosen the blueberry jam, his favourite. Emergency rations before he tightened his belt the whole day for Ramadan.

"You're always saying me and Noah only ever listen to gangsta rap, so we thought we'd make you happy," he said, the three silver rings on his hands flashing as he waved them around.

Farid never took the rings off. During the raids, they were hidden under his gloves. They meant a lot to him. But what exactly?

"Yo, man! What we like most of all is making people happy," Noah said.

"But Mistinguett remixed is an idea to keep on the back burner," Farid added, with another gracious sweep of his hands.

Farid was proud of his hands, but he could be equally proud of his looks. The good looks of a twenty-year-old who has no worries because tomorrow doesn't exist. Beside these two, Jean-Luc felt old. Old, at twenty-six. He forced a smile.

The Siamese twins finished eating; Jean-Luc could only manage a coffee. Then the three of them went down to the garage to pick up the Kalashnikovs, the sledgehammers and the bags. They climbed into the Mercedes 4×4. The automatic doors lifted, to reveal a B.M.W. parked across the way. Menahem started the engine at once. Young Menahem was one of the best: he always supplied in time and on time. He was the one who had stolen the 4×4 and the B.M.W. in Asnières. He was Noah's kid brother, and Noah looked out for him. No way was he to get involved in a raid: they all understood that all he would ever do was supply the cars and be their driver.

While they were speeding through Saint-Denis, Noah switched on the radio. The news soon turned to Palestine. People killed in a suicide bombing. Sharon says this, Arafat says that, and meanwhile Ramallah in ruins. Farid changed stations. Whenever the talk grew serious, he always changed the radio station, the T.V. channel, the subject, or left the room. And he never read a newspaper. The same went for music. Farid didn't like French hip hop because it forced him to listen to the words, to open his mind to others. And all Noah had learned from the American rappers was the "Yo, man!" he was always coming out with.

Jean-Luc took another antacid tablet. He had to talk to forget the way his guts were heaving; and besides, whatever was going on between Farid Younis's ears interested him. He couldn't just be some guy who blew all his dough on gear and C.D.s. Farid was as shut tight as an oyster. But a pearl oyster. Jean-Luc thought for a while, then asked, "D'you have a problem with reality, Farid?"

"None. My reality is money."

"Yo! Me too," Noah said.

"You see, Jean-Luc, my best mate is a dirty Jew, and his reality is money as well."

"You're my favourite towel-head of all time," Noah said, ruffling Farid's hair.

"I don't get it. You never talk about things."

"There's enough people talking shit already," Farid said.

"Too right, man," Noah said.

"If I were in your shoes, it'd do my head in. Brothers killing each other. It could be you two. On opposing sides. Hasn't that ever occurred to you?"

Dense silence from the Siamese. The tranquil silence of unshakeable bravado. The 4×4 was entering Paris. Noah headed towards Boulevard Ney, the B.M.W. and Menahem still in his slipstream.

"It's a nightmare, spiralling out of control," Jean-Luc went on. "Those people hell-bent on tearing each other to pieces over a miserable bit of land that was promised so long ago no-one can even remember who to. And no-one can see an end to it."

"Yo, man!" Noah said. "A nightmare . . . spiralling out of control? What the fuck you talking about?"

"About piles of dead bodies. About things getting worse and worse. That's what I'm talking about, Noah."

"It's true that it concerns us," Farid said, "and I'll tell you why, Jean-Luc."

"Go ahead, I'm listening."

"Because it's bad for business. They screw up the whole planet. That's why terrorists terrorise and people everywhere are shit-scared. So here and elsewhere, they vote for the Right. And suddenly the Feds are all over the place, especially in Paris, and it gets harder for us to do our job. You see, the dirty Jew and me do think of these things. We know it's all connected, don't we, Noah?"

"Course we do, man," Noah replied, stifling a giggle.

"Respect, Farid. Comparing terrorists who terrorise with us and our hold-ups is one way of looking at things."

"You wanted to know if I had a problem with reality. Now you know. I look reality in the eye."

Jean-Luc silently gave up on the twins' lack of awareness. A lack he now realised he envied. Perhaps if he'd been Jewish or Arab or both, the Siamese would've really been his brothers; that level of complicity must help them feel less fear when it came to crashing into the wall. All he knew was that he was in fact circumcised. Before abandoning him, his mother had made sure his foreskin was snipped. God only knew why.

Adopted by a family in Normandy, Jean-Luc had grown up in a

small town where the kids went to catechism without a murmur. One day he had explained to the Mediterranean Siamese twins that he was a bit like them, without going into it too closely. The missing foreskin had no more interested them than the ruins of Ramallah.

He still had his terrible stomach ache.

A deserted Paris rushed past their car window. Even the Eastern European whores had gone home to bed. Autumn felt increasingly like winter. Jean-Luc's desire to be sailing freely across the Mediterranean grew stronger with every day. A few more jobs and he'd be able to buy the sixty-footer of his dreams. A bargain at 1,200,000 euros. The deal would be done through a broker in Palma de Mallorca. Easy: you say you prefer to pay cash, and the money goes through a bank in the Virgin Islands, a tax haven where boats change hands as easily as the wind changes direction.

Out at sea he would listen occasionally to French songs to remind himself of Paris and perhaps of Normandy a little as well. After all, it was thanks to his Norman childhood that he had become a sailor. Jean-Luc wondered why Farid never talked about Algeria, where his parents were from. In Paris, the Younis family lived in the Stalingrad neighbourhood, but Farid never visited them because he wasn't on speaking terms with his old man. Neither was his sister, and she and Farid didn't speak either. A real hornets' nest.

They were getting close. Noah drove past Saint-Philippe-du-Roule church. Jean-Luc read the banner on its façade. *Come unto him, Jesus is here to listen.* Something seductive like *Jesus gives himself to you* would have been better, he thought. That was what people needed right now; their funkometer was off the scale. Jean-Luc had heard a study about people's fears on the radio. The French needed no encouragement to be scared shitless. Terrorism, unemployment, the threat of war, oil spills, apocalyptic viruses, Frankenstein maize, human cloning sects. Everything scared the life out of them. Really, it was only at sea you could find peace. Provided you avoided the pirates. As long as all this keeps going through my head I don't feel so scared, Jean-Luc told himself. They were almost there, a matter of seconds . . .

The Champs-Elysées were less empty than the boulevards. Here, a group of party-goers was leaving a night-club. Elsewhere, a few outcasts were pounding the pavements in the chilly dawn. The few cars visible sped along the wide avenue towards the Place de la Concorde and beyond. A fluid Paris . . .

They were there.

Farid put on his gloves. His hands weren't shaking. On the ground floor of a modern block, a brightly lit shopfront with an electronic door, two employees behind the tills. And, damn it, two customers. A boy and a girl with backpacks.

"What are those asshole tourists doing at a bureau de change at five in the morning?" Jean-Luc growled, putting on his ski mask.

"They're after a bit of cash the same as us," Farid said.

Noah slowed down. They all put their seat-belts on. Farid passed Noah his mask before slipping on his own. Noah swerved the 4×4 onto the kerb, and accelerated.

"PARIS IS A BLONDE!" he shouted.

"THAT EVERYONE ADORES," Farid added, chortling.

It's unbelievable, they're like little kids having a laugh, thought Jean-Luc. The 4×4 smashed into the bureau de change window. The sound of an iceberg cracking. Huge splinters in the glass. Relieved, Jean-Luc said to himself: it's giving way, we'll do it. Noah hit reverse. Accelerated again. A gaping hole in the glass window – it was collapsing. And no sirens, no police. A miracle that never ceased to amaze him.

The three men leapt out of the vehicle. Kalashnikovs slung over their shoulders, Farid and Jean-Luc used their sledgehammers to widen the hole while Noah covered them from the roof of the 4×4. They could hear the girl screaming.

Jean-Luc pointed his gun at the cashiers, Farid covered the customers. The girl was sobbing, she looked ridiculously clean for a backpacker. Farid slapped her. She fell to her knees, blood pouring from her nose. Farid stuck the gun-barrel to her temple. Paralysed by fear, her partner looked as if he was about to faint. The cashiers didn't move, except to put their hands in the air. They seemed accustomed to it. Jean-Luc pulled the bags from his jacket, threw them over the counter. Farid told the younger cashier, "Hand over everything in your safe. Be quick about it."

He did as Farid demanded. Jean-Luc pointed his gun first at the tourists, then at the other cashier, who still had not moved. The money flowed on and on. It's the biggest heist of my life, Jean-Luc thought. The girl started to moan, "Please, don't shoot, please . . ."

"Shut up!" Farid barked.

Jean-Luc had no idea Farid could speak any English. It must have come from listening to all that hip hop.

As they charged out of the bureau, Menahem was pulling up in the B.M.W., doors half open. Jean-Luc jumped in the front, Farid slid in the back alongside Noah. Menahem sped up towards the Champs-Elysées roundabout, then turned down Avenue Matignon.

"A nice, fresh miracle," Jean-Luc thought. At first glance, there must be over a million euros. At the very least. Noah had started counting the bundles. Farid was smiling into empty space.

It was worth scaring yourself shitless. Jean-Luc had always known Farid would bring him good luck. In prison, he had developed a technique for seeing inside other people. You had to concentrate as hard as possible on the person you wanted to see into. So hard you ended up in a trance. Then you could see the same way a medium does. Shortly after he got out of Fleury, Jean-Luc had concentrated on Farid. Against a sky streaked with orange, a sky on the verge of tearing open with rage, he had seen a dark angel. An angel with huge, floating wings that made a soft, unnerving sound.

As long as Farid's power remained focused on money, everything would be fine. But beware if it was turned against you . . . Farid had it in him to kill.

The American backpacker had no idea who she was up against. Perhaps because she was a woman. All men instinctively knew you had to respect Farid if you didn't want the swollen, angry sky to split in two and pour down on the world.

"Hey, guys – roughly speaking we've nabbed about a million and a half euros," Noah said, without any trace of emotion. "Plus a small bundle of dollars. And a few yen."

Menahem allowed himself a quiet whistle. Farid was unhurriedly stuffing the bundles of notes back into the bags. It looked to Jean-Luc as if he were calculating something.

"Drop me off at Passage du Désir," Farid said to Menahem, closing one of the bags. "I'll take the metro back to Saint-Denis."

"What are you doing, Farid?" Jean-Luc asked.

"I'm taking my share."

"Man, it's crazy to walk around with all that cash on you!" Noah protested.

Jean-Luc tried to read Farid, but Farid avoided his gaze.

"For that sister of yours?"

"No, not for Khadidja. For Vanessa."

"Your sister's friend?"

"That's right. I'm giving her my share."

"You what?"

"You heard me."

"Why give her all that cash? She isn't even family."

"Who says she isn't, Jean-Luc?"

There was no edge to his voice, but Farid was staring straight at him. The angel's wings are rustling, thought Jean-Luc. He weighed his words:

"I was just curious. Besides, now we've pulled this off we should be thinking about the future . . ."

"I'll do what I like with my share."

"I never said you shouldn't. We all do what we like. That's the least we can hope for after all the risks we run. But take time to think about it, all the same."

Menahem pulled up in Rue du Faubourg-Saint-Denis. Farid got out without a word, and disappeared off towards Passage du Désir. Jean-Luc let Menahem drive on for a while before he took up the topic again. Just a few harmless phrases to whet Noah's appetite. He knew Noah, he always ended up talking, especially with Farid out of the way. Jean-Luc had never bothered to go into a trance over Noah. It wasn't worth it. What was there for him to see? An angel's assistant, a shark's pilot fish, or even better, a weasel teamed up with a jackal. Noah had a clingy side to his nature, heaven knows why.

Jean-Luc and he had met in prison, where Noah had been happy to find a hulking friend to protect him from the loonies and queers. When they got out, Noah had met up with Farid again, and his friendship with Jean-Luc had cooled. Jean-Luc had not lost any sleep over that. Farid and Noah had teamed up with him because of the house he lived in – a perfect hideaway they didn't want to pass up. The

Siamese twins lived in a tower block – too many dealers and too many police. But Jean-Luc thought Farid could be tamed. Provided he was handled properly. From all points of view.

"Do you get why a guy would give money to a girl who's finished with him?"

"He's proving he respects her," Noah replied.

"He's paying a high price for a kilo of respect," Jean-Luc said. Menahem guffawed.

"Yo! You're here to drive! Keep your nose out of everything else," Noah said. Then, turning to Jean-Luc: "Farid gives everything away. To prove he's not a fucking accountant. That he's cool. That's all there is to it, man. And if he wants to win Vanessa back, it's not such a bad idea."

"Why does he need to sweeten that chick? If it were you or me I could understand, but with Farid's looks?"

"Farid doesn't settle for the ordinary."

"Is she that beautiful then?"

"No idea, man."

"You're his best friend, and you don't know?"

"No."

"Oh come on, Noah!"

"I swear, I've never seen his missus!"

"But he can't be scared you'll steal her from him!"

"Farid is like Menahem. He's my brother, I tell him everything and he tells me everything, but he never talks about Vanessa. And I respect him. I accept that. The day Farid talks about Vanessa, I'll listen. For the moment, I keep my trap shut."

He's my brother. The sky ahead of them was full of purple clouds on a background that was more charcoal grey than black night. Paris was slowly waking up, and it seemed like hard going. The rain had stopped, but the truce was not going to last: the sky looked threatening. It was cold, the last traces of the Indian summer were slinking off, tail between their legs. Menahem was driving smoothly, the pavements were slick with rain, the streets were empty of people, of police: they would reach Saint-Denis in no time.

My brother.

Jean-Luc admitted that understanding Farid wasn't enough. In reality, he had always wanted Farid to show an interest in him. For Farid to call him his brother with a hint of the accent he sometimes had. The accent that was all that was left of a country he had nothing more to do with. My brother. My circumcised brother from Normandy. Yo! Man!

2

Resurrection is a matter of willpower. That's what Maxime Duchamp's body was telling Ingrid Diesel's expert hands that morning. She had dreamed of this moment so often. Before discovering his body for real, she had imagined it, not that big but perfectly proportioned, the strong chest, the perfect outline of shoulders and biceps, buttocks to die for, nice legs, nice hands and feet: and she was not wrong. But she had not foreseen the stigmata on his flesh. *How can you imagine the kiss of death?* Maxime's back and part of his right side were a mass of swellings and scars that spoke of how death had held him to her and liked what she saw.

Maxime had just begun to tell the story in that calm voice of his: the scars were a souvenir. 28 February, 1991. The last day but one of the Gulf War. And the last day of his career as a photojournalist. Of course, Ingrid was anxious to know more, but Maxime took his time. His eyes closed and his body relaxed, breathing gently, he seemed to be listening to the rain, which had finally made up its mind after a long hesitation. They could hear it streaming down the glass canopy over the front of the studio, bouncing off the ground in the Passage du Désir. It's nice and warm in my place, thought Ingrid, the storm has broken but only its fragrance manages to steal in through the cracks, a fragrance heavy with the smell of dead leaves. Oh yes, we're cosy in here. The only difference between us is that Maxime thinks in French and I think in English, but for the moment at least our thoughts in step. *We are safe at home even if the fragrance of rain plays with our minds . . .*

"O.K., Maxime, turn over."

He obeyed, opened his eyes, eyes that were midway between green and blue. He smiled at her. She could have talked for centuries about his face. A face that was easily moved, astonished, laughing, thoughtful, but stubborn as well. His extraordinary face, slightly the worse for wear, rising from a powerful neck and framed by short hair that was just beginning to thin. The first time she saw him, Ingrid had been reminded of a sailor, a little helmsman who had steered his ship towards the four points of the compass in turn, and had seen all there was to see, taken everything in, stored it all up, until the entire world was imprinted between his forehead and chin. And she was not far wrong. Instead of merchant ships or fishing boats, it had been aircraft carriers.

"They lied, you know, Ingrid."

"What do you mean?"

"It wasn't a smart war. There was nothing surgical about it. It was sickening. There was blood, burnt flesh, cries of terror, tears. And I was busy photographing it all."

"Until February 28."

"Yes. But if I hung up my camera that day, it wasn't because I'd been wounded."

"No? Why then?"

"I was taking pictures of a convoy on a highway when it was bombed. We were in the press jeep. Our driver was killed on the spot. I took some shrapnel in my back. Jimmy, my colleague from *Newsweek*, escaped with only a few scratches, and I'm sure he'll spend the rest of his life wondering how he was so lucky. We were evacuated. I can still see myself in that chopper. I couldn't move; my back was mincemeat. Opposite me was a wounded twenty-year-old marine; he was weeping. And his best buddy. Dead, laid out in a body-bag. His armoured vehicle had been accidentally hit by an American missile. Between them lay another soldier, his face covered in a blood-soaked bandage. And there was I thinking what an amazing photo this would make, a photo I was unable to take and which Jimmy would shoot instead. You could blame it on the sedatives messing with my head. You could . . ."

"But it wasn't that."

"No. Later, I analysed the situation calmly and told myself I had to stop before I became completely hardened. Or completely crazy. Lots of people in my circle were surprised when I quit. Jimmy won the *World Press* for his photo, and I was pleased for him."

Ingrid was working on Maxime's arms. Although he still felt quite relaxed, his body had tensed. It was obvious they were no longer listening to the rain together. Just when she thought the spell of the moment had been broken, Maxime spoke again, "What strong hands you have! I never imagined a Balinese massage was like this."

"Like what?"

"So vigorous. It hurts, and yet it's good."

"If it's too delicate, it's no use."

"I'm not complaining. Keep going!"

Ingrid Diesel did not chase after clients. She was a qualified masseuse, but not officially registered, and so practised discreetly in Passage du Désir in the 10th arrondissement. There was no brass plate advertising her services: word-of-mouth was enough, and she reserved the right to choose her customers. Only those with enticing skin whom she thought she could get on with. Maxime Duchamp definitely fell into both categories. Except that in his case Ingrid could have wished there were more to it. That their feelings could grow and blossom in their hearts until the only solution was to fall into each other's arms. But that didn't seem to be how things were turning out. None of the compass points led to the little helmsman's embrace.

Maxime already had a figurehead on the prow of his ship. Ultra-feminine, mane of hair, a good figure with a tight little backside. Khadidja Younis knew how to make men want her with a savviness that Frenchwomen seemed to have patented.

Frenchwomen. When it suited them, they talked about the equality of the sexes, but whenever necessary they knew only too well how to lay on seduction. Even their voices were different at moments like that. They spoke softly, although they were also capable of saying nothing, to allow the male to think he was steering the ship as well as the conversation. You had the impression that history was furling up, like a piece of old carpet, as if the feminists had never burned their bras as a symbol of liberation. That it was all an illusion and that the passionate militants of women's rights had been nothing more than a club of charming ladies who simply wanted to exchange recipes for lemon sponge over cups of tea. That none of them had ever said: men are from Mars, women from Venus.

Girls like Khadidja were born and bred in Paris. They wore push-up bras and men fell over themselves to hold open doors, rushed to light their cigarettes, buy them flowers, pay them compliments that were accepted with a fluttering of fake eyelashes. It was like a Balinese massage. It promised to be painful; it already felt good.

Ingrid thought of her own physique. Of her genes. Russian on her mother's side, Irish on her father's, a combination that had first seen the light of day in Brooklyn in 1972. The best definition for a physique like hers was "atypical". Tall (a good few centimetres taller than Maxime), muscular, not an ounce of fat, cropped blonde hair, skin as white as could be, eyes almond-shaped and icy, prominent cheek-bones, generous mouth, strong teeth, a giraffe's neck, and crowning all that and reinforcing the work of Mother Nature, a magnificent tattoo running down from her shoulders to the top of her right buttock. Nothing to do with the kiss of death this time. The tattoo showed a woman leaning over an iris-ringed pool in which carp were gambolling, with one of them leaping from the water for joy.

From an aesthetic point of view it was wonderful (an authentic *bonji* carried out by a Japanese master from Kamakura) but erotically speaking it was perhaps not so successful. At least as far as Maxime Duchamp was concerned. Ingrid had strong hands, with clipped nails that were nothing like Khadidja's talons. Khadidja's were always varnished, and always adorned with golden rings, which did not seem to bother her when she worked as a waitress in *Belles de jour comme de nuit*, the restaurant in Passage Brady. Maxime Duchamp's other life. Ingrid already knew all about his convalescence in Le Quercy with his family. A return to the source that had acted as a trigger. Maxime had been reunited with his grandmother, who owned the only inn in the village, a few kilometres outside Castelsarrasin. He had spent hours helping her in the kitchen just as he had as a boy. And his reflexes had returned and he had been resurrected, dressed now in a starched white apron and accompanying chef's hat.

Ingrid asked another question on a very different but equally interesting note. Maxime was on form this morning. She had to take advantage of it.

"Have you never been married?"

As she expected, his blue-green eyes opened wide. He stared at her in surprise.

"I'm sorry, I'm being nosy. That's how we are in the States. Strangers get on a bus, and five minutes later they're discussing the intimate details of their marriages, divorces and illnesses. But it doesn't mean anything . . . Besides, you and I aren't strangers any-more, and—"

"It's no secret. Yes, I've been married. Once."

"So you're divorced?"

"A widower. Rinko is dead."

"Rinko?"

"She was Japanese. We met during the Falklands War. She'd travelled to Buenos Aires for a script."

"She was a film-maker?"

"No, a manga artist."

Shortly afterwards, even Ingrid had to admit that the Balinese massage was coming to an end. She informed Maxime, who thanked her with a brotherly tap on the shoulder, got dressed, and picked up his sports bag. He refused her offer of a coffee. He had to get back to the *Belles* to help Chloé and Khadidja take in the deliveries. They kissed chastely on both cheeks, and Ingrid watched as he opened his umbrella to face the deluge. He turned back towards her, understood she was still curious, and shouted so that she could hear him above the rain bouncing violently off his black umbrella, "Rinko was murdered."

"What?"

"She let the murderer into her studio. Well, it was our apartment as well, on Rue des Deux-Gares. He was never caught. That was twelve years ago."

"I'm so sorry, man! I'm so dumb sometimes . . ."

"No harm done, Ingrid. That wasn't a secret either. Rinko's ashes are still at my place. One day Khadidja asked what the urn was. So I told her."

Ingrid would have liked to dig deeper. To ask whether Khadidja had shown any compassion. She would have liked to know if Khadidja had stopped thinking about her *look* for just two seconds, and taken Maxime's face in her hands and told him how much . . . That's exactly what I want to do right now, Ingrid thought, but I can't. I can pummel Maxime Duchamp's body from the roots of his hair to the tips of his toes, but I can't take his face in my hands, and I can't press my lips to his and give him a kiss. Fuck!

Ingrid had to make do with returning his wave. She watched him walk off towards Rue du Faubourg-Saint-Denis and Passage Brady. A few steps from here. Light years away in reality. She had wanted to hear his secrets, and boy had she heard them.

Ingrid made herself a coffee, put on some music, and stretched out on the pink sofa in the hallway that was her waiting room. Maxime was her only client that morning. For a while she listened to The Future Sound of London, soaring techno sounds that went well with the rain and the bucket-load of misery that had just been poured over her. But as soon as she had finished her coffee, she leapt up and went to sit at her computer. She was going to e-mail Steve to tell him about her talk with Maxime. Steve, who knew how to make her feel better. He had the gift of empathy, of making you feel you were not alone in your little worries. After the Twin Towers attack, Ingrid had felt particularly anguished. Her e-mail correspondence with her compatriot in Miami had helped her cope.

Ingrid had plonked her suitcases down in France two years earlier. The American globetrotter, who had learned Balinese massage in Bali, Thai massage in Bangkok and shiatsu in Tokyo, who had contacts from Sydney to Solo, from Koh Samui to Hong Kong, from Luang Prabang to Manila, from Vancouver to New York, had finally taken time out in Paris. Where she had no friends, only acquaintances, no love, only expectations. She kept in touch with her scattered friends via e-mail. Her computer was hardly ever switched off.

Paris – a city far too beautiful for any traveller to get to know properly in a few months. A place where the cliché about life being sweet was true, whatever the locals might say – people whose favourite hobby was to complain, and who for the most part couldn't see how lucky they were to live in one of the most beautiful cities on the planet.

And fate had brought her to live in Passage du Désir. Steve had thought that was great. What was less endearing was that Khadidja lived in the same building. One of life's little ironies. "Somewhere on top of you is the body of the other, this rival of yours who tramples on your head and crushes your heart. It's quite a perverse situation," Steve had written. He often had the words "perverse" or "perversity" on his tongue or on the keyboard, but that didn't matter, he was also an intelligent, funny guy.

Khadidja shared her apartment with her friends Chloé and Vanessa. Plump little Chloé was the other waitress at Maxime's restaurant. Vanessa, a blonde girl with a serious outlook, worked in a shelter for street kids. Ingrid would have preferred to be the only one in Maxime's entourage to live in Passage du Désir. Such a good metaphor: both poetic and direct. But that's how things were; metaphors don't belong to us any more than anything else.

After writing to Steve, Ingrid decided to roam Paris. To walk always did her the world of good. Walking for hours even in the rain, even in the cold that was taking hold day by day. This morning the pavements had the grey-black colour of wet tarmac, a dark gleam speckled with tiny glints of quartz. And in certain neighbourhoods, next to parks and along tree-lined avenues, the fallen leaves decorated the bitumen with a thousand gold dots. Ingrid liked the plane tree leaves best, the way they had of spreading harmoniously as though governed by chaos, a magnificently ordered disorder. Then there was the restless sky – suddenly the leaden clouds would be swept away to reveal a glimpse of blue. The houses turned from grey to honey-coloured. Free of the swarm of vehicles, the city sang its soft song.

Paris tasted so sweet on Sundays.

3

The body of the other on top of hers. Hands on her throat. No luck. Too strong. A beast howling inside her. A beast sweating with fear. I never thought I wanted to live so much! If only I'd known . . .

Her head was turned towards the shelf.

The book was there.

All she could see was the book . . .

Hans Christian Andersen . . . the hours spent listening . . . my mother reading . . .

Nobody knew . . . all the beautiful things she had seen, in the midst of what splendour; no-one ever dreamed of the splendour in which she had entered with her grandmother in . . . the . . .

Chloé Gardel and Khadidja Younis got back to their apartment in Passage du Désir around four in the afternoon. Khadidja usually stayed on at Maxime's after lunch, especially on Sundays. But today she had a casting she didn't want to miss. She wanted to make herself up and dash off to try her luck. As soon as they arrived, Khadidja headed for the shower, which meant it was Chloé who found the body. She was about to shut herself into her room to finally sit down to some cello practice when she noticed that Vanessa's door was ajar.

Her flatmate lay stretched out on her bed, in her pyjamas. Chloé thought she must be feeling lazy, day-dreaming with her eyes wide open, head turned towards the books and teddy bears cluttering her shelves. Going over to her, Chloé felt herself being pulled in by Vanessa's staring eyes. She saw the red marks on her friend's white neck, then realised her socks were wet. She was standing in a sticky pool of blood. The idea that the murderer might still be in the apartment didn't even occur to her. Her brain switched off for the seconds it took her to imagine her oesophagus becoming a warm volcano, and she began to throw up.

It was the unfamiliar shape etched on the far left corner of her eye that eventually brought her back to reality. Turning her head, she saw a large, black zip-up bag nestling on the yellow armchair.

Khadidja meanwhile, in only a plastic shower cap and bathrobe, could not work out why their vacuum cleaner was taking a bath in her tub. With a ton of bubble bath. At that moment, Chloé pushed open the bathroom door. Pale-faced and wild-eyed, she was clutching an open sports bag full of banknotes that tumbled out in a seemingly endless stream. Despite the look of terror on her friend's face, Khadidja couldn't help smiling. She had never seen so much money.

4

Lieutenant Jérôme Barthélemy loathed his new boss. Commissaire Jean-Pascal Grousset. He detested everything about him, including his Christian name. Barthélemy had always found double-barrelled names ridiculous, especially when they were Jean-something. The first name always spoilt the second, or vice versa. Officially, they all called the commissaire J.P.G.; unofficially, most of them referred to him as the Garden Gnome. Short-arsed and equally short on ideas, Grousset was endowed with a chin-strap beard he trimmed obsessively, a head of pepper-and-salt hair cut to regulation length, a pipe, and a pipe-smoker's breath. Whenever he ran out of ideas, he stuck the pipe in the corner of his mouth.

For the moment, the Garden Gnome was making the pretty little Arab girl who had called the police and opened the door to them repeat her story all over again. A girl who did not look particularly stupid, but whom Grousset was addressing as though she were a mental retard.

"So, you take in the deliveries at the restaurant, wait at table, then come home. You start to have a shower. Without worrying about where your friend was. Run that past me again, will you?"

"I had a casting."

"Where?"

"At M6."

"So tell me again, are you a waitress or an actress?"

Khadidja Younis had known the Garden Gnome for twenty minutes, but had already got the measure of him. She gave only desultory replies, while her friend, completely out of it, sat on a kitchen chair in her blood-soaked socks, a trembling finger tracing a circle on the oilskin tablecloth for the fifty-second time. The girl needed emergency psychiatric treatment, but the Garden Gnome preferred to continue to interrogate her flatmate. That was no surprise, she was a real stunner. And beautiful, self-assured young women always aroused Grousset. It was more to do with nerves than sex.

"How about your friend? Is she an artist too? A musician?"

"She studies at the conservatoire. And she's a waitress. At *Belles*."

"Like you."

"Like me."

"And at the time of the murder she was at the restaurant three hundred metres away, waiting for deliveries, like you."

"Like me."

"And neither of you left the restaurant at any time?"

"For the third time, no. Neither of us came back here to murder Vanessa. And we didn't murder her together either. Because that's what you're thinking, isn't it?"

"Answering a question with another question won't work with me."

Disgusted, Barthélemy went to see what the forensic people were doing. They were working in silence; the kind of intense silence they reserved for very young victims.

She was not yet twenty. Her birthday would have been in February. Stretched out on her back, with her long blonde hair forming a tousled halo, the perfect arches of her eyebrows, almond pale-blue eyes, her china-doll face, she looked as though she were resting. The problem was that she no longer had feet. The photographer prowled round the body, forced into complicated contortions by the tiny room. His camera flashed at regular intervals. The forensic expert Philippe Damien was waiting patiently for him to finish taking photos.

The bruises on her neck showed she had been strangled, but unlike the other cases of strangulation that Barthélemy recalled her features were still intact. No swelling to the face, no cyanosis, no traces of blood. Vanessa Ringer had been pretty, and she still was.

"Her face looks untouched," he said to Damien.

"Yes, it was a quick death. Continuous pressure on the carotid arteries for fifteen to thirty seconds is enough. Strangulation with the hands is more likely to produce a cardiac arrest than if some form of cord is used. The pressure of fingers on the arteries is more precise. And those scratches on her neck were made by her. Trying to struggle free."

"Which means her killer was strong."

"Stronger than her, in any case."

"And he cut her feet off *after* killing her."

"Correct. At first glance, he mutilated her with a powerful implement."

"Some sort of chainsaw?"

"More like a butcher's cleaver. The incisions are precise, and he even borrowed a chopping board from the kitchen. It's over there. But he took the cleaver away with the feet."

"No sexual violence."

"A cold, calculated crime."

"Meticulous."

"Down to the smallest details. Did you see the vacuum cleaner in the bathtub?"

"I did."

"Methinks I won't find much D.N.A. Either in the bedroom, or in the vacuum filter."

"That seems to be the conclusion."

"I just hope it's not a serial—"

The forensic expert was interrupted by shouts from the kitchen. Khadidja Younis was screaming at the Gnome. Barthélemy and Damien exchanged weary smiles.

"I never thought I'd miss our old boss so much," said Barthélemy. "I can't stand this guy."

Damien gave a sympathetic shrug of his shoulders and murmured:

"Maybe he won't last long. In the meantime, good luck my friend, especially if it is a serial killer."

Khadidja Younis was kneeling beside her friend. Slumped against the wall, her legs splayed out, the small plump girl's eyes were staring wildly, and she was gasping for breath as though there was not enough air in the kitchen. As though she wanted to melt into the wall. The Garden Gnome had just taken out his pipe to give himself a superior air. He was staring at the two girls as if their presence offended him.

"I'm telling you, you have to phone her shrink! He lives just round the corner, on Rue du Faubourg-Saint-Denis. Doctor Antoine Léger. It's not that difficult, for fuck's sake!"

"Watch your language, young lady."

"But can't you see she's having a panic attack! I'd like to see you cope with one."

"These little crises are a luxury we policemen cannot afford. In spite of all we see and hear! But I'm more interested in knowing why your friend here is throwing a fit. And why you are being so aggressive. You're keeping something from me, but you're going to have to spit it out sooner or later!"

Help! thought Barthélemy, as he went to rummage in the medicine cabinet. When he got back to the kitchen, the situation had not changed one iota. Chubby Chloé was seriously losing it, and the Arab girl Khadidja was fending off the Gnome as she tried desperately to revive her friend. It looked like a *pietà* with a very fat baby Jesus. Barthélemy put the box of valium on the table with a discreet gesture towards Khadidja.

"She's not going to tell you anything in this state, is she? And neither am I, for God's sake!"

"Oh, I'm in no hurry. I've got enough tobacco to last the whole day. And I don't need anything more."

"Are you for real or is this a nightmare?"

Damn and blast it, Lola, this is all your fault! Why did you run out on us, eh, boss? Why?

"Barthélemy?"

"Yes, boss."

"Go and interview the neighbours, and take Vernier with you. That kid could do with some practice on the ground."

Barthélemy didn't wait around for his boss to change his mind. He took the youngster outside with him, then left him with a capable uniformed officer and passed on the order for them to talk to everyone in the building. Then he went off in search of Antoine Léger, the shrink on Rue du Faubourg-Saint-Denis. A few metres away. Not difficult. Except that this was Sunday.

As he walked along, he imagined what this Antoine must look like.

From the thousands of different witness statements he had collected, he had developed his own little theory about first names: if it's not unusual for a person to look like their dog, it's not unusual either for people to resemble their first names. It was clearer for some – Antoines for example. Antoines often have fair, curly hair, and an almost naive expression, which makes them look young even if they are old.

Lieutenant Barthélemy found the brass plate easily enough. The psychiatrist was also a psychoanalyst.

Two floors up and: bingo! The doctor had curly fair hair, and his kindly face had a childish aspect. His apartment must also serve as his consulting room: everything in it was beige and light-blue so as not to upset his clients.

"How can I help?" Doctor Léger said in a fine, deep voice.

"There's an emergency, doctor. One of your patients. Chloé Gardel. A panic attack. She's not good. Her flatmate Vanessa . . ."

"Vanessa Ringer?"

"She's been murdered."

A slight tremor in his blue eyes, a deeper blue than the décor, but apart from that, nothing: the shrink was obviously used to crises.

"And you are . . . ?"

"Lieutenant Jérôme Barthélemy, from the 10th arrondissement police."

The shrink nodded and his eyes narrowed as if the officer had just put his finger on a nice, juicy suppressed memory.

"Alright, doctor, I'll let you finish whatever you were busy with, but get a move on because in a few minutes my boss is going to cart her off to the station."

He was about to turn on his heel when he saw a Dalmatian. A splendid animal with big black eyes. At first glance, it didn't look much like its owner. Mind you, it stared at you silently, without getting excited, when it could have allowed itself a bark or a growl, could have sniffed your shoes, or slobbered on your trousers.

"We'll be there," said Léger.

"We?"

"Yes, Sigmund and I. My dog doesn't like being left on his own."

"As you wish, but you'll have to leave him out on the landing. On account of the blood: there's quite a lot of that. And because of the D.N.A. samples. Do you understand?"

"Yes, I know the score, lieutenant."

As he left the building, Jérôme Barthélemy hesitated between returning to Passage du Désir or letting his feet take him to Rue de l'Echiquier. It was from number 32 of that unremarkable thorough-fare that Lola Jost looked out with contempt on the world. Because it must have been contempt that made her quit a well-knit team overnight, a group that had seen everything and more, but knew still how to enjoy themselves in the good times. She had no right to leave, throwing bad memories and the fleeting moments of elation into the same dustbin. Especially when she was the boss, someone no-one would have dared dismiss with the nickname "the fat lady" or "the bitch" or "the pain in the neck" or "the old cow" or "the big pain in the neck" even if some days you really felt like doing just that. With good reason: Lola Jost was not an easy woman, Lola Jost had a foul temper and Lola Jost was no beauty queen.

Almost unawares, his footsteps had already taken him south, towards a weak sun trying to break through a barrier of grey cloud, managing only the appearance of a faint lantern behind tracing paper. Lieutenant Barthélemy and his thoughts had just gone past Rue d'Enghien. If his memory did not fail him, Lola's street was the next. He slowed down. What if she sent him packing with nothing but a resounding curse for a greeting? What if she left him out on the landing on the other side of the spyhole, ringing and ringing like an idiot? What if she had left Paris to go and warm her old bones somewhere less damp and less crowded, since she could no longer stand people . . . No . . . not her style. In the past, Lola Jost used to repeat to anyone who cared to listen how much she detested pointless changes of scenery, all the opportunities for a break offered by short and long weekends, holidays, sabbaticals, bank holidays. With just one exception: when the boss went to visit her son and granddaughters in Singapore. But then she travelled for family reasons, not for any exotic pleasures. Never that. She never even talked about those holidays she had south of the Equator, however hard they tried to worm it out of her.

Oh yes, she led us a merry dance, every single one of us. Talking of changes of scenery, she did that alright when she heaved her huge frame out of her tiny office, never to set foot there again, Barthélemy told himself as he climbed the stairs in a building that had no lift or caretaker. No fool, the boss lived on the first floor.

Her name was written under a brass bell linked to some ringing mechanism that set off who knew what chain reaction. Outside a flimsy-looking door that was little more than a single sheet of laminated wood, Barthélemy shifted uncomfortably. Unable to move his feet, unable to speak, and yet he knew he was going to have to. Until now, he had been simply chewing on his rancour. Not a good start, but he rang the bell. Several times. Nothing happened. Something had snapped in the chain reaction. Tough luck. But in the stairwell, with its comforting smell of toasted bread and Sunday morning breakfast, Barthélemy smiled as he took out a mobile he had almost forgotten about, carried away on the waves of his resentment. Of course, the boss's number was saved under "Lola", a familiarity he would never have allowed himself beyond the confines of an electronic address book.

What's really funny is that she's not even called Lola, thought the lieutenant as he pressed the keypad. Her real first name is Marie-Thérèse. And of course she looks more like a Marie-Thérèse than a Lola. O.K., that's her only foible . . . although some evenings, fag dangling from her lips, arms folded, skirt raised up to her knees to reveal legs that were astonishingly attractive considering the rest of her physique, when she was describing the details of a case to you in that gravelly voice of hers, with the slight drawl that gave her words a certain Swiss flavour, and her sharp eyes darting everywhere, then Marie-Thérèse Jost could well have been a Lola.

When she replied after five rings, Barthélemy's heart leapt. How good it was to hear that gruff voice again, still sounding as if stacked with a lorry-load of cigarettes. The almost asthmatic voice that radiated authority.

"Hello, boss, this is Barthélemy. I'm on your doorstep."

"What's my doorstep ever done to you?"

"Er . . . I'm on a case in the neighbourhood with the Gnome and . . . I came to take a breather at your place, and perhaps a coffee, if you have one on the go, that is . . ."

"What you did was wake me up, my lad."

"You were still asleep at this time of day! I don't believe it, boss!"

"Apart from you, I don't see who that concerns."

"Well, what I meant was that naps aren't your kind of thing . . ."

"O.K., cut the crap, Barthélemy. You can have your coffee! Give me two seconds to jump into my dressing gown."

Like the Foreign Legion parachuting on Kolwezi, thought the lieutenant, as he waited patiently for a good five minutes. The door opened on a Lola with a puffy, creased face wearing an expression as welcoming as a police baton. The dressing gown looked as if it had belonged to Clark Gable in "Gone With the Wind", but at least it appeared to keep her warm. Now that the days were growing colder . . .

Barthélemy had already been inside the boss's lair a couple of times. A badly designed two-bedroom flat, with a corridor that was too long and a kitchen that was too small. All of it decorated in green and salmon pink to stay Zen while the pizza-delivery boys on the ground floor despatched their takeaways at all hours of the day and night. He took off his shoes to stay in the boss's good books, and followed her into the living room. Most of the space was taken over by a table with its leaves extended. On it was a board, and on the board was a jigsaw puzzle that gave you a headache just looking at it.

"The Sistine Chapel in five thousand pieces," said Lola. "In other words, the height of vice. Last night I was puzzling like a madwoman. Thanks to that damned Michelangelo I got to bed at three in the morning."

"It's very impressive," said Barthélemy.

"Do you really want coffee?"

"No."

"So much the better, because I feel queasy from last night. I kept myself going thanks to some fifty-year-old port. The face of Eve being banished from paradise gave me a hell of a time. I'm making a peppermint tea, are you up for some?"

"Always, boss."

"Oho, you sound like someone who wants something."

"I don't want anything, boss. It's just that perhaps . . . I'm out of sorts, and it's not the flu."

"That's terrible, at your age."

"You like studying the Sistine Chapel, but I can't stand to look at the Garden Gnome. He depresses me, his methods make me want to shoot myself, his stupidity leaves me speechless."

"*In vain is good a good for us too high. When hope has died, desire too must die.*"

"Is that by a Zen monk?" asked Barthélemy, refusing to be put off.

He was used to Lola's quotes: she'd been a French literature teacher in another life, one in which generations of schoolkids must have had a really hard time.

"No, it's an elegy by Bertaut. My way of saying that you need to get used to the idea: I'll never set my blasted feet in the police station again."

"That hardly seems reasonable when you haven't been retired a year yet.".

"I didn't join the police for the bureaucratic perks. And my reasons for leaving are my business."

"Everyone knows what those reasons were," Barthélemy retorted courageously, defying his boss's look, which was fast becoming glacial. "Your reasons have a name: Toussaint Kidjo."

Lola eyed her former colleague disdainfully, then headed for the kitchen without a comment. Relieved he was still persona grata, Barthélemy could hear her banging pots and pans. She came back, stiff and erect, her expression set in stone, carrying a steaming teapot and two cups on a tray, her hideous dressing gown dangling down like a royal train:

"Take that board off for me and be careful you don't spoil the Sistine."

Barthélemy obeyed with the renewed enthusiasm of someone reunited with the one person capable of blowing away the fog and clearing the horizon. A chief, a manageress, a sweeper-away of nothingness. Of course this was an illusion, but still, it was heart-warming. Not a single piece of the puzzle fell onto the green carpet.

"O.K.," Lola sighed, "tell me. It'll do you good and it might amuse me."

So Barthélemy told her about the blonde Vanessa and her two friends from Passage du Désir. Girls who did not appear to be rolling in money, who shared a small apartment so they could live in the centre of Paris. He described the victim's pale but intact face, the quick, brutal strangling, the story of the vacuum cleaner, no hint of anything sexual. And the feet, supposedly cut off with a cleaver; Barthélemy attached great importance to those cut-off feet that had vanished into thin air. He insisted on the lack of clues: D.N.A., potential enemies, motive, meaning. And the contrast. An unfathomable contrast between a straightforward strangling and a perverted mutilation, an intact face and two gory stumps. All this had happened to an unremarkable girl with a modest job and, according to her flatmates, no boyfriend either. No diary, no letters, nothing apart from a shelf stuffed with books, most of them children's books, like *The Little Match Girl*, in amongst dolls and teddy bears.

Lola wrapped her hands round her steaming cup; the vapour clouded her glasses, so that Barthélemy could not gauge her expression. By blurting out about the mutilation, he had run the risk of reviving memories of Lieutenant Toussaint Kidjo. His sudden, violent death had marked the start of their problems, the spark of a fire that grew and grew until only ashes remained. Under the boss's guidance, the cops of the 10th arrondissement had formed a close-knit team. Now it wouldn't be long before it all went up in smoke: each day, the Garden Gnome threw fuel on the fire like a sadistic simpleton, a miserable wretch bent on destroying what little reason remained to get out of bed in the morning. Depressing. And then people wondered why everyone went running to a shrink. Whether his name was Antoine or Jean-Gédéon. Whether he had a Dalmatian or a proboscis monkey from Borneo.

"I know Khadidja and Chloé," Lola said, breaking the silence.

They're waitresses at *Belles de jour comme de nuit*. I think they're good kids. Grousset will give them a hard time for a few hours, then let them go."

"That's not how he seems to see it. There's no sign of a break-in. Either the killer had the keys, or Vanessa let him in."

"You know that more than seventy per cent of homicides are committed by people close to the victim, Barthélemy. And if you know it, so does the Gnome. He's working on Vanessa's flatmates. Anyone would do the same."

"The Gnome's thought processes worry me far less than his style."

"A piece of good advice, Barthélemy: give it time. It'll all sort itself out, you'll see."

"That's not what my nerves are telling me. And they rarely get it wrong, the swine."

"Do you know the metaphysics of the jigsaw puzzle, Barthélemy?"

He contented himself with shaking his head from left to right.

"All it takes is one piece, and suddenly the universe becomes whole. Provided of course you are satisfied with a universe that makes sense. A universe within our reach. When you can't take on something far too heavy for you, you have to lighten up, Barthélemy."

"I don't understand what you mean, boss."

"My, my . . . you used to be much sharper in the old days. What I mean is: I can't go through the front door of the 10th arrondissment cop-shop anymore. I find it physically impossible. I can't sit at my desk as though nothing has happened, and lead you useless lot with an iron fist in a velvet glove, or a morning-after face beneath a carnival mask. I was, and am no longer. I've given, and have nothing more to give. So I do jigsaw puzzles, and that simple activity satisfies me. Completely."

"That's hard to believe."

"I'm not asking you to believe it. Contrary to what you might think, I'm no guru, my lad. Now it's Jean-Pascal Grousset, a.k.a. the Garden Gnome, who's in charge. He's not as stupid as he looks. He's letting you find the missing piece."

"What piece?"

"The piece of the puzzle, you ninny. The one you're possibly going to fit into the right place to bring your investigation to a conclusion, and to make the world whole for five minutes. That's your glory and your calling, my boy. But to do that, don't you think you'd better make a start on interviewing the neighbours?"

Barthélemy raised a sceptical eyebrow at the same time as he raised the cup to his lips. It had started to pour with rain again. He could see it lashing down in silvery – or, more precisely, grey – torrents against the front of the building opposite. He was going to have to get a move on. That was true. And inevitable. To question all those people to find out if they had seen anyone, learned anything, if they had an opinion concerning Vanessa Ringer, Chloé Gardel, or Khadidja Younis. Before Lola had walked out, Barthélemy would have relished a painstaking task of that kind. He was like a bloodhound, muzzle in the dirt, and that didn't bother him. Quite the opposite, because the boss also stuck her nose in every gutter in the neighbourhood, without ever missing a single one. But that was over. He was alone again.

Barthélemy said goodbye with a heavy heart. He had come to settle his doubts, and was leaving with a certainty. *When hope has died, desire too must die.* Lola Jost had been a splendid pain in the neck, her invisible sword raised threateningly over the neighbourhood, her elephant's feet making the ground tremble. Now she was just an old woman who did jigsaw puzzles.

*

Once her former colleague had left, Lola Jost stood watching the rain fall and tried to recall Vanessa Ringer's face. She remembered a pretty young girl who always seemed cold or sad. From time to time she ran into her in the shops, dressed in dark colours that only made her lily-white face stand out all the more.

Lola abandoned Vanessa and her window. She ate two slices of gingerbread and a banana – magnesium: good for the brain cells, even more so for jigsaws. She coughed as she smoked a cigarette and did the washing-up while she listened to the news on France Info. The presenter was describing a hold-up on the Champs-Elysées. Three masked men carrying assault rifles had emptied a bureau de change in a matter of minutes, shortly before five in the morning, and got away with the tidy sum of a million and a half euros. They had disappeared just as they had appeared, abandoning their vehicular battering ram at the scene. The raid ended with a Canadian tourist in a state of shock, and an expert from the Anti-Gang Squad declaring that times were changing. They were dealing with a new generation of criminals, very different from the old-fashioned thieves who had a code of honour, professional experience and an awareness of the risks they were running. Nowadays, these young delinquents, who often came from the housing estates ringing the capital, would indiscriminately raid jewellers, bureaux de change or auction houses, equipped with military firepower and an unfailing nerve. They struck quickly, took ludicrous risks, and didn't hesitate to squander the fruits of their raids blindly, with no thought for the morrow.

"Well of course, my lad, they're not your typical investors, are they?" Lola growled at the radio, before turning it off.

5

Jean-Luc had spent part of Monday cleaning and tidying his place. He liked order, and these chores helped him reflect. In fact, he had never stopped thinking about Farid and that incredible story about the dough. He had done well to stay cool. Better to allow Farid to pursue his dream. Logically, seeing all that money, the famous Vanessa must have welcomed him with open arms.

Now Jean-Paul was following the Route du Rhum yacht race on television. The competitors must be tired of feeling sick, because the sea had been particularly rough that year. He was gobsmacked at Ellen MacArthur's exploits. That brown-haired young woman might even win. They were the same age. He could give half a million euros to a woman like that, he told himself. That made sense: Ellen MacArthur was a heroine. Jean-Luc could imagine all she had to endure on her solo yacht. He concentrated very hard to try to read her, but it was impossible. At that moment, someone rang the doorbell. Jean-Luc sighed. Trust some asshole to show up right on cue.

"You've got to come."

Noah looked a changed man. Hard to say why. Then suddenly Jean-Luc realised this was the first time he had seen Noah out on his own since he had met Farid. The Siamese twins had been separated. Without Farid, Noah was no more than a shadow of himself.

"Farid's refusing to come out. Get a move on."

"So what if he doesn't want to leave your estate? Haven't you noticed the weather? He's better off at home."

"No, I mean he won't come out of his flat! He won't even answer the door."

"What's going on?"

"Yo! I've no idea, man. First Farid smashed everything up, now he's barricaded himself in, and . . ."

"Wait a minute. You say he's smashed everything. That must have made quite a racket."

"You're telling me, man."

"Why didn't you say so straight off? The neighbours are bound to call the Feds!"

"Perhaps not. The old geezer on the left is gaga. And the ones on the right are ganjas."

"What?"

"Yo! Listen up. Blacks who smoke ganja."

"So? That doesn't make you deaf. And there are more than two neighbours in the block."

"Let's go, Jean-Luc. Are you coming?"

"Wait, I have to think this over."

"Can't you think in the car?"

"Noah?"

"Yes?"

"Focus for thirty seconds, will you? If you couldn't get in, it's because there's a problem with Farid's door."

"That's right, man. It's reinforced. Of course it is! There are too many nutters on that estate."

Thanks to the Route du Rhum, Jean-Luc had a brainwave. He went to look in the cupboard for his red oilskin cape and his full-face helmet, which he had kept when he sold his bike. Bombarded with questions from Noah, he put on the oilskin and went down into the garage to find a can of spray-paint. He had touched up the chrome on one of the cars Menahem had delivered with some silver paint. Noah, who had finally realised he was not going to get any answers, watched him spraying the helmet without a word. That was something at least. Pleased with his work, Jean-Luc ordered Noah to bring the sledgehammers from the workbench, and threw them in the car.

Noah and Jean-Luc got out of the lift on the tenth floor and walked up to the eleventh. Before putting his silver helmet on, Jean-Luc noticed the ganja-haze floating through the air to the rhythm of a Youssou N'Dour number. The music was coming from the door to the right, but the left-hand neighbour was much more clued-in, and extremely interested in what was going on around him. One of his ears was stuck to Farid Younis's door.

"SAINT-DENIS FIRE SERVICE!" Jean-Luc bawled.

The old man jumped.

"Oh! I was just about to call the police. The young man must be drunk. I think he's smashed everything in his flat. I hope he hasn't killed himself."

"We'll get him out of there. Go back inside, please. We have to break the door down. It'll be very noisy and could be dangerous."

"I'm used to it, you know. My neighbours love music, and the drunken young man always slams his door when he comes in, whether it's noon or midnight. That's what the new generation is like, you have to get used to it. I've lived on this estate for thirty-seven years. My name is Sébastien Hopel. I'm pleased to see that firemen still respond so quickly. That's not the case with a lot of other services."

Farid lay bare-chested on his bed. He had downed a bottle of gin. Before that he had destroyed his few sticks of furniture and torn down the blinds. He appeared to be fast asleep. The bathroom was a wreck. The medicine cabinet and its contents had joined the wash-basin mirror in the tub. A copy of *France-Soir* was floating on top of them. Jean-Luc turned it over and read the front page headline: IS ANYONE SAFE? Beneath it a photograph of a pretty young blonde woman. "Vanessa Ringer, aged 19, a social worker, was murdered in her own home yesterday morning. In Passage du Désir, in Paris's 10th arrondissement, Sundays are only peaceful on the surface . . ."

For the first time in his life, Farid had read a newspaper, and it hadn't done him much good. Jean-Luc folded up the dripping pages of the newspaper and slipped them into the pocket of his oilskin. Then he studied the medicines floating in the bath. Nothing too worrying: aspirin, paracetamol, throat pastilles. No antacids. Of course. Farid the fearless didn't need any.

"Yo! And he never touches alcohol."

"I just hope he hasn't had a cocktail of gin and sleeping pills."

"No! He never kept any pills here."

"So it seems."

"Definitely not! Farid never goes to the quack. And I don't remem-ber us ever holding up a pharmacy."

"Wrap him in the blanket, Noah, we're taking him with us. While you do that, I'll make sure we're not leaving anything valuable behind."

"What do you mean? The bag with his share?"

"Bravo, you're a mind-reader."

"I never thought Farid would demolish everything around him like fucking Attila the Hun. Did you see? He's even torn down the blinds."

No, it's the angel who got his wings caught up in them, thought Jean-Luc:

"Yes, he did a good job," he replied.

"Do you think the old dodderer took you for a real fireman?"

"He doesn't look as senile as you seem to think. Anyway, he can take me for Flash Gordon or Spiderman, I couldn't give a fuck. Now we've found Farid; the most important thing is to get him off the estate."

And to get it into your thick skull that you won't be coming back here any time soon, thought Jean-Luc as he lifted Farid in his arms. He was a lot heavier than he would have imagined.

Posted at his friend's bedside, Jean-Luc spent a long time watching over him. The curtains in the room filtered the daylight, and Farid's sleeping face was in semi-darkness. From time to time, he muttered something and stirred. His brain must be scrambled, and his heart bled dry. The prince had just lost his Scheherazade, and no longer had a clue what to do with his thousand and one nights.

Jean-Luc had tried to wake him up by forcing him to drink coffee through a funnel. Noah had lent a hand, but they had only succeeded in staining the wallpaper and armchairs. As long as Farid didn't slip into a coma, they would just have to let him sleep it off. He would pull out of it. Besides, on a boat he'd experience worse. He'd feel drunk every day without touching a drop. Jean-Luc had taken two decisions. First, to christen his boat *The Dark Angel*. Second, to convince Farid to buy it with him and head out to sea. Jean-Luc had already put money by, and it would be easy to do the deal. Farid needed a goal, a life he could live beyond the day-to-day. Jean-Luc would teach him to sail. As for Noah, they would see. If Farid really wanted to take him with them, Jean-Luc would do his best.

Obviously the mess in Passage du Désir had to be cleared up first. But Jean-Luc had learned to be patient, like a yachtsman ready to risk his life and boat for thirteen days and twelve nights on the ocean, from Saint-Malo to Pointe-à-Pitre, for example. In any event, whether or not Farid had killed Vanessa, Jean-Luc was determined to take him away. There remained only one not-so-simple problem: to find out what Farid had done with his loot. Jean-Luc had been to the newsagent's and leafed through all the available newspapers. He had zapped through the T.V. channels: none of the reports mentioned a bag full of money in connection with the Vanessa Ringer affair. That could mean either that the police were keeping the information under wraps, that Vanessa's flatmates had spirited it away, or, best of all, that Farid had stashed it somewhere. There was no shortage of possibilities.

While he was waiting, Jean-Luc had tried several times to see what the angel was doing. In the end, after many attempts, he had seen him, head lowered, clinging by his feet to a big black tree that had shed all its leaves. His wings folded across his body exactly like a giant bat. Jean-Luc took Farid's hand and twisted it gently to make the silver rings gleam in the dim light.

"You don't know who you are anymore, do you, my friend? Well, that's something I've never known. That means we have something in common now. Whether you like it or not."

6

At about eight o'clock that evening, the Sistine Chapel was at a standstill, and her packet of cigarettes looked equally unrewarding, so Lola decided it was high time she went out to eat. Knowing Maxime Duchamp as she did, his restaurant would probably be open despite the catastrophe that had unfurled around Khadidja and Chloé's young heads. He was a past master at offering an oasis of well-being, a modest rallying point for the band of regulars who were tempted by the modest prices. *Belles de jour comme de nuit* was a small, unpretentious restaurant. Good, simple, and not too expensive. In other words, a rarity in Paris.

Lola donned raincoat and boots, slipped a fresh packet of cigarettes into her pocket, took her umbrella out of the china stand decorated with dragons (a gift from her son, who had only one failing: he liked chinoiseries) and headed for Passage Brady. As she walked up Rue du Faubourg-Saint-Denis, Lola thought that if it kept on raining like this the doom-mongers who were predicting the Seine would flood worse than in 1910 would soon be proved correct.

As she plunged into the covered passage, the wind brought with it the usual smells, above all of curry. The *Belles* was the only establishment of its kind at the heart of an arcade lined with Indian restaurants. Despite the blustery rain, Lola paused to consider the slate outside the restaurant. Brawn vinaigrette, selection of crudités, andouillette A.A.A.A.A. (Amicable Association of Amateurs of Authentic Andouillette), beef *à la mode*, Barbary duckling, and desserts. But desserts had never interested Lola. She was all about savoury and spirits.

Through the window she spied Edouard, the newsagent's son. He was wearing a big black apron and was waiting at table in place of Chloé and Khadidja. A catering student, the lad often filled in at Maxime's. Which meant the Gnome really had arrested the two young women. Fine, that wouldn't kill them, and it might give Khadidja inspiration for her auditions. What doesn't kill us makes us stronger, blah, blah, blah.

Lola recognised several of the regulars, among them a blonde giraffe with cropped hair, shoulders like a female wrestler and an American accent. She also seemed to appreciate this little haven. Lola suspected her interest was not exclusively gastronomic; she had noticed what she was up to with Maxime. Whenever he left his stoves to come and pay court to the customers, she gazed at him with smouldering eyes. Despite being short in stature, Maxime Duchamp had always attracted women. The look he had, of someone who had seen the world but had not grown tired of the sight, made it hard to grow bored of him.

Edouard showed her to her usual table, the one she had so often shared with Toussaint. Facing the mirror through which she could observe her world without being seen, Lola was horrified to see once more how closely she resembled a beached sperm whale. A broad face framed with grey hair with a frumpish cut, a size twenty-two or twenty-four body, depending on the label. It always felt like that when Toussaint's ghost came knocking on the door.

"What lousy weather, Madame Jost! It's brave of you to come."

"We shouldn't complain all the time, my boy. In 1910, the Seine rose more than six metres. The Zouave soldier statue on Pont de l'Alma got his moustaches wet. The revellers who weren't drowned had a high old time of it in the restaurants. Compared to then, we're doing fine."

"On the radio this morning they said the rain might be back again."

"We'll shed our tears when the moment comes, Edouard. While we're waiting, I'll have an andouillette with chips, accompanied by a house red. And tell Maxime I'd like a word with him. Understood?"

"Understood, Madame Jost."

The andouillette was tasty, the chips as well, and as the last drop of the house wine expired in Lola's glass, Maxime came to sit at her table. He stared at her for a moment without saying anything. He was very good at that.

"Hello there, Maxime," she said, because somehow she had to break the spell and bring him back to the here and now.

"Hello, Lola."

"When I got up this morning I remembered that my real first name is Marie-Thérèse and that I'm a hundred-and-twenty years old."

"I refuse to call you Marie-Thérèse. To me you will always be Lola."

"Well, alright," Lola said. "But I'm thirsty."

Maxime raised his arm to catch Edouard's attention and sketched a magic sign in the air. The two of them fell silent again until the wine arrived. Maxime knew Lola was thinking of Toussaint, but was tactful enough not to mention his name; he was waiting for her to do so. But Lola was not in the mood to bring him up. She let the silence hang in the air, then opened a fresh packet of cigarettes, without offering one to Maxime. That was not one of his vices.

"Who is that Viking?"

"The tall blonde in the sailor's jersey?"

"Yes."

"Ingrid Diesel. She's a masseuse from Passage du Désir."

"Heavy stuff indeed."

"Thai, shiatsu, Balinese."

"What's that nonsense?"

"She does all kinds of massage."

"Have you tried it?"

"Yes, Lola."

"Was it any good, Maxime?"

"Fantastic."

"How did you get to know her?"

"In the gym on Rue des Petites-Écuries. She's something else: she never misses a session."

Lola emptied her glass, Maxime did the same, then poured them another. Lola reflected that this was exactly what she wanted. For him to serve her wine, and drink with her. For him not to tell her she smoked too much. To listen to her talk or say nothing. To tell her what was on his mind – or not. She always felt relaxed with Maxime. And this Monday evening, he wanted to talk.

"I'm sure you know Khadidja and Chloé have been arrested."

"Yes, I heard."

She listened to him talk about the girls. Chloé, who had weight problems, took refuge in playing the cello or contacting her invisible friends in cyberspace. Khadidja the brave little soldier who Maxime was sure would be more than capable of keeping up their spirits. But it was tough on such young girls: Chloé, Khadidja and Vanessa, the inseparable trio who had known each other since schooldays. Chloé was scared to death. Khadidja was on her mettle, but sick at heart.

Neither of them had the slightest idea who could have butchered their friend. Either Vanessa had opened the door to her killer, or he had got in using the keys. That was all Chloé and Khadidja had to say, but the police, in the shape of a small, dim-witted commissaire, didn't think that was enough.

"I'm doing all I can to reassure them. But I don't like the look of it. The killer cut her feet off, you know."

"Yes, I know: a former colleague told me."

"That wasn't in the papers this morning."

"A trick. Grousset wants the murderer to know more than the public, in order to catch him out in the interrogation."

"What if we're dealing with a crazy guy who wants to try again with Khadidja or Chloé? That's Lieutenant Barthélemy's theory. Do you think he's right?"

"I don't think anything. Especially as I'm no longer on the force, remember?"

Lola said this with more regret in her voice than she would have liked. She smiled at him to compensate. Maxime patted her hand before saying mischievously, "You know what you need?"

"No idea."

"A nice session with Antoine."

"Who might that be?"

"He's a regular at *Belles*, Chloé's shrink. Perhaps if you go and stretch out on his couch you'll feel better. And his dog's name is Sigmund."

"No way!"

"Yes. Besides, Antoine is a great guy. Do you know why shrinks make their patients lie down on the couch and then sit behind them?"

"So they can have a bit of a nap now and again?"

"Not even close, Lola. Clients open up more if they are facing the void, that's to say facing themselves."

"You find that reassuring?"

"I think accepting the void is a good place to start."

Lola felt better for having talked to Maxime, and had gone back to her puzzle. She had overdone the house wine, but couldn't care less: it would help her sleep. When the doorbell rang, she thought it must be Barthélemy, and got up muttering to herself. But the only person she could see through the spyhole was Ingrid Diesel, the versatile masseuse. Lola looked at her watch: twenty-five to eleven. Despite the hour, she opened the door to the disrespectful intruder, who was smiling like someone who has too big a favour to ask. Lola looked her up and down without a word. An attitude that had unsettled quite a few in her time.

"Madame Lola Jost?"

"That depends . . ."

"My name is Ingrid Diesel. It was Maxime Duchamp from *Belles* who sent me."

"Oh yes, I know Maxime. What is it?"

"Can I come in?"

Lola made way for her without bothering to hide her lack of enthusiasm. The wrestler muttered a few words of apology, took her shoes off so as not to dirty the carpet (a point in her favour) and went to drape herself on the sofa. Less of a point in her favour. Her socks were grey-blue, she was wearing a pair of faded jeans and a striped jersey she peeled off without a second thought, complaining how hot it was. Lola found herself facing a muscular young woman in a tank-top, with a tattoo creeping over the top of one shoulder. She lit a cigarette, unsuccessfully offered one to her visitor, then went to sit in her favourite armchair, closing her dressing gown round her innermost thoughts and her outermost bulk.

"Maxime told me you used to be in the police force."

"That was long before you were born. The dinosaurs were only just thinking of setting up shop."

"I'm well over thirty, you know."

"And might one know what brings you here at such a late hour, Ingrid Diesel?"

"Oh, it's not even eleven yet. Well, I live in Passage du Désir, in the building where Vanessa Ringer was . . ."

"Yes, I know about that."

"Your colleagues have already questioned me at home. I had nothing bad to say about my neighbours. When I saw they were being taken down to the station, I followed. After we got there, I tried to back them up, and one of your colleagues was very rude."

"It's so easy to forget that a police station isn't a tropical resort. The people there are stressed out, and not very friendly towards tourists."

"I think you can help me. Well, all of us. The people in the neighbourhood. Because the death of a young girl concerns everyone."

"This conversation began on a rational basis. You used the past tense when you mentioned my police career. You hit the bull's-eye with that. Now you're veering off target, which is a shame. Especially since it seems to be becoming a habit: you're the second person to sing me this nostalgic song. Get used to the idea: nowadays Lola Jost does jigsaw puzzles at home. At least she does when she's allowed to."

"But puzzles must be so . . ."

"So what? So bloody boring?"

"Er . . . yes. But forgive me if I try for the bull's-eye again. Maxime told me I could talk to you, that you were a really exceptional woman."

"An 'exceptional woman'. That sounds like a cliché if ever I heard one. I would prefer *Maxime told me you were an exceptionally real woman.* I can accept that. I enjoy being a woman. Or what remains of the woman I was. I've given and given and given, and now I have the right to stay home and do puzzles or cut carrots into rose shapes if I feel like it. Or do the crossword. I do that when I'm fed up with puzzles. It's my right."

"No."

"What do you mean, 'no'?"

"If you do nothing, they'll arrest an innocent man, and the bastard who killed Vanessa will remain free. That's inadmissible."

"I also know some big words, and not all of them cross ones: 'intolerable', 'incontrovertible', 'inconceivable', and even 'injustice'. So don't flaunt your big words at me, I'm not impressed."

"But surely there's more to life than staying at home and forgetting everyone else."

"Life, young lady, is a stone soup, and if you haven't understood that by your age, there's nothing I can do for you."

"Maxime told me you were an incredible cop before your colleague was killed."

"You're starting to get on my nerves."

"Why don't you snap out of it and come and help the neighbourhood instead of just stewing in self-pity in that hideous dressing gown of yours?"

"Right, that's enough. I won't have a tattooed shaven-headed lunatic in stripes being rude about my dressing gown. Out you go."

"No."

"On your own head be it. I'm calling my so-called colleagues so they can cart you off. And this time I can assure you, they'll give you their full attention."

"You're not an exceptional woman at all. Maxime was wrong, and I insist: your dressing gown is hideous. Totally ugly. When you're properly settled into your cushy little life as a pensioner, when you've given up, you really won't interest anyone anymore. And it won't be long now."

"The door hasn't moved, and nor has the police station. You have two seconds to choose your destination."

The Yank did not need to be told twice, and so Lola was finally able to slam the door on the shameless hussy. She stood for a moment staring at the door and the spyhole; a brief image of a rectangular, cataleptic Cyclops flashed through her mind. The sort of character who could have been in "Les Shadoks". But "Les Shadoks" hadn't been on T.V. for ages. Then she realised the tattooed wrestler had left her jersey behind. She went to the window and saw her silhouette storming towards Passage du Désir. With athletic strides. Half naked in the cold November night, but with her seething anger to keep her warm. People were incredible when they didn't realise they were being watched.

Absent-mindedly, Lola read the label on the jersey. A make that sounded Breton. Size twelve. Lola remembered the days when she had been a size twelve. The days of "Les Shadoks". She took the pullover with her into the bedroom and stood in front of her wardrobe mirror. It's true that this dressing gown is ugly, but so what? At least it's warm. When she held the sailor's jersey up to her melon breasts it looked like something out of the children's department. Thanks to some Darwinian process gone haywire, mermaid-Lola had slowly mutated into an old sperm whale. So slowly she had not seen it coming. And thousands of years after the wreck, along came a little hussy waving her jersey like some naive pennant, or flag of convenience, as if everything were that simple. As if it was enough to say *Yes, oh yes, let's just do it.*

O.K., come on, stop your nonsense, Lola. You've had too much to drink, my girl. Time to go to bed.

And that is what Lola did. But no sooner had her head hit the pillow than she sat up again. A few words had lodged themselves in her ear, something that Diesel girl had said. "If you do nothing, they'll arrest an innocent man . . ." And she had apparently gone to Rue Louis-Blanc to vouch for Khadidja and Chloé.

Lola got out of bed and went to call Barthélemy. The little idiot seemed overjoyed to hear her, and immediately started with his "Yes boss, no boss", as tedious as a Monday morning with no jigsaw puzzle. She soon hacked a path through with her machete, and the lieutenant told her what she wanted to know: the Garden Gnome had already had enough of toying with the two waitresses. Now his interest had shifted to their boss. Being Khadidja Younis's boyfriend, Maxime Duchamp had access to the keys to the girls' apartment. And on the morning of the crime, he was in the neighbourhood. Being massaged by the Diesel woman. Lola dressed in a hurry, grabbed the sailor's jersey, and set a course for Passage du Désir.

7

FEAR IN THE CITY! THE DOGS ARE LOOSE! THEY HAVE TO
BE HOUNDED!

Someone had sprayed their views in red paint on the window of
the antique shop next to the budiling where Ingrid Diesel and the
girls lived. Lola touched one of the exclamation marks with her
finger: it was still fresh. Then, inside the window, in the middle of the
O of LOOSE, she saw a bottle containing a tiny ballerina with jointed
legs, dressed in a tutu and ballet shoes. The key setting her in motion
hung down to the right. Lola peered along the passage, but it was
empty, apart from a cottony mist and a fellow sleeping on a pile of
cardboard boxes. She rang the bell marked i. DIESEL.

"I took off my dressing gown and brought back your blue-striped
or white-striped pullover, I'm not sure which anymore."

"What I really want to know is if you've changed your mind."

"There you go, straight to the point. You haven't changed your
style, have you? Well, are you going to allow me into your ground-
floor reserve or simply leave me out here to work on my rheumatism?"

Diesel stepped back, and Lola entered a room that looked like a
waiting area. A psychedelic version. An orange sofa stood opposite an
identical one in pink, with summer-sky-blue cushions scattered on
both; a yellow and mauve shaggy carpet looked like a mutant tiger's

skin. A lava lamp exhibited the floppy dance of wax blobs in a purple liquid. An L.S.D. landscape. And there was music: a catchy little repetitive number no doubt composed by a neurasthenic robot.

"Shall I stop the music?"

"Not at all," Lola said, sitting in the middle of the orange sofa. "But I'd like you to stop your music-hall act."

"What do you know about my act? What are you getting at?"

"It's not for the sake of the neighbourhood or Khadidja or Chloé that you came to see me. It's for Maxime."

"O.K., I admit it."

"And it wasn't Maxime who sent you. If he had wanted me to stick my nose in this business, he would have asked me himself."

"I admit that too. Maxime simply told me one day you were a cop. And tonight, when I saw how relieved he looked after talking to you, I followed you."

"Good, that's saved some time. Now, tell me what comes next, I'm all ears."

Ingrid Diesel fluttered her long hands a little, then went to open a pink fridge that Lola had not noticed, and took out two bottles of beer, which she swiftly opened. She automatically handed one to Lola without offering her a glass, then started to swig from her own. Lola looked at the bottle with its long neck and drank from it as well. When in Rome . . . she said to herself, searching for her pack of cigarettes.

"Don't you have an ashtray?"

"I don't smoke."

"I'm not surprised. Pass me a glass, I'll put my ash in the bottle."

Instead of getting up, Ingrid tore a page out of a magazine and carefully fashioned a little boat out of it. She put it in front of Lola, indicating that it was now an ashtray.

"On the morning of Vanessa's death, Maxime was here. It was his first massage. He stayed about an hour."

"Did he have a bag?"

"Yes, his sports bag. Maxime had just left the gym. Why do you ask?"

"No reason. Go on."

"That bearded cop who questioned me thinks Maxime could have killed Vanessa before or after the massage session."

"The bearded cop is called Grousset. He may be a bit dim, but not to the point where he would share his theories with a witness."

"He didn't tell me what he was thinking. It's what I deduced. Then there's the question of the keys."

"The spare set to the girls' apartment. Which is kept in a drawer behind the counter with all the other restaurant keys. That's not good when it's a case of a murder with no break-in."

"Oh, you know about that?"

"Of course. Don't forget, I'm a regular at *Belles* and a friend of Maxime."

"And there's something else."

"Keep going."

"Maxime was married to a Japanese woman. She died about twelve years ago. In their studio-apartment on Rue des Deux-Gares. Murdered. The killer was never found."

"*Bougre de coquinasse!*"

"What on earth . . . ?"

"Don't worry, it's Provençal. My grandfather was from Gardanne. It comes out whenever I get emotional. But how did you find all this out? I've known Maxime much longer than you have, and—"

"I just asked questions."

"You're not backward in coming forward, are you?"

"It's a question of mentality. In France you're too fond of secrets. But I confess I did insist a bit. You know, when you massage people, little by little you become very close. Well, anyway, I asked him a few questions, he replied quite frankly, I excused myself by saying that in the States, when strangers meet on a bus, it's quite common for them to exchange confidences, and . . ."

At that precise moment the two women heard voices and the sound of smashing glass.

"Is that part of the music?" Lola asked, standing her beer on a pile of magazines.

"No."

They rushed outside. Two figures were running towards Faubourg Saint-Martin. The man on the cardboard boxes was wide awake: he was cursing the two jokers and trying to chase after them, but his arms were moving noticeably quicker than his legs. The antique-shop window had taken a hit. The crack spread in a spider's web that seemed to have trapped the little ballerina figurine inside. Lola saw Ingrid take off after the fleeing men. Still holding her Mexican beer, she was shouting, "MOTHERFUCKERS! I'LL KILL YOU!" Lola ran after her, but at a much slower pace. Her lungs wheezed. Her knees as well. She saw the quicker of the two hooligans jump on a scooter and ride off. Diesel had seized the other one by the neck and was bashing his shoulders methodically with the beer bottle. First to the right, then the left; right, left, right, left. The tearaway on the scooter turned to charge Diesel, who would not let go of her prey. Lola yelled, "POLICE! NOBODY MOVE!" and the scooter spun around and disappeared at the end of the passage. Lola could not read its number plate.

His accomplice was lying flat like a gun-dog, moaning: "Stop hitting me! I surrender! Stop hitting me!"

"O.K., stop massacring him and tie him up with this!" Lola told her, handing Diesel her raincoat belt.

"I know where to hit," Ingrid said, panting. "It hurts but it doesn't break anything."

"That's not the impression one gets," Lola replied, then called Barthélemy on her mobile.

This was the second time she had woken him in the space of an hour, and yet the young lieutenant seemed just as happy to hear from her.

"You have to come and pick up a client as quickly as you can. Then you have to grill him to find his accomplice, who escaped on a scooter."

"Goodness, for a retiree you certainly keep busy, boss!"

"That's right, Barthélemy. Every night I don a black mask and body-stocking and roam the streets looking for a juicy crime I can get my teeth into. It's keeps the old ticker going."

"There's been a development, boss."

"O.K., let's hear it."

"Vanessa Ringer kept her toys and kids' books on a shelf. I pointed out to Grousset that one of the dolls was too new to come from the victim's childhood. It's a Bratz. A brand that's made a fortune."

"Are you interested in dolls now, Barthélemy?"

"My daughter asked for one for Christmas. I've already bought it to avoid the crush in the shops. And boss, you ought to know that dolls aren't what they used to be. They're cool and sexy. Nowadays they look like the singers out of 'Star Academy' or the girls in 'Big Brother'. Make-up, jewellery, bare belly-buttons, slinky dresses and detachable feet."

"Did I hear you say 'detachable'?"

"Yes, you did. The shop assistant told me you don't change the shoes anymore. You change the feet with the shoes on them. And little girls don't even think they look like artificial limbs. Strange times we're living in, eh, boss?"

"What does the Bratz doll look like? Don't tell me she's blonde?"

"Not only is she extremely blonde, but she's wearing a white uniform with a cross and a heart drawn on it in red felt pen. I think that's a pretty good image of a social worker, don't you?"

Barthélemy came in person to pick up the trouble-maker. He cuffed him and gave the boss her belt back. He stayed a while in the midst of the group formed by Lola, Ingrid, and the victim, a long-haired tramp with a beard and nose hair, his forehead swathed in bandages thanks to the close attentions of the intrepid masseuse. Barthélemy had seen her at the station squaring up to the Gnome. A memory to savour.

The tramp was busy eating a ham and cheese sandwich – also provided by Diesel. He was complaining because there was only American soda to drink. The hooligan, who looked like a man who had been battered with a Mexican beer bottle, was wondering why he was being forced to camp out with two ogresses and a hobo instead of going to a nice warm cell. A retard like him could hardly be expected to understand. He couldn't imagine what it meant to redis-cover the great Madame Jost, who now turned to address the tramp.

"What's your name?"

"Antonio, but my friends call me Tonio. Tonight, and forever, you've won the right to call me Tonio, my Good Samaritan."

Barthélemy told himself that certain theories are threadbare. You decided almost all Antoines looked angelic, and this was what you got.

"When you arrived, sweetheart, those bastards had just woken me up. They smashed the window. An' they wanted to rearrange my mug, throw my boxes away, but I've been in the Legion. Those jokers don't scare me."

"We've arrested one of them."

"I can see that, and he looks in a right mess, the stupid idiot, but what about the other guy? This one's a coward. He came first on his own to do the graffiti. I gave him a rollicking because that spray paint stinks. He wanted revenge, so he returned with his pal on that put-put-putting machine of his."

"Barthélemy will sort it all out. Won't you, Barthélemy? And he'll ask the vigilante graffiti artist to explain his theory about FEAR IN THE CITY, just in case he has any first-hand information about the Vanessa Ringer case."

"No problemo, boss."

After that, they all had to go their own way. Lola followed Ingrid home, leaving everything up in the air. Did she want to lead the investigation under the nose of the Garden Gnome? Had she considered the consequences of a possible return to the 10th arrondissement? Were her thoughts keeping her awake at night, leading her to spend her time with a street-fighting masseuse? Unable to find a response to the mysteries of the world, which seemed as dense as the fog that did not seem to bother the tramp (who had already rebuilt his cardboard bed), Barthélemy told himself he might find the answer to at least one question that night.

"Tell me, Tonio, when you were little you didn't have blond curls did you, like an angel?"

"You bet your life I did, my friend. Whenever they tried to give me a parting, for first communion and so on, it never stayed. Because of all the curls."

"Please, sir, if it's not too much trouble, I'd like to be taken to the police station," the graffiti artist said.

At that moment, Maxime was walking back from the police station on Rue Louis-Blanc along Quai Valmy, which was almost deserted at that time of night. He had gone to take Khadidja a sweater. As he walked along the Canal Saint-Martin, inhaling the odour of drizzle mixed with stagnant water, his feet scuffing through the dead chestnut tree leaves, he momentarily forgot the two girls' problems and thought of Rinko. She had made dozens of sketches of this neighbourhood, looking for inspiration for a manga that would begin peacefully in Paris and end badly in Tokyo. Rinko only liked violent, desperate stories, adventures from which none of her heroes emerged unscathed, even if they had fought like lions; cruel stories that left you feeling wretched. She would have been really intrigued by Vanessa's death. For many reasons.

Yet Rinko had been a fragile woman. A wife who found it increasingly hard to cope with the knowledge that her husband was far away at one of the four corners of the planet, risking his life for a photograph. That was why she kept postponing the moment to have a child. They had married so young. It had been pure passion, for a while.

When he reached *Belles*, Maxime went upstairs to his apartment and then headed straight for his study. He hadn't looked at his photographs for at least two years, ever since meeting Khadidja. They were filed in chronological order. He quickly found his series on Romanian children in the orphanages or on the streets. Black-and-white prints. The first were dated 22 December, 1989, the day of the fall of Nicolas Ceausescu's regime. He went through them, taking his time. Each image brought back emotions, sounds, smells. The faces of child convicts, heads shaven to keep away lice, skinny bodies that no-one had ever given anything to, least of all love. These grubby kids dressed in rags who slept on pavements, in train stations, or anywhere they could, eating out of dustbins, sniffing glue. There was the child who continually beat his head against the wall, another who had almost reverted to being a wild animal, and had bitten a nurse so hard he had drawn blood.

Christmas 1989: Maxime would remember it for the rest of his life. He was supposed to work no more than a week and be back for New Year. He stayed a month, held in thrall by those kids, by their suffering. He no longer knew whether it was compassion or excitement, or both. He no longer wanted to know. He was completely immersed in what he was doing. He had never been so caught up in his work. For once he wanted to slow down, to get to grips with his subject and bear witness. Not simply to take photos but to show them. Rinko called every day. He tried to explain, but she didn't understand. She wanted him to come home. She said she was afraid at night without him. She wanted his body alongside hers, his reassuring body. He told her: "I'm not your teddy bear." That was what he really thought. He had found her calls ridiculous.

Then he slowly came to his senses, recovered his sense of time, remembered his responsibilities to the agency. His boss, Lionel Sadoyan, had urged him to "disconnect". He had complained, but had come back. Paris in January 1990. He arrived on the last plane at night, without telling anyone. In the taxi on the way home, he was not even thinking of Rinko. Everything seemed to him incredibly clean, organised, smooth. Rich.

Maxime Duchamp closed the portfolio, put it away. He stretched out fully dressed on his bed with the light off. He listened to the rain. He usually liked its music, but tonight everything was different. He could feel the effects of Ingrid Diesel's strong hands. She had worked on his body and his memory. He could still hear her asking him "Have you never been married?"

For many years, Maxime had told himself that if he had come back from Bucharest on the agreed date, Rinko would still be alive. After the cremation, he had walked around in a mental coma for quite a while. The ever-efficient Sadoyan had taken care of everything. The photos of the Romanian children had reached newsrooms all over the world. The ever-efficient Sadoyan was discreet. He had called after a decent length of time. And Maxime had picked up his cameras again and set off to war.

It had taken him several months to realise that his heart was growing a little colder with each passing day. Until 28 February, 1991.

8

They had walked as far as Rue des Récollets. The sky was an incredible blue. Ingrid found the Paris climate far more droll than its inhabitants. Four days of rain, then all of a sudden, an Indian summer. Well into November. But the locals did not seem to find that odd; in fact, the locals seemed blasé about everything. At the shelter, Ingrid was sitting next to Lola in the office of Vanessa Ringer's boss, whom she found neither friendly nor co-operative. Guillaume Fogel seemed unable to tear himself away from his computer. Incomprehensible columns speeding down his screen seemed to interest him more than his visitors did. The figures gave him an excuse to avoid answering questions from a woman who after all was nothing more than a retired police officer. Lola had been open about that, which Ingrid thought a mistake. And yet when she put her mind to it, Lola knew how to be convincing. The previous evening she had laid her cards on the table: "Ingrid, I have two rules. First, I don't work for free. Second, I don't work alone. So you can pay me in kind. I want a weekly massage, but above all, I want you to lend me a hand." Ingrid, who had other sources of income besides her massages and so had some free time, had found the "boss's" authoritative tone impossible to resist.

"Did you notice anything strange when Vanessa worked for you? Did she have any problems here?" Lola was asking the shelter director.

"None at all. It's as I told Commissaire Grousset. Vanessa got on with everyone. And she was good with the kids, she knew how to treat them."

"Could you be more precise?"

"She was gentle, but she won their respect. I think Vanessa had found her vocation with us, and believe me, this is no picnic."

"Never any arguments with her colleagues or the kids?"

"Not that I know of."

"I'm sure you need training to work here. And Vanessa didn't have any."

"In theory you do, but for me what really counts is motivation; believe me, commissaire, if everyone thought that way in this country, there'd be fewer young people out of work."

"Is it mostly young Romanians you take in here?"

"Not entirely, but mostly, yes. In fact I've had to teach myself Romanian. Fortunately I spent some time with an N.G.O. in Bucharest. That helps."

"Have you never had trouble with the Albanians who run these kids?"

"No, those bastards know how to keep a low profile. When the police started to react over smashed parking meters, they were quick to recycle the kids into pickpocketing and prostitution."

"How old are the eldest?"

"I'd say around fourteen, but it's hard to tell because none of them has identity papers."

"Did Vanessa have anything to do with them outside work?"

"Definitely not. I advise my team to keep a strict separation between their work and private lives. Otherwise, they couldn't cope."

"Did Vanessa follow your advice?"

"I assume so, given how sensible she always was. Her attitude was of someone always keen to learn and help. Vanessa was a brave little soldier."

"Can you give me an example?"

"I remember a very troubled boy. Vanessa was extremely patient with him. She spoke no Romanian. He must only have known a few words of French. But they got on well together . . . she brought him round."

"Can we see the boy?"

"That reminds me, I haven't seen him for two days."

Lola gave a slight sigh. She waited for Fogel to offer more details, but none were forthcoming.

"Could his disappearance have anything to do with Vanessa's death?" she asked, the tension mounting in her voice.

"The children know nothing about that. The social workers have been told not to say anything for now."

"Don't forget that Vanessa's face has been on the front page of several newspapers."

"Ah."

"You didn't think of that."

"No, but you know – we're rather busy here."

"What's the boy's name?"

"Look, I'm really not sure I can—"

"I can understand your reticence, Monsieur Fogel. Call the 10th arrondissement station and ask to speak to Lieutenant Barthélemy. That should set your mind at rest. And you'll be really helping us."

"Helping who, exactly?"

"Vanessa's family, her friends, yourself when you look in the mirror in the morning."

"Really, madame!"

"Don't take it as an insult, Monsieur Fogel. Jean-Pascal Grousset is a very mediocre officer. He worked under me long enough for me to see that. If nobody else dips their oar in, the murderer will still be free when the statute of limitations comes into effect."

Fogel looked up from his columns. That was something gained at least. He seemed to be struggling with his conscience, but finally said, "He's called Constantin. He's about twelve years old. Blond. Wears a black hoodie. He was a member of a gang who robbed from parking meters, then he took refuge in our shelter because they wanted him to work as a prostitute. But we don't know his real name, his real age, or the name of the people he was stealing for."

"Any idea where we might find him?"

"Vanessa told me one day that Constantin was dazzled by the Champs-Elysées. He lived in poverty but was always hanging around there. The bright lights of the shop windows, tourists from all over the world, money on display everywhere, all that . . ."

"I'm sure it makes a change from Bucharest."

★

Ingrid's attire consisted of a well-worn, fur-lined leather jacket and a Russian fur cap that made her look like a young airman from the now defunct Soviet armed forces. Not wishing to draw attention to them, Lola almost asked her to leave it in the car before they went into the 8th arrondissement station, where she had kept contact with Captain Huguette Marchal. Better still, she was unaware that Lola had taken early retirement. On the telephone, Marchal had mentioned that three kids had been arrested for pickpocketing on the Champs-Elysées that afternoon.

The youngest was wearing a thin black cotton polo shirt. The two others wore only T-shirts, and their trainers were full of holes. Lola thought of the heavy rain that had started to teem down again over Paris in the past few minutes. The gentle October weather was but a memory; autumn was beginning to bite, and the kids would soon be feeling the cold.

She went over to the little blond boy. Questioned him. He refused to tell her his name and pretended not to understand French. He had a mischievous smile, with eyes to match. He kept telling incomprehensible jokes to his pals, who guffawed as they chewed their gum. They think I'm a hoot, Lola reflected. How come children always find it so simple to laugh? Even when their families have sold them to modern-day ogres, even when they're out on the streets on a damp, cold night in nothing more than T-shirts? Then she thought of Toussaint, who would have taken the plight of these children of the night as a personal affront. He had the gift of making himself loved by almost everyone who came near him. A truly remarkable phenomenon. Probably because he never judged anyone. Lola had to admit that since she had started this investigation with the unlikely Ms Diesel, the images of him did not come back to haunt her so often. The black shell of remorse was beginning to crack, allowing some good memories to surface.

"I recognise the eldest," Marchal said. "We've already arrested him several times. And I know he speaks French."

"Do you know Constantin?" Lola asked him, but he pretended it was all Chinese to him, opening his eyes wide and raising his hands as if to say: *I know nothing, lady, absolutely nothing.*

9

Ingrid was at the wheel of the Twingo. Lola no longer liked driving at night, and her new teammate was bound to be good at it. She was clever with her hands. Whether she was massaging or dishing it out to layabouts. It reminded Lola of her night patrols with Toussaint. He always took the wheel and drove quickly and smoothly, often with background music from Senegal, where his father was born. Strangely enough, that sunny music went well with a starry sky. Or at least with the idea you had of one: stars were an increasingly rare sight in the capital's sky.

For an American, Ingrid knew Paris well. She drove towards Porte Dauphine without hesitation. Obviously, she drove with her window down, to make it plain that smoking was an outmoded habit practised only by a handful of Neanderthals . . . But Lola had never felt the cold.

It was almost eleven o'clock. They passed a few vehicles on Place Charles-de-Gaulle, then Ingrid headed down Avenue Foch. Wide as could be, greenery galore, beautiful buildings. Then at the far end of one of the finest avenues in the world, a black hole, a vortex that swallowed kids whole, thought Lola, recalling her own son and two granddaughters, who she reckoned had turned out rather well.

Slowing down, Ingrid slipped in among the cruising cars. Lola thought she would have made a decent officer. And in the present situation, her androgynous appearance was a definite plus. The jacket and the Russian hat had stayed on the back seat. But the sailor's jersey looked good. Beneath the airman, the seaman.

"Drive round slowly so I can see if I recognise anyone."

After circling for a while, they parked with the engine still running, but the locals kept their distance. Of course they did, what was Lola thinking? That the two of them looked like potential clients? Beyond the stink of Lola's disgusting cigarettes, there was the damp smell of the Bois de Boulogne – too damp for Ingrid's liking; then there were the figures on the edge of the pavement, on the edge of the world. Which of these ghostly shadows could point them in the right direction?

Ingrid thought she spotted a teenager. He smiled at them, but no, he was a fully grown man, his teenage years a long way behind him. The expression in his eyes makes him seem ten thousand years old, thought Ingrid. Then it was Lola's turn to wind her window down and ask someone if he knew Constantin. He didn't, but offered them his services. Ingrid bit her tongue to stop herself from insulting him, and decided to take the car round again, leaving his smile suspended in mid-air. There were many similar others, hanging in the moist air, in the smell from the woods. Ingrid instantly thought of leeches.

"Him, over there!" Lola said, almost joyfully.

Ingrid turned towards the kerb, wondering how many years it had taken her colleague to feel at ease in an environment such as this. The youngster can't have been more than twenty-five. He was wearing a suit, a dazzling white shirt that was almost a beacon in the darkness. His blond hair was artfully tousled, his thin face good-looking. He did not have the look of a cheap trick. He was something different. He was trying to look like David Bowie, and had almost succeeded.

"He's called Richard," Lola said. "He was one of my informers. A real viper's tongue, but always with a touch of class."

"Yes, I can see he's not bad-looking. So why does he do it? Drugs?"

"Exactly. He's got plenty of lovers, but his faithful wife is dope."

To Ingrid, his suit was no different from the ones worn by men working in the business towers at La Défense. He looked nothing like his colleagues here, who all went for jeans or leather.

"Good to see you again, Richard. I really am."

"Commissaire Jost, it's been an age! And you're still going round in that rotten old jalopy. The pay isn't up to much in your line of business, is it? After all these years, the skinflints."

"That's as may be, Richard, but the replies to my questions are free, so I'm going to take full advantage."

"That's my lot in life anyway . . . go on, ask away. What can I do for you?"

"Help me find a Romanian boy. Constantin. About twelve years old. Very blond, a black hoodie."

"Wow, that's some ask. And I've no answers in stock."

"I never thought I'd strike lucky the first time. I simply wanted you to point me in the right direction so I won't be here all night. I know how much you want to be loved."

"No, you don't. Anyway, I don't know any Constantins. Those young kids are usually controlled by other kids of around fifteen or sixteen from the same country. They sell their arses too. You need to find someone like that."

"If you think you're teaching me something, it's a bit thin."

"Your colleague hasn't said a word. Is she shy? She's got the same hairstyle as Jean-Paul Gaultier. And the same jumper. It's cool."

"Of course, it is Jean-Paul Gaultier."

"I thought it must be."

"O.K., Richard, are you going to enlighten us? Or do Gaultier and I have to take you in? Seeing you're as beautiful as a fallen angel, you'll miss a good few tricks. And the nights are soon going to be longer and longer and colder and colder. Think quickly."

"Oh, you're such a flatterer! You know how to persuade a guy. Well sweetheart, go down this side path and back up towards L'Étoile. Not the North Star, the one we have here in Paris. Somehow I've never been able to call it Place Charles-de-Gaulle."

"Richard, you're straying off the point."

"You'll see a parked Mercedes with a Diplomatic Corps number plate. Inside there's a kid with bad hair busy looking after the diplomat. Kid's name is Ilie. It sounds like a bird's name, but he's a guy. Get a move on, because even if the nights are long, it doesn't take long to suck someone . . ."

The fallen angel's final words were lost as Ingrid sped off to the centre of the square.

"Is your little sailor's jumper on fire, or what?" Lola said.

"I don't like that kind of talk, that kind of guy, or that kind of place . . ."

"That's a shame. Because despite appearances, the night is just beginning."

Ingrid pulled up ahead of the side path. They left the car and walked towards the Arc de Triomphe, shining beyond the mass of dark trees. The Mercedes was a couple of metres further on. They waited for the door to open and a small blond boy to appear.

"Take my arm, so we'll look like a grandmother and her grand-daughter out for a constitutional."

"Throw away your cigarette, you don't look like a respectable grandmother."

"O.K. then."

"How about me, do I look normal?"

"If you don't crack him over the head with a Mexican beer bottle, you'll do. Watch out, we're going to nick him . . ."

"What?"

"Cop speak. We'll nab him, pull him. Come on, Ingrid, get up to speed. WE'LL NICK HIM! LET'S GO!"

Lola was a good head taller than the boy, and so could easily push him up against the side of a van. To play her part, Ingrid shouted: "Police! Don't move!" The youngster muttered a few words, rolling the *r*s. His eyes rolled as much as his *r*s; he was looking for his protectors. The older boys. Richard might have a viper's tongue, but he knew what he was talking about.

"We know who you are. Your name is Ilie."

"I haven't done nothing!"

"Who says you have? Don't worry, everything's fine."

Ingrid thought he must be around seventeen. He had acne, and the beginnings of a moustache.

"Listen carefully, Ilie," Lola went on. "We don't mean you any harm. If you answer my questions, we'll vanish. Like ninja warriors in the night. Now you see us, now you don't. O.K.? Understand what I'm saying?"

Ilie nodded. Lola told him she was going to let go of him, and that he had to stay calm. He straightened his jacket and his hair. He had a stray lock that dangled down over his face, but the back of his skull was shaven.

"We're looking for little Constantin. The last we heard, he was somewhere around Faubourg-Saint-Denis. And don't tell me you don't know him. I know you do. Someone told me so."

"What you want with him?"

"Answer my question, Ilie. Do you know where Constantin is?"

"Constantin disappear. I know nothing. Nothing at all. He not like work here. He vanish. I swear to police. Is true."

"If he's vanished, your bosses must be looking for him. And they must have started somewhere. Tell us where."

"I swear to police I know nothing."

"O.K., you're coming with us," Ingrid said, playing the tough cop.

"I know nothing, I swear, I swear."

"Is there anyone who knows him?" Lola insisted. "Anyone who would know where he is?"

"Perhaps cook."

"What cook?"

"Not know his name. Know restaurant. Cook gave eat sometime. That why Constantin go there. In Passage Brady."

"If you're telling me lies I'll be back tomorrow and have you deported. And perhaps that would be the best thing for you."

"I swear, I swear. I tell everything. The cook, is true."

"O.K., Ilie, you can go. If that's what you really want."

It was what he wanted. Ingrid and Lola watched him head off towards Porte Dauphine.

"Do you get the impression we're back where we started, Lola?"

"No, Ingrid; as I told you, the night's just beginning."

"By the way, d'you know who we remind me of?"

"Jean-Paul Gaultier and Mae West?"

"No, the *Belles* . . ."

"Night and Day?"

"Exactly."

10

Passage Brady was plunged in darkness. But the murk was pierced by a gleam of light from the restaurant. Lola saw it as a symbol, but was soon disappointed. As well as the light, there were shouts: a couple was busy arguing. Or more exactly, a woman was hurling her wrath at a man who was trying to keep his self-control. The voice was Khadidja's. Ingrid and Lola shot each other a quick glance, and took up position as close as possible to the restaurant.

"All you're worried about is having missed a casting because you were arrested. That's what you're really upset about, isn't it?"

"SO YOU SAY!"

"I'm simply stating a fact."

"DO YOU WANT ME TO TELL YOU WHAT THE FUCK THIS IS REALLY ABOUT?"

"Yes, but without the screaming and swearing."

"What this is really about sticks in my craw. You told me your wife was dead alright. The only thing you carefully avoided telling me is HOW SHE DIED!"

"Tone it down a bit, will you? If you'd been interested for more than two seconds, I'd have told you."

"You couldn't give a fuck about how stupid I looked in front of that slimy cop."

"We're back with you again. How sad."

"I'm not talking about me. I'm talking about us, Maxime. I was disowned by my parents and brother because of you."

"Oh, you've got a brother, have you? First I heard of him."

"That's not the point. My brother is bad news, but when he says I'm shacked up with a guy who's far too old and will never marry me, he's not far wrong."

"What's marriage got to do with it?"

"I don't give a fuck about marriage, that's not the problem. I can take you not making any promises. It's your little secrets I can't bear. It's also thanks to the slimy cop that I learned you go and get massaged by that Yank who looks like a drag queen."

"That's no secret."

"It isn't?"

"Ingrid Diesel is just a friend, and she's a wonderful masseuse. It relieves stress. You should try it."

"Now you're making fun of me."

"Me, me, me. That's the only word you know, Khadidja."

"You really don't get it, do you, Maxime? I've had it up to here with your bullshit. I'm out of here."

"You're a free woman."

"That's so easy, isn't it? And it suits you fine."

"What do you mean by that?"

"I've nothing more to say to you. Bye."

Ingrid and Lola crouched low behind the privet bushes on the terrace – especially Ingrid. Khadidja went off like a bomb, the high heels of her ankle boots exploding across the pavement.

"A forceful personality," Lola whispered.

"I call it bad-tempered."

"Favouritism."

"What?"

"Your weakness for Maxime. I'm not that wet behind my ears, you know."

"Unlike your glasses. They're covered in raindrops. They need a good wipe."

"You're changing the subject, Ingrid. Leave it where it is, it's a perfectly good one, and it doesn't mean you any harm."

"I'm telling you, your glasses are wet. Are you going to wipe them or not?"

"Yes, yes, I'll wipe them."

"So what do we do now? Do we go in or not?"

"We go in."

"Good. Let's move."

They pushed the door open. Maxime was behind the bar, and had just got out the bottle for special occasions. And for great disasters, like the one written across his face. The storm abated a little in the breeze that blew in with the two newcomers. Lola went over to the bar, to the bottle. On the blue-edged label someone had written in their own handwriting: "ENGLESQUEVILLE 1946". She remembered it. Firewater that burnt your gullet and impregnated your flesh with the scent of glazed apples.

"We've arrived in time for the calvados. I'm sure Ingrid has never tasted anything like it."

Maxime put another two glasses on the copper counter. And filled them.

It felt really good in the restaurant. Lola left her raincoat on the back of a chair. Maxime raised his glass, "To women. With no hard feelings."

Lola clinked glasses too. As she did so, she cast a sideways glance at Ingrid. Her teammate was devouring Maxime's face with her eyes. And the morsel was hard to swallow. People think Yanks are big children, but that's wrong, thought Lola. This one is growing up fast. She wet her lips in the warm bronze liquid. Ingrid drank a mouthful and almost choked. Maxime smiled: it was good to see.

"Oh, my gosh!"

"Yes, it's a bit wild," Lola said. "You can't jump on it like a cowgirl on a mustang. You have to approach it gently, my girl."

They finished their calvados in cautious little sips, but as Maxime was about to serve them all another one, with the air of someone who has decided to make a night of it, Lola put her hand over Ingrid's glass.

"Not for her. Tonight she's driving my Twingo."

"What are you doing out in this foul weather?"

"Saving your hide, Maxime."

"What are you talking about, Lola?"

"Ingrid and I have formed a Protection Society. With one person to protect. You. There's no way I'm going to let Grousset pin Vanessa's murder on you."

"That's very kind of you, but I'm big enough to protect myself, especially as I've done nothing wrong."

"That argument won't stop the police mill grinding away. Grousset is the stubborn sort of fool. He doesn't let go. Especially if he has something to grind. The key to the girls' flat in the bar drawer, for example. Or – at the moment the crime was committed – your massage with the Yank. Sorry, Ingrid."

"You're welcome, dear."

"And then there's the hacked-off feet."

"With a kitchen cleaver. And a chopping board. The clinching detail," Ingrid added.

"Not forgetting Rinko's death," Lola said.

Maxime refilled his glass and gulped it down. After a long pause, he looked at both women, and asked, "Do you really want me to tell you about Rinko?"

Lola nodded calmly, whereas Ingrid seemed to be paralysed, was staring at Maxime as if all knowledge of the French language had suddenly gone out of her head. Picking up his glass in one hand and the bottle in the other, he walked towards the staircase leading to his apartment. Halfway there, he turned and signalled for to them to follow. Lola felt as if Maxime were a book, and she had just turned the first page.

11

"What's the matter, Chloé, can't you sleep? Hey, you're trembling!"

"Some guy phoned twice. He wanted to speak to you."

"What guy?"

"I don't know."

"Did he mention the money?"

"No. Perhaps we should get out of the apartment and ask Maxime if we can stay with him. I'm scared, Khadidja!"

"There's no point being scared. Besides, I've had a bust-up with Maxime. We're going to have to fend for ourselves."

"But we've got nowhere to go!"

Khadidja thought of Chloé's mother. Lucette had lived in the apartment until her car accident. A single mother and a chronic depressive, she had never been a steadying influence, drifting from job to dead-end job. Even so, she was a lot better than Vanessa's parents. A pair of diehard Catholics as blinkered as they come. When they learned that Vanessa was going out with Farid, they made her life impossible, and eventually threw her out. My parents are pretty much the same, Khadidja thought, irritably. "Religion, snare for the unaware".

"Tell me, Khadidja, who do you think this guy is?"

Khadidja stared at Chloé for a moment, then took her in her arms and held her tight. She stroked her hair and rocked her. She led her into the kitchen; and as she made a hot chocolate she explained the theory she had come up with, while Chloé drowned her fear in Bach's *Cello Suites*.

"I'm sure my brother's behind this. Whenever there's trouble, Farid isn't far away."

"But it wasn't Farid on the phone."

"It was one of those guys he always has around him. Farid may be a wolf, but he's not a lone wolf, believe me. And he has two men inside him: one is hellish, the other a charmer. He switches between the two. It was the same all through my childhood. My brother's a nutcase, even though he seems normal."

"Stop! You're not exactly reassuring me."

"There's something you need to know, Chloé."

"What?"

"I'm not afraid of Farid. We share the same blood, and I have the same strength in me. Besides, I was born before him. We fought inside our mother's belly, but he was the one who came out second. And that's how it will always be."

"I thought people were bound to love their twin."

"The worst of it is I do love him. That doesn't stop me seeing what he's like and being on my guard."

"What if it was him . . . ?"

"With Vanessa?"

"Yes. Would you go to the police?"

"I'd never hand my brother in to the police. Whatever happens."

One foot in Maxime's private world; Ingrid was thrilled. What she glimpsed delighted her. The only surprising thing was that there was not a single photograph on the walls. She would never have imagined that in an ex-photojournalist's apartment. As for Lola, she seemed oblivious to the décor. All she had eyes for was her objective: an answer to her questions. At the same time, her anxiety was almost palpable.

Maxime pulled a large portfolio out of a cupboard. He opened it on the table: it contained the original drawings for a graphic novel. Black ink drawings, with flowing, powerful lines. Adolescents in a mega-city where tradition and modernity were jumbled together. Ingrid recognised Tokyo, its express highways, its trains, its electric pylons weaving their web of cables above narrow alleyways, its mushrooming tower blocks, ugly but fascinating, its urban villages, its inhabitants going about their daily lives, cyclists on the pavements, street-sellers offering sweet potatoes. And crowds everywhere. In the train stations, the stores, at intersections. And solitude. It seemed Rinko Yamada-Duchamp had a real talent for depicting solitude.

"*Otaku* is Rinko's masterpiece," Maxime said. "She wasn't afraid of tackling uncomfortable issues."

"What does '*otaku*' mean?" Lola asked.

"It means 'he who seeks refuge at home'. An *otaku* is a young man who refuses to grow up. He shuts himself in, forgets the real world, and lives only to feed his obsession."

"What kind of obsession?"

"Making models, collecting watches, schoolgirls' knickers, porno videos, and so on."

"Do I detect a certain penchant for fetishism?"

"Exactly. And there's a whole market devoted to their idols. Photos, discs, dolls that look like young singers, actresses."

"We have that here too."

"In Japan it's more complex. The *otaku* may choose to reject the constraints of life in society, but Japanese society doesn't forget the *otaku*, it sells him what he wants. It's this cynical merchandising that Rinko's manga is attacking."

"What's the story?"

"That's difficult to sum up. It stretches over fifteen books. It starts with a schoolgirl in a bikini being photographed in a studio; her image will be used to create marketable figurines. She is to become the centrepiece of a collection. The collection of an *otaku* who is completely deranged."

Maxime shut the portfolio. Then he filled his glass. Ingrid realised he intended to get drunk. She would have liked to join him, but Lola wasn't in the mood. She was waiting for Maxime to add the finishing touches to his description. The ex-commissaire and the ex-photojournalist stared at each other for a moment without speaking. Lola's big round eyes showed tenderness but also determination. Maxime blinked first:

"You wanted to know who Rinko was. Now you know."

"All you've done is show us a portfolio . . ."

Maxime smiled again, but he looked distraught. If Lola hadn't been there, Ingrid would have taken him in her arms. She was almost trembling with the desire to do so.

"By following me here, Rinko made a great sacrifice. She drew her inspiration from the lives of her fellow countrymen and women. She went on drawing in Paris, but it wasn't the same. She was no longer at the heart of things. The story ended with her finding death in Paris. What's left is her work and, as I was telling Ingrid the other day, her ashes on the mantelpiece. And her collection of dolls, the likenesses of schoolgirls she used for *Otaku*. If Commissaire Grousset wants to find a link between my memories and Vanessa Ringer, let him look."

"How did Rinko die?"

"She was strangled."

Lola sat down, and Ingrid followed suit. She felt weak at the knees.

"I can tell you now, Maxime, that a second strangulation, even after twelve years, doesn't look good."

"Perhaps, but that's the reality. What do you want me to do about it?"

"To give me as much information as possible, so I can keep Grousset at bay. Like for example, how did you get on with Vanessa?"

"Wow, this is really turning into an interrogation, isn't it?"

"Make an effort, Maxime."

"She often came to eat with us."

"Us being?"

"Khadidja and Chloé. We always have our meals in the kitchen before the customers arrive. Vanessa would join us. I enjoyed seeing the three friends together, and I knew Vanessa wasn't made of money. Besides, I thought she looked a bit on the thin side; at least with us she could eat properly."

"Conclusion: you saw her often."

"Very often."

"That's not good either."

"You think so?"

"Yes, I think so."

"I can't see what's wrong with opening your door to people."

"We absolutely must do our damnedest to find a witness, a young Romanian boy. He disappeared following Vanessa's death."

"Constantin?"

"So you know him?"

"Vanessa brought him here. After that, he used to come and see me from time to time. He liked watching me work, and to eat something here and there."

"Do you have any idea where he might be?"

"No, because I never asked him questions. Constantin had been in Hell, a place I know only too well, and I had no wish to rub his nose back in that slime. I fed him, chatted to him. In fact it was more with gestures than words."

Ingrid and Lola walked towards the edge of the liquid curtain pouring down Rue du Faubourg-Saint-Denis. Unlike their investigation, the weather was constantly on the go. Lola raised her head to the rain bouncing off the glass canopy over Passage Brady.

"In a deluge like this, the kid must be sheltering somewhere."

"I hope so for his sake. But can you tell me why human beings live like that, especially young kids, Lola?"

"After the fall of Ceausescu, the world realised that thousands of children were rotting away in orphanages that looked dreadfully like concentration camps. Casualties of the fertility policy of a dictator who wanted to double his country's population to celebrate the third millennium. Contraception forbidden. Five compulsory children per family. The State promised to take care of all those the family abandoned for lack of money, or love, or whatever. A whole generation was sacrificed due to the megalomania of a sad despot."

"Is nothing being done about it?"

"Yes, there are charities trying to help. But they've got a lot of work on their hands. An enormous amount. Two-speed Europe, isn't it called?"

They both fell silent for a long while, fascinated by the sheets of rain sweeping over the street and managing even to wash Lola's car clean. Eventually the drumming on the glass canopy above them slackened to a gentle tapping sound. Now what do we do? wondered Ingrid. She was about to ask Lola the same question, but her partner got in before her.

"Maxime talks and keeps quiet at the same time. Did you notice?"

"What do you mean?"

"He doesn't want to tell us everything. That's crystal clear. Oh, what a nightmare!"

"Maxime doesn't want to think about his past."

"The problem is, Maxime's past really wants him to think about it."

12

Chloé Gardel was dreaming her body was a cello and that a gnome armed with a teaspoon was trying to stuff it full of food. He was trying to push the gruel in through the instrument's sound-holes. His other hand was clamped over her mouth.

She gulped for air and woke up. She could sense the presence of a man she could not see. She tried to scream.

"Don't make a sound."

In spite of her fear, she recognised the voice. Calm but icy. The voice on the phone.

The light flashed on, revealing a face. Shaved head, a devilish goatee, staring eyes. All of a sudden, she heard Khadidja, "Let go of her, you retard! What the fuck are you doing?"

The man took his hand away, and Khadidja appeared.

And Farid.

Chloé huddled against the wall. She had hoped he had vanished. *Whenever there's trouble, Farid isn't far away.* Khadidja was right.

"I'm stopping her rousing the neighbours. And you'd better drop that retard shit."

"All you had to do was ring the bell, not come through the wall like fucking Fantômas!"

"Excuse me, Farid, but your sister is incredibly rude," the man with the goatee said.

"O.K., everyone into the kitchen, we need to talk," Farid said wearily.

Chloé pulled a sweatshirt on over her pyjamas and followed them. She was trying to take deep breaths in order to collect her thoughts. No use: a thousand confused images were dancing around in her brain. She made a detour via the bathroom and took one of Doctor Léger's pills. She was surprised to find herself hoping he might arrive, in the middle of the night. He would manage to persuade Farid and his friend to leave. He had stood up to the bearded commissaire who wanted to haul her in even though she was having a panic attack, and won her some respite. Doctor Léger was not like these aggressive sorts who only knew about violence. All these guys made him sick.

"If madame would be so kind, there's a meeting in the kitchen."

"I'm just taking my medication."

It was Farid's friend. He must have been at least two metres tall. What a fright he had given her, the great brute. Her anxiety came flooding back: her hands had started to shake again. She hated it when they did that. She was worried her system might get stuck on "continuous vibration" – if it did, how was she going to play the cello?

"I hope you didn't try to call anyone."

"We only have one, and that's in the entrance."

"You can use mobiles anywhere . . ."

"I don't have the money for a mobile."

In the kitchen, Khadidja was tearing a strip off her brother, but he didn't seem to be listening. He had the vicious look of his bad days, and was staring down at his hands. Chloé remembered his silver rings. That night by the canal, they had shone. And then the blood, all that blood. Chloé stifled her desire to throw up, and forced herself to sit down opposite Farid; he did not even raise his eyes towards her. She blessed Doctor Léger; his pills started to take effect after only a few minutes. She felt better already.

Khadidja reminded Jean-Luc of Mistinguett. She looked a bit like one of those feisty Parisian dames who made your head spin with their constant chatter. Who don't hesitate to call you a retard, hands on hips. He didn't like hitting women, but he wouldn't need to be asked twice to slap that one. Chloé was different. She was a lost soul, living in her friend's shadow. But you couldn't trust those shy girls either, Jean-Luc told himself, the dumpy ones who think they're ugly, the short ones, the ones that don't wear make-up, the frumps. This one looked vaguely like Ellen MacArthur, with short brown hair, chubby cheeks, and a snub nose. Perhaps there was more to this Chloé than first appeared.

He tried to concentrate so that he could read her, but it was difficult with Khadidja going on and on. And yet Farid had only asked her one simple question: "Where's the money?" For the moment, he was the Angel perched high up on the cathedral, a magnificent gargoyle waiting for ordinary mortals down below to finish their idle chat before he took to the air. He was in the heights, in that dark silence of his, head drooping, eyelids half closed, hands at rest. Chloé kept stealing glances at him: she was obviously scared stiff, that was as plain as Ellen MacArthur's spinnaker in the centre of the T.V. screen. Chloé had understood who she was dealing with. Or Chloé knew. She knows something about Farid that I don't, Jean-Luc thought.

"You creep in like a burglar, you make us almost die of fright, and all you can come up with is: 'Where's the money?' I've got a question too, Farid: was it you who killed Vanessa?"

Farid turned towards her. Then he said, "No." Just that. Perfect.

"And I'm supposed to take your word for it!"

He did not even respond to that, just stared at her with his menacing eyes, oozing contempt. Jean-Luc recalled an argument between Farid and Noah about Khadidja. Farid was furious because his sister was sleeping with a non-Muslim, some guy a lot older than her who had no intention of slipping a ring on her finger. And on top of that, she wanted to be an actress or a singer. Funny how old-fashioned Farid could be, he thought.

"Our door wasn't forced. How do you explain that? You got in with a key just now, didn't you?"

"I don't owe you any explanations. I'll say it again: where's the money?"

"What money are you talking about?"

Farid sighed, then smiled almost regretfully. The last time Jean-Luc had seen him do that, it had ended badly for the person concerned.

"We pulled off a big heist. I decided to give my share to Vanessa."

"So it was you who did that hold-up on the Champs-Elysées?"

"That's not your problem. Vanessa refused my money. I insisted. She said she was going to give it to a charity for Romanian kids."

"Is that true?"

"Yes."

"And you left her the money?"

"As if you didn't know."

"I not only don't know, I can't even begin to understand why you wanted to give her that money."

"You're right, don't even try. Anyway, it's none of your business."

"Oh yes it is. Vanessa was my friend, and you're my brother. What I don't get is why you come here and question me about money when she's dead. I thought you were madly in love with her. Was that just an act?"

"I couldn't give a fuck about the money. What I want to know is if you killed her to take it."

"ARE YOU SICK OR WHAT?!"

"Hey! Not so loud!" Jean-Luc said.

"Answer me," Farid said icily.

"Go fuck yourself," Khadidja hissed.

Farid's slap lifted her out of her chair. She groaned as her head hit the floor. Farid kicked her in the backside. Then kicked her again. Jean-Luc was keeping an eye on Chloé, in case she took it into her head to either make a run for it or scream. But Chloé sat like a great lump on her chair; her only reaction was to blink back her tears.

Farid went on hitting his sister again and again.

All of a sudden, it was Chloé's voice that could be heard. A faint voice at first, drowned out by Farid calling his sister a whore and Khadidja moaning:

"It's not her, stop, it's not her! I beg you! STOP, FARID!"

Farid straightened up, and looked menacingly at Chloé. He took her by the shoulders and started to shake and shake her. There was no point, she was talking, talking like a gushing fountain. The dark angel had the knack of making them gush like that, just as he did with money.

"We were coming back from the *Belles*. I found Vanessa dead on her bed. Khadidja was in the bathroom. I went to tell her and she said we had to call the police at once. They searched everywhere. There was no money. Whoever did it must have taken it with him. And I think he stole Vanessa's diary too. But don't hit her anymore, please! Stop! Khadidja didn't do anything. She wouldn't have mutilated Vanessa. And she's never said anything to anyone, ever. Nor have I. So stop, I beg you."

"Mutilated! What are you talking about?"

"The murderer chopped Vanessa's feet off."

Farid turned to stone. Intrigued by his friend's face, for a brief moment Jean-Luc no longer heard the girls moaning and sobbing. He turned towards Chloé, who had gone as limp as a rag. It's true, Chloé knows something I don't. She's never said anything to anyone, ever. Khadidja, the same. *She's never said anything to anyone . . . nor have I . . . stole Vanessa's diary . . .*

"How far have the pigs got?" Farid asked.

"Nowhere," Chloé said. "They're investigating those who were close to her, and interviewing people all over the neighbourhood, but they've got nothing."

"Was there someone in Vanessa's life?"

"No."

"You'd better be sure."

"There was never anyone after you. I don't think Vanessa could stand men anymore. The only thing that interested her was her work."

"I'm beginning to wonder whether she wasn't right," Khadidja said in a faint voice.

She was a pain, but you had to admit she had guts. Jean-Luc thought this was a good time to butt in: "O.K., but who else besides a boyfriend could have got in so easily? He saw the money, and without thinking twice, decided to clear off with it. Vanessa tried to stop him, he strangled her, then made it look as if a maniac had done it. That's all there is to it."

"If the Feds find him, I'll kill him," Farid said.

"Fat chance of that," Khadidja retorted, straightening up. "Vanessa had scratched him, so he cut off her fingernails. Then he did the housework. He drowned the vacuum cleaner in the bath. So no D.N.A. He cut her feet off with a cleaver, on a chopping board, and used the bedcover to soak up the blood. So you can imagine, they're going to have their work cut out to find such a well-organised guy."

"If they don't find him, I'll take care of it," Farid muttered, as if his sister had not said a word.

Shit, it's more complicated than I expected, thought Jean-Luc.

When Farid had eventually recovered from his drunken stupor, Jean-Luc had moved cautiously. He had sent Noah in and then listened, his ear pressed to the door of the friends' room. Farid had told his "brother" everything.

He had entered the girls' apartment using his keys. He had sat on the bed watching Vanessa asleep. He stroked her hair, her face, until she woke up. As Jean-Luc listened to him, it occurred to him that the Angel must be an expert in bed. But Vanessa had treated him like a stranger. Farid had opened the bag, shown her the money: "It's for you . . . I can't live without you . . ." No reaction from Vanessa, a real ice cube. A girl who no longer gave a damn about anything. Then she started to say over and over: "Take your money, I don't want it." Farid had left the bag on a chair and cleared off to avoid saying things he might regret, to give her time to think it over. Vanessa's last words had been: "I'm going to give it all to a charity for abandoned Romanian children. When I was little, my favourite story was *The Little Match Girl.* I thought misery like that was only for the nineteenth century, but I was wrong." Farid had burst out crying in the street like an idiot, like an idiot on the metro. People were staring at him, but he couldn't give a shit. It was the first time he had cried since the days when his father used to thrash him with a belt as a kid. An interesting admission, that. A father who was a foreman in a factory that fashioned dark angels.

Step one: he knew what had happened in the bedroom between Vanessa and Farid. Not a lot. Step two: he had no idea how he was going to get him to go to sea with him to appreciate the bigger picture. For now, his friend was adrift on the waves of his inner storm. And it was blowing a gale, the hull was taking a battering. Farid wanted to get his hands on the bastard who had killed the love of his life. Fair enough. The problem was that this was bound to take time. Mutilation, manicure, housework, dousing the vacuum. All very complicated, but manageable. All you needed was patience and strength of character. Just like on the Route du Rhum.

13

Finally they left. Chloé found the words to comfort her friend. What an odd situation, she thought. Before, of the three of them, Khadidja had been the strong one. Now for the first time, it's my turn to console her. Khadidja was lying on her bed, and Chloé was rubbing her buttocks and thighs with arnica cream. Farid had been careful not to leave marks on his sister's face. Chloé guessed it was so as not to arouse police suspicion.

"First thing tomorrow, remind me to change the locks," Khadidja said. Her beautiful tresses were buried in the sheets. She was exhausted, but added: "I'm proud of you, you really had him fooled. You said exactly the right thing."

"I amazed myself. I'd never have believed I could lie to your brother like that."

Chloé wondered if her lies would be enough to keep Farid and his giant at bay. It all depended on what Khadidja decided about the money. She tucked her into bed; when she sensed her friend was falling asleep, she tiptoed out of the room and sat down at her computer.

She had never felt such a strong desire to talk to Peter Pan as she did now. A boy her age, born in Paris, who liked music, comics, the cinema. He lived in Tokyo, where his father had been posted a few years earlier. His mother stayed at home to look after him and his two brothers and sister. Of course, Peter Pan was an alias, but that was the rule on the net, it helped you feel freer. Chloé had a mental picture of him based on his modest description: *brown hair, blue eyes, average height.* Within a few weeks, he had become her confidant. She had dared tell him about her bulimia, the way she forced herself to be sick after eating so much she felt ill.

Following Vanessa's death, their exchanges had changed in tone. Peter had become even more sympathetic. He wanted to be a writer, and was interested in everything to do with the human soul.

That night, she wanted to tell him about Farid and the hulk's visit, and the story of the bag stuffed full of banknotes. Peter's friendship was easy and risk-free. Concealed behind her own alias, Chloé changed names and places. She was Magdalena (a nod towards Bach, her favourite composer). Khadidja had become Jasmine, her brother Farid was Karim. It was exciting to disguise reality. It made her feel closer to Peter, who wanted to transform life, to turn it into his creation. And it meant she felt less frightened.

Chloé opened her mailbox. There was a message from Peter Pan.

"Hi Magdalena! Here in Tokyo, the fans of the imperial family are grieving. Friday was when Prince Takamado was cremated, after he died of a heart attack. I went to the cinema and discovered Takeshi Kitano's latest film. No more gangster films. 'Dolls' is a violent love story that revolves around dolls, poor human puppets . . ."

Even while she was reading this, Chloé was thinking of her reply:

"Hello Peter, tonight I thought I was crossing to the other side of the screen and taking part in a real gangster film . . ."

"The boy's called Constantin. He's about twelve. He wears a black hoodie, and he's very blond."

Lola was questioning a streetwalker on Boulevard Ney. The girl was wearing silvery thigh-boots and a fluorescent pink coat displaying a decidedly unseasonable dress. She looked anywhere between twenty and thirty years old. She was at least the fiftieth streetwalker Lola had interrogated with Ingrid as they traversed the ring of boulevards named after field marshals on the outskirts of Paris. Lola had decided they ought to ask the girls pimped by the Albanians. But none of them could or would identify the little Romanian boy. The new girl Lola was talking to had a strong Parisian accent.

"I see so many people I no longer even notice what they look like."

"What's your name?"

"Everyone calls me Barbara. You wouldn't have a fag, would you?"

"Yes. Take the packet while you're at it. I'd better stop, I can feel the flu coming on."

"You ought to get a jab."

"Right . . . Constantin is hiding. He's scared. He only has a few words of French. He's just a kid. So Constantin isn't like the youngsters you see round here. But there's a strong possibility he's been taken on by the Albanians."

"I don't work for them."

"I don't suppose you do, but ten metres further on, all your colleagues have Slavic accents."

"And at least ten years less on the clock, I know. Believe me, I don't find that funny. But I still have no idea who you're talking about. Hey, it's true you don't look well. Vaccines work on the police as well, you know."

"I don't have the time right now."

"And you think I do? But listen, while I think of it . . . why don't you ask Java?"

"Who's that?"

"She goes round the boulevards with her boys in a van."

"Is she a colleague with wheels?"

"No, she drives a charity bus. The Helping Hand, it's called. They hand out medicine, give vaccinations. They're the ones who gave me the jab. And they have condoms, jelly, aspirins and coffee. The girls call her Java, that's coffee in their language, because her skin's a milky coffee colour. We talk sometimes. They're a nice enough lot, and for once they're not heavy with it."

"But I don't want to get vaccinated. I'm looking for Constantin."

"No, I'm not talking about vaccinations now. Java drives around the whole night in her van. She might have seen your Constantin."

"So where do we find this helping hand?"

"It's usually her who finds you. Cruise round the boulevards and you're bound to run into their white van. Or you could stay here. They haven't been by yet tonight."

"Do they come past every night?"

"No, I never said that."

"Yes, that would be too good to be true, Barbara. Far too good."

So Ingrid sent the car into orbit around the field marshals' boulevards. Lola had stopped smoking, and they drove along with the windows up. This was a significant improvement, but Lola did seem the worse for wear. It was four in the morning; the fog and rain were bringing out her flu. She might look as tough as old boots, but Lola Jost was the same as everyone else. Ingrid wondered if she had a temperature.

"Don't you think we should go home, Lola? We can come back again tomorrow."

"*I have seen nights more beautiful than days, which led me to forget the sweetness of Dawn, the glare of noon.*" *

"What?"

"Don't bother. I used to be a French teacher. Some people collect schoolgirls' knickers, I collect quotes."

"Do you know many?"

"Loads."

"Why did you join the police?"

"For the same reason I do puzzles. I'll explain one day when we get to know each other better."

"Have you ever been married?"

"Yes, to an Englishman."

"Oh yeah? You speak my language then?"

"Not as well as you do mine, but I understand it perfectly."

"What happened to your English hubby?"

"We were divorced a long time ago."

"Why?"

"Hey, Ingrid, you're in a Twingo in Paris, not a bus in Oklahoma City."

* Pierre Moreau de Maupertuis, *Abrégé du système du monde.*

14

Lola held out her hand to Guillaume Fogel, who responded unenthusiastically, but climbed into the car. She repeated what she had told him on the phone: she had found Constantin in the Helping Hand van. She thanked him in advance for agreeing to act as interpreter. The charity offered decent coffee and sympathetic listeners, but none of them spoke a word of Romanian.

Now they were out on the Périphérique, Lola reflected that she had made every effort to be agreeable. She had gone to Fogel's home in Rue de la Grange-aux-Belles to fetch him. She had stopped off at a chemist's on the way. With the flu under control, she had tried to keep the conversation going as she sped along; the flow of traffic kept increasing almost imperceptibly. But ever since they had set off, Fogel had deigned to give her only curt replies.

She felt tempted to stop pussyfooting around and start asking the hard questions. What exactly was your relationship with Vanessa Ringer? Where were you on Sunday, 17 November between nine and eleven in the morning? But it was better to keep on the shelter director's good side.

Lola left the Périphérique at Porte de la Villette. The dark blue of the buildings in the Cité des Sciences stood out against the sky's pink and grey backdrop. It was quite beautiful, but sad too. Then everything became sadder and less beautiful as they approached the Canal de l'Ourcq. The only pleasant sight to be seen was Ingrid. Left behind to keep an eye on things, she was walking up and down the dreary boulevard, her blonde hair gleaming in the morning light.

"Is the kid alright?" Lola asked her.

"He's eating with Java."

"Has he talked to you?"

"I left him alone while I waited for you to arrive. But it's cool. He's not afraid of me. I gave him my Russian hat."

Constantin was sitting at a table with a woman and two men. Under the strip light in the van, his hair looked almost white. Lola went forward cautiously, only too aware of her size in the cramped space. A hot chocolate had painted a brown moustache on Constantin's face. When he caught sight of Lola, he shrank back, put down his bowl, and lowered his head. He gave a hoarse bark, like a little dog. Then he saw Fogel and realised his escapade was over. He almost looked relieved. Lola in her turn was relieved at this, that he was willing to return to the fold. The only one they could offer him. She pondered over what she was going to say, lost for words for once. What exactly could she say? She thought of Toussaint, of her granddaughters, of her own son, of Constantin's mother, who had abandoned her child or left him in the hands of the mafia, of how afraid she was of losing her friend Maxime, a fear that was mounting because exhaustion can push our fears right up into our throats. *Ah coquin de diou!* how exhausted she was.

"Can I talk to you?"

Lola found herself facing a girl who could not have been more than a metre and a half tall. Her round, caramel-coloured face was sprinkled with freckles, and behind her glasses her eyes were an unusual deliquescent green. Entranced, Lola stared at her for a moment. She had an air of Toussaint Kidjo about her. Either that or the night's fatigue is playing with my mind and making me see things. But no, no. Toussaint, Toussaint, you're softly coming back to me. You have a strange way of choosing your moment, my lad. But that's fine, I'll always be here for you.

"He needs to see a doctor," the young woman said firmly. "I think Constantin has a throat infection. And he probably hasn't eaten in ages. Plus, he's scared. There are too many people in here."

"I completely agree with you, mademoiselle. So everyone is going to get out of the van, including me, and Guillaume Fogel will be the one who talks to Constantin. My colleague Ingrid will just listen. We'll do everything softly, softly. Is that O.K. with you?"

When Ingrid emerged from the van, Lola was waiting in her car under an insolently beautiful sky. A great expanse of intense blue, with small, freshly washed clouds drifting across it. A sky that heralded winter, shimmering with cold light. In this luminous glacier-like glow, the violet bodywork of the Twingo seemed to come alive. Lola lowered her window, and Ingrid came to a halt outside the car.

"He ran away because he liked Vanessa. When she died, Constantin felt completely lost. But he's sure Vanessa never had anything to do with the mafia."

"I have to say that's not good news."

"Why?"

"Vanessa mutilated by Albanian mafiosi with a justified reputation for extreme violence would have been plausible. Now though we can be certain: we're dealing with a madman. Anyway, what else, Ingrid?"

"Fogel's stayed inside. He's going to try to convince Constantin to go back to the shelter with him. The kid has agreed to see a doctor."

"Don't tell me that's all, Ingrid!"

"No, wait! Vanessa and Constantin used to talk about things."

"I thought she couldn't speak Romanian."

"She always found another kid to translate. It seems she was trying to boost his morale."

"Alright, but I guess if Vanessa felt threatened, she wasn't going to confess her worries to a kid already scared to death."

"That's right. But she taught him that whenever you had problems, in order to feel better, you should talk, draw, or write. And that's where this becomes interesting. Vanessa told him she had kept a diary for many years and that it had helped her. Helped her to get by."

"Could we be getting somewhere?"

Whereupon, Lola called Jérôme Barthélemy. Ingrid heard her call him "my favourite mole". When Lola finished the conversation she looked thoughtful, then passed on to Ingrid what the lieutenant had told her: that a personal diary was not among the items recovered from Passage du Désir; that the tramp's attacker had nothing to say about the Vanessa Ringer affair apart from "Nobody is safe!" and that Maxime Duchamp had been called in for questioning.

"Let's go and see Chloé and Khadidja. They didn't mention the diary to the police. I can see it now: buried deep, the name of her boyfriend, written for all to see. And perhaps also the key to this Pandora's box, some clue as to how it all began."

"Who's to say that this boyfriend exists, Lola? Why do all women have to have one?"

"Vanessa was uncommonly pretty."

"So what?"

"It's odd, but something tells me I'm not going to have the last word on this. Let's go to Monoprix instead."

"Which one?"

"The one on Rue Saint-Martin, of course. We're going home. Come on, jump in."

Lola's flu had lost the first round. Following in the wake of her indomitable companion, Ingrid veered right, then left, left and then right, climbed the staircase, right and left again – how quickly she could walk when her mind was made up! What was she looking for? *Ladies: dare to be different with our new designer lines. Go for the silk look with bold tartan patterns. A vamp's stockings with trainers! Turn your wardrobe upside down!* The voice intended to seduce female shoppers whispered its dynamic attractions in between adverts and two bursts of muzak. Lola pulled up sharply, declared that the French were beginning to talk as crudely as the Yanks, winked at Ingrid, and shot off again. They finally came to a halt in the office supplies department.

"Which colour?"

Lola was holding up two notebooks with a serious, extremely serious, expression on her face.

"What's this for?"

"A surprise, Ingrid. So, which colour?"

"Er . . . red. Like your dressing gown."

"Ouch, low blow."

The restaurant was not yet officially open, but they installed themselves at Lola's usual table. Maxime was at his stoves, Chloé was setting places. No sign of Khadidja.

"She has a casting," Chloé explained. "She'll be here later."

"Bring us something to eat then," Lola said.

"O.K., but what?"

"Whatever's ready. And heat up some coffee."

"Of course, Madame Lola."

Chloé came back with two plates of salted pork with lentils. She had not forgotten the house red.

"If we drink, we'll fall face first into our plates," Ingrid said.

"*To eat is a requirement of the stomach, to drink, a requirement of the soul,*" Lola said, filling their glasses.

"Who said that?"

"Brillat-Savarin."

"Never heard of him."

"That doesn't surprise me. Come on, let's drink a toast. To the *Belles* – in other words to Ingrid Diesel and Lola Jost. And chew your food properly, my girl, it'll wake you up."

"Lentils for breakfast is a bit odd, Lola."

"Don't exaggerate, it's already a quarter past eleven. However, a purple and yellow Peruvian hat at breakfast is very odd indeed."

"It was on sale at Monoprix."

"That doesn't surprise me either."

"I'm not taking it off just yet, my ears are still cold."

Some time later, Lola seemed to succumb to a torpor that made her eyelids droop. The carafe of house wine was empty thanks mainly to her, and she had ordered a third double espresso. Despite her own fatigue, Ingrid kept a close eye on her, and concluded that their investigation was about to come to a halt, that Lola had forgotten the red notebook slumbering in her pocket. But a sudden command from her comrade rapidly changed her mind:

"Come and keep us company for five minutes, Chloé. Come on!"

The young girl approached reluctantly. She stood next to the table, unsure what to do.

"Sit down," Lola said.

"But the customers are arriving, madame . . ."

"This will only take two minutes."

Chloé sat beside Ingrid. Lola took the red notebook out of her pocket and waved it in the air, before placing it on the table and trapping it under her ample hand.

"Do you know what this is?"

"No, Madame Lola."

"Vanessa's diary."

Ingrid had her eyes fixed on the girl. She had only flinched for perhaps a quarter of a second, but she had flinched. Chloé tried to recover, but it was too late. Ingrid felt nothing but admiration for her stout companion.

"In it, Vanessa talks about her boyfriend."

"She does?"

"You know him."

"No."

"That wasn't a question, Chloé."

"But I don't, madame, I really don't!"

"But you know he exists."

"That's not what I said."

"Your eyes said it for you."

"I honestly don't know who you're talking about."

"You know I retired from the force, don't you?"

"Yes, Maxime told me."

"Do you trust me?"

"Of course, Madame Lola."

"So what are you afraid of?"

"Nothing, it's just that with everything that's happened in the past few days, I'm on edge."

"I can understand that, but I have no intention of arresting you, or your flatmate or your boss, for that matter. Did you know he's been summoned to the police station? Maxime is my friend. *Belles* is my canteen. At my age, you get used to your little habits. Think carefully, Chloé. By helping me find who did this, you'll be helping Khadidja and Maxime. And you'll be helping yourself."

Darn! Holy smoke! Ingrid cursed under her breath as she saw Khadidja pushing open the door to *Belles*, returning from her casting or whatever it was. Flowing locks, short black jacket over a clinging leopard-print jumper and faded skinny jeans with smart ankle boots, she greeted the three of them without a smile, made to head for the kitchen but noted Chloé's expression and veered towards their table.

"What's going on?"

"Madame Lola has decided to conduct her own investigation."

Ingrid noticed that Khadidja's arrival had a soothing effect on Chloé. She found her words more easily, was suddenly more confident. Lola noticed it as well. She presented Maxime's petulant girlfriend with her stony silence. Perhaps that would impress her.

"There's no point, Madame Lola. We're already besieged by your colleagues as it is. You don't want to make our lives completely unbearable, do you? Come on, Chloé, we've got work to do."

"Gently does it, my girl," Lola said. "You're not going to get off the hook that easily."

"Lola, you're a friend of Maxime's, so I owe you respect, but allow me to say that to me, retired or not, you're still a cop. Yesterday, for the first time in my life, I had dealings with your colleagues, and it wasn't pleasant. I think all of you deserve the reputation you have."

"Madame Lola has found Vanessa's diary," Chloé said in a faint voice.

Khadidja thought this over for a moment, studied Lola's impassive face, then pulled out a chair for herself and sat astride it. Ingrid had to admit she had style. You could almost have believed she was about to launch into something very Parisian, but a rap or funk version. Then she laughed out loud, a brief cackle devoid of any gaiety that ended as abruptly as it had begun.

"Wait a minute. You *recovered* Vanessa's diary . . ."

Lola simply stared at her without blinking. Ingrid loved it when she did that; she wished she herself could always stay just as unruffled. But Khadidja seemed unimpressed.

". . . whereas neither me nor Chloé told Grousset it had disappeared."

She could have said "neither Chloé nor me", Ingrid thought. Maxime was right to suggest Khadidja only thought of herself always. In full flow by now, she backed up her words with vigorous hand gestures: "You're bluffing. I don't know by what miracle you could have found that diary. Unless it was you who strangled Vanessa."

"But Madame Lola showed it me," Chloé said.

"O.K., then I'd like to see it too."

Lola took the red notebook from her pocket and showed her the blank pages.

"I told you she was bluffing."

"Perhaps, but that bluff allowed me to find out that you didn't tell Grousset everything."

"Who would want to talk to an animal like that?"

"Did you know he's summoned Maxime?"

"No."

"Well, now you do. The ball's in your court, my girl."

Ingrid did not like what she saw: Khadidja seemed to take the news badly. She turned a worried face towards the kitchens, towards the aroma of what Maxime was carefully cooking, towards Maxime's concentrated face as he cooked.

"Before she worked for Fogel, Vanessa was an usherette at the Star Panorama, on Boulevard Magenta. A cinema specialising in gore films. Grousset is bound to find that out, but I'm giving you a head start."

"Good. That's the spirit," Ingrid said jovially.

Khadidja shot her a fiery look, no doubt choking back her desire to ask her what business of hers was this affair. But she was not one to show weakness. When Khadidja left her chair to go into the kitchen, Ingrid felt her heart sink. It was obvious just looking at her that the previous night's argument had vanished like rainwater after a storm, swallowed up by the gutter. Ingrid imagined her removing her jacket, tying on her apron, flinging her arms round Maxime to give him a kiss.

15

Ingrid and Lola were walking up Boulevard Magenta. Nice name for a boulevard: Ingrid pretended to believe it was a homage to the purply-pink colour, and enjoyed listening to Lola correct her by evoking a battle against the Austrians, who preferred spiked helmets to Peruvian hats. After that barbed exchange, Ingrid had touched on the topic of fatigue and the limits of the human body. Lola's in particular. More than once she asked her valiant partner if the nap she had taken was really enough, if it wouldn't have been better to have a proper sleep, to put off until the morrow what they were intending to do tonight. Obviously there was real concern behind her questions, but also a slight problem of her own. That night, Ingrid had things to do, and didn't know how to break it to Madame Lola.

It was a fine building that must have dated from the fifties. Carefully restored, the Star Panorama did not stint on gilt or velvet. Ingrid tried to play for time before Lola pushed open the glass and bronze door and launched into one of her stubborn interrogations. She pretended she was interested in the photographs advertising the films being shown. In one of them, a woman as dusky as she was voluptuous was screaming, enveloped in a green mist while an incandescent stream of blood poured from her neck, descending like rosary beads towards her snow-white breasts. Ingrid wondered why the image of a rosary had come to mind, then realised that on the other side of the boulevard opposite the cinema stood a church with a small square next to it.

"It's no coincidence that surgeons wear green. There's a close relationship between green and red, one that's organic and spiritual, yet hard to define."

"If you say so, Ingrid. O.K., shall we go in?"

"Lola, you know I enjoy working with you, but I have an appointment. I really must go. I'll see you again tomorrow."

"I hope your appointment isn't with your pillow, my girl. That wouldn't be worthy of you."

"Of course not!"

"And yet I made it clear I don't like working on my own."

"That may be, but it's always you who leads the dance when it comes to interrogations."

"Exactly, and in a dance you need a partner who can encourage you. I don't like playing the lonely old cop, Ingrid. Stay at least for the lead-off?"

"Alright! Alright!"

The owner of the Star Panorama was called Rodolphe Kantor. He was a stocky man with thinning, slicked-back hair and a pencil moustache. He was dressed in a pinstripe suit, as sharp as the ones in "Scarface", with a white cotton handkerchief as an added touch. When he placed a cigarette in his tortoiseshell holder, Ingrid realised he was imitating the father in the Addams family.

She soon identified the cashier and the two usherettes. They looked as gothic as their boss: the cashier was wearing a skeleton T-shirt, and the two girls were in pretty jet-black dresses that showed off their pale Vampirella faces, coal-black eyes, and purple lips. Fishnet stockings and high-heeled shoes completed their outfits. All three seemed completely unperturbed by the screams coming at more or less regular intervals from the auditorium. Ingrid asked whether this was a special performance, but Kantor explained that on the contrary, their get-up was perfectly normal; they had to make an effort, particularly when it came to their clothes, to create an atmosphere and keep the customers happy.

"I came to talk to you about Vanessa Ringer," Lola cut in.

Kantor remained as tightly shut as Dracula's coffin when struck by the first rays of dawn. Several seconds of silence drifted around the three of them, before they were shaken by cries muffled by the old-fashioned bronze-edged doors. Star Panorama really was a fine cinema, thought Ingrid. And it's getting awfully late.

"Can you confirm she worked for you?"

"No doubt about that."

"For how long?"

"About three weeks."

"Goodness, that's not long."

"You're right. But why all these questions? Are you from the police?"

"Not exactly."

It's getting later and later, thought Ingrid, desperately searching for an excuse to sneak away.

"Are you from the police or not?"

"Think of me as an officer who took early retirement, and is now employed in a private capacity by the victim's family."

"I agree to talk. But only to the real police."

"The police are not very interested in this affair. In fact, I bet they won't even come to see you. So rest assured, you'll only have to tell your story once."

"I doubt if the police lack interest, but you certainly don't lack cheek. Now, excuse me, but I have work to do."

"Do you know Dylan Klapesch, Monsieur Kantor?"

Lola glanced at Ingrid with surprise, at Kantor with close attention. The American had just swept off her Peruvian hat; she was not unaware of the effect her cropped, post-modern Joan of Arc hair would have on such a lover of sartorial extravagance as Kantor.

"Obviously! He's the rising star of French horror cinema. I'm a big fan of his."

"I know Klapesch well. His real name is Arthur Martin."

"No kidding."

"As sure as my name is Ingrid Diesel. And if you agree to help my friend, who has told you nothing but the truth, I'll get Dylan Klapesch to come here for a talk."

"But he has the reputation for being terribly temperamental."

"Do you want Klapesch or not?"

"You bet I do!"

"Deal!"

"Not so fast. I also want a piece of paper. Signed by you."

"O.K., but get a move on."

The manager disappeared for a moment, and Lola took the

opportunity to question Ingrid discreetly. She found it hard to believe in this fortuitous friendship between a film director and a masseuse.

Kantor came back with a typewritten sheet and a biro. Ingrid read the document and signed. She stood poised for a second, contract and pen in hand, a vague smile on her lips. Eventually, she took a Swiss army knife out of her pocket, pricked the end of her thumb and pressed her bloody print onto the document.

"Now I have to rush, Lola. And you, Kantor, be nice to her, O.K.?"

"Whatever you say."

Kantor's eyes followed Ingrid's athletic silhouette until it dissolved into the night. Then he gazed at the piece of paper decorated with its fine scarlet thumb-print as though it were a Hollywood contract, and turned towards Lola, whose face betrayed no emotion.

"Your friend is a real eccentric. Peculiar but not annoying. I really appreciate folk like that."

"Eccentrics?"

"Yes, they're sadly lacking in these grey times of ours. In the seventies, there were a lot more per square metre."

"O.K., let's start again. Why did Vanessa only stay three weeks?"

"She didn't deign to give me an explanation. I found myself with only one usherette slap in the middle of a Dario Argento festival. And you may not be aware of it, but Dario Argento fills cinemas."

"Had there been a problem?"

"Not that I know of. I treat my employees correctly."

"No trouble worth mentioning with the customers?"

"What d'you mean?"

"They're a rather special assortment. You must get lots of eccentrics, but of a more annoying sort than Ingrid Diesel."

"My clients are no stranger than the ones who go to art films. Gore has its dignity, madame."

"How did you come to hire Vanessa?"

"It was my son Patrick who introduced her. If he hadn't, I don't suppose I'd have taken her on."

"Was Patrick close to her?"

"Yes, a friend."

"Her boyfriend perhaps?"

"No idea. This generation does as it pleases, even if many of them still live with their parents. As for confiding in us, forget it. And they're not even amusing with it."

"Does Patrick live with you?"

"Oh, yes. He can't afford to do otherwise. He passed his end of school exams in June. Since then, he's been helping my wife Renée. She runs a bookshop."

"Where is it?"

"In the neighbourhood, on Rue des Vinaigriers. You can't miss it. It's called *Le Concombre Masqué*."

"That's original."

"Not especially. Have you never heard of the kitchen garden adventures of the Masked Cucumber, a comic by Mandryka?"

"Was that from the seventies too?"

"It certainly was. Renée specialises in comic books."

A heart-rending cry split the air. Lola turned to look at the staff. The cashier was chatting lackadaisically to one of the usherettes. Standing on one leg as she massaged her ankle, she looked like a wading bird in mourning.

"Did those two know Vanessa?"

"No, they're new here. As you can imagine, I find it hard to keep my staff. They have to be here around five in the afternoon, and seldom leave before one in the morning. In between, they don't have the imagination to keep themselves busy. So they get bored. It's the modern malaise. You'd do better to question Elisabeth, she's outside taking a cigarette break."

The usherette's silhouette stood out against the backdrop of Saint-Laurent church and its square, both of them now lit by spotlights. She was staring into space, the tip of her cigarette glowing in the dark. Lola squinted, and for a second imagined Vanessa alive, looking even slimmer in that black dress – and those ridiculous shoes, the heels far too high even for a homage to Dario Argento. The young woman saw her and hesitated before coming over. She was a redhead, with pale skin and green eyes. And a worried look.

"Haven't they found the person who killed Vanessa yet?"

"No. Did you know her?"

"Not very well. Vanessa wasn't exactly talkative. All I knew was that she wasn't going to stay here long."

"Are the conditions that bad?"

"No worse than anywhere else. Kantor is an alright boss. But I think Vanessa was bored. It was like she was killing time here and didn't want to make friends. I read in the paper that she was working in a children's shelter. I wasn't surprised. She needed to do something she believed in."

"In general, how are things between you and the customers?"

"There are lots of young people. Students, I reckon, if they can go to bed so late during the week. Generally they're no trouble. They barely notice us. To them, we're just usherettes."

"Any rude remarks?"

"More like indifference."

"Did Vanessa have contact with any of them in particular?"

"It's funny you should ask me that. I was just thinking about it as I stared at the church. There was a young guy who was always going on at us to appear in his first film. So much so that we ended up calling him the Spieler. One evening I was having a smoke when I saw Vanessa sitting in the church garden, in the glow from the spotlights. She was talking him."

"What about?"

"We weren't close enough for me to ask her."

"So why was she talking to Spieler rather than her workmates?"

"Perhaps because he was amusing. Working here gets to you after a while. I don't know if it's from having your head stuffed with all these horror flicks. I don't understand how anyone can enjoy watching a guy being hacked to pieces by a zombie. If you've got an explanation, I'll buy it. I used to look at the customers without seeing them, but after this I'll be more wary. Have you heard about that teenager who killed a girl in the Nantes region?"

"After he saw 'Scream'?"

"That's right. What if the person you're looking for is a sicko like that?"

"We were talking about the Spieler. Does he fit the picture?"

"No, he seemed nice. To me, the weirdos aren't the people who make this kind of film, but the ones who enjoy them."

As if agreeing with the mournful tone of Elisabeth's words, the sky began softly weeping. Hey you up there, it's been at least five minutes since you pulled that one on us, Lola thought, wiping off the raindrop that had crashed into her glasses.

"Do you know where we can find him?"

"Not the slightest idea. Sorry."

"When did you last see him?"

"Two or three weeks ago. But the Santo Gadejo festival starts tomorrow – the Chilean director. Spieler loves his work. He's bound to be here."

Lola thanked the usherette, and left in search of Kantor.

"I've another favour to ask of you."

"What now?"

"Think of Klapesch, Kantor. Think very hard of Klapesch. A favour."

"Just one, I warn you."

"I'd like to be free to slip into the cinema whenever I like with my friend Ingrid Diesel. At least during the Santo Gadejo festival. Don't worry, I'll pay for our tickets. But I'd appreciate it if you avoided *recognising* us."

"What do you intend to do? Sniff around among my customers?"

"That's the general idea. Does an amateur director your usherettes have christened 'the Spieler' mean anything to you?"

"Nothing at all. It doesn't ring a bell."

"Then as you can see, I'm going to have to find him myself."

"But you're going to destroy my business with your infiltration techniques."

"I'm an old hand at subtle infiltration."

"That isn't the impression one gets before one has the pleasure of knowing you better."

16

The sky was still weeping when Lola left the cinema. She crossed the boulevard and walked over to the church and its illuminated square. It occurred to her she must look like a giant firefly drawn to the light as it flew through the night. She pushed open the iron gate and went to sit on the bench where Vanessa Ringer had been seen with the Spieler. From there, the view of the Star Panorama was interesting. Its gilt and velvet décor and its roster of goths were clearly visible. Is that why Vanessa had come here? To gain some perspective? To observe her colleagues and her job in a detached way? Before detaching herself completely? Lola realised that just like Elisabeth the usherette and so many others, she herself didn't know much about Vanessa. She was investigating the murder of a girl whose main interests and habits were a mystery to her. Even Maxime, who took such a great interest in his fellow human beings, had little to say about her. Why did she laugh at the Spieler's jokes in the halo of light beside a church? Could he be her boyfriend? And where was this young freak to be found?

When her shoulders began to feel cold from the rain, Lola unfolded her mental neighbourhood map and ran over the journey back. She would take Rue de la Fidelité, then go down Faubourg-Saint-Denis. She would pass by the entrance to Passage du Désir where Antonio the legionnaire was probably fast asleep, and Ingrid the masseuse possibly was not. Where on earth could she have got to on this rainy November night? She would find out one of these days. After that, Lola would walk past Passage Brady, sparing a thought for Maxime, who was back from the police station and was sleeping in Khadidja's arms. A moment of tenderness snatched from the harshness of life.

But when she reached Passage Brady, Lola had no time to think of Maxime, because she saw a man out walking his dog. He was tall, still young, and had fairish hair. Like her, he was strolling along without an umbrella, but was clutching a small plastic bag. To clear up after his Dalmatian? Lola inwardly registered her approval: of all the urban pests, the two kinds she most hated were reckless drivers and those who fouled pavements. One day she had even given a sixty-year-old a face-pack with it after he allowed his pooch to soil the threshold of *Belles*. Which had led to Maxime collapsing with laughter. He had taken her over to the sink to wash her hands, and they dissolved in hysterics while the delivery men looked on in astonishment. She had laughed with Maxime exactly as she had once done with Toussaint. It was almost painful to think of that now. There ought to be a way to immortalise the feeling, to invent a machine that could be plugged into the brain to reproduce memories that would be like holograms, which you could smell and touch too, why not? You would be able to appreciate them in the flesh. Smell them, hear them, and touch them: smooth, rough, silky, hairy, spongy, any way you liked. Oh, I could do with a drink, thought Lola. I'd invite the shrink to *Belles*, wake up Maxime, and I'd be happy to drink the boss's tipple with the two of them until dawn.

She shouted, "SIGMUUUND!"

The Dalmatian reacted gracefully; he stopped sniffing at a tyre and glanced for a second at the woman who had called out to him. Then he looked round at his master, lifted a leg, and peed.

"Do you know my dog, madame?"

"I know you too, Monsieur Léger. I'm a friend of Maxime's. My name is Lola Jost. I think I need to talk. To talk to you."

"Do you need to talk or to talk to *me*?"

"Both. All the cafés round here are closed. You're going to have to invite me to your place for a moment."

The shrink smiled, which brought out wrinkles around his pale-blue eyes. Despite appearances, this fellow had to be around forty. He was standing under a street-lamp, with the rain glinting off him just as it did around Sigmund's metal chain, which he was holding nonchalantly. He was wearing cord trousers and a waterproof jacket.

His hair was plastered against his skull because he had not bothered to raise the hood. Léger looked like a man to inspire a great desire to talk on a night glittering with rain that seeped into your soul.

"Yes, I would very much like to talk to you, Antoine Léger."

He had shown her into his consulting room, offered her a cigarette, and sat opposite her across a dark hardwood desk from the 1940s. Léger had taken off his jacket and offered Lola a generous measure of good-quality Scotch; he served himself a more modest amount. Sigmund stretched out on the carpet but was not asleep.

She spoke about Vanessa Ringer and all the things she didn't know about her. About Khadidja Younis and everything she did know about her: her love for Maxime, her dreams of success. Léger listened, in a top-quality silence. As smooth as his Scotch. Lola settled comfortably into the warmth of his silence. She went on describing the young women who lived on Passage du Désir; Léger was a perceptive man, she had to sail with him on a sea of words until they reached a creek where they could land. And finally set foot on sand. At the same time, Lola was only too aware of how much she wanted to sleep.

"Kha-di-dja. That's a good name. Did you know that was what Mohammed's first wife was called? A rich widow, older than him. She was the one who encouraged him to become a prophet. She sponsored him, as it were."

"That's history for you," Léger said at last.

Lola liked his voice. Deep and musical, effortless. A preacher who was saving his energy. Lola found herself struggling, because the charm of his voice only increased the temptation to sleep.

"Maxime told me you're Chloé Gardel's doctor."

"That's correct."

"Since when?"

"For several years."

"But how can she afford to pay you?"

For the first time, she heard him laugh. Very elegant: nothing like the snigger of someone trying to conceal their nerves.

"You're an extraordinary woman, Madame Jost. Maxime warned me as much."

"It's on Maxime's behalf I'm carrying out this investigation. So that he doesn't end up in jail."

"You know very well I can't answer all your questions," he answered with a smile.

"I understand. Like priests, you are sworn to respect the sanctity of confession. But my first question was of a financial nature. It won't compromise you."

"Chloé first came to see me when she was at secondary school. She was bulimic. After her mother died, I went on seeing her. Free of charge. She insisted on giving me her dog in payment."

"And you accepted?"

"He was only six months old. I rechristened him Sigmund."

"But why did Chloé give you her dog? That's absurd."

Lola looked across at the Dalmatian. He had raised himself on his hind paws and was staring at her with his imperturbable gaze.

"Chloé couldn't bear to have him around anymore."

"Did she tell you why?"

"No. At least, not yet."

"Chloé and Khadidja hid from the police the existence of a diary that was probably stolen by Vanessa's murderer. That made me think the girls didn't want to reveal something from their shared past. We're not going to find that diary any time soon. On the other hand, we can discover Chloé's memories here. In your files."

"Possibly, but why would those memories be related to Vanessa's death? And who's to say they're accurate? People often disguise things unconsciously."

"Oh well, since you've no wish to talk about either Chloé's memories or why she abandoned her Dalmatian, let's discuss something else. Let's talk about bulimia in general."

"What would you like to know, Madame Jost?"

Léger looked amused. He seemed to be enjoying himself: either that, or he had been brought up to be a perfect gentleman.

"Call me Lola. I'd like to know what leads to bulimia."

"Well, Lola, bulimia is violence directed against oneself. It usually affects young women. Girls inflict this violence on their own bodies, boys against the social body. The result is the same. They both have problems feeling they are an active part of society, or finding their place in it. Whether by joining or opposing it. Opposition to parental authority is an important step in building one's own identity. In a single-parent family, or when a parent is out of work, it's difficult to rebel. Young people in that situation haven't the heart to rise up against an adult who is already struggling. The consequence is that some of them have trouble finding themselves, and increasingly lose their bearings."

"Is that what happened to Chloé Gardel?"

"Chloé's mother was a chronic depressive. A woman who brought her daughter up on her own. Before dying in a car crash."

"It all sounds very tragic."

"As you say."

"What do you think of the way Vanessa was mutilated? You saw what was done to her, didn't you?"

"Yes, I saw. I'm not qualified when it comes to criminal psychology. I can only tell you about the symbolism of mutilation."

"That's a start, Antoine."

"Mutilation can mean disqualification. In the Celtic tradition, a king was deprived of his throne if he lost an arm in battle."

"So the killer wanted to knock Vanessa off her pedestal . . . ?"

"It's only an interpretation, and as such has no scientific value. Besides, there are many others."

"I'm all ears."

"Instead of concentrating on mutilation, we could focus on 'foot'."

"Not bad, go on."

"Freud and Jung agree that the foot has a phallic significance. For certain fetishists it has an erotic fascination."

"So cutting off a woman's feet would be the same as negating the sexual attraction she exercises?"

"Why not? Although you could turn the hypothesis on its head, like turning a glove inside out, and fly from the realm of sex to that of the spirit."

"O.K., let's fly, Antoine."

"Angels, Lola."

"Angels, Antoine?"

"Mercury, the messenger of the gods, is the forerunner of our angels. The wings on his feet symbolise his ability to rise towards the divine. Then there's the footprint. In many cultures it's regarded as the mark of the divine in the world of humans. Buddha measured the universe by taking seven steps in every direction; we are reminded of Christ's footsteps on the Mount of Olives, and of Mohammed's at Mecca."

"What about the question of cleansing? Is it to do with purification?"

"Exactly, Lola. Whirling dervishes' feet are washed to rid them of the impurities they have picked up on the erroneous paths they have trodden in the past."

"Mutilation is the most extreme example of that."

"Your theory is a little audacious: but then again, why not?"

Lola talked with Léger for a long while. Her fatigue helped conjure up strange images in her mind. Even as she asked questions and listened to his answers, she let them float around. The image of a dog that had devoured two pretty white feet boiled in a saucepan. Leaving no trace of them. No flesh, bones, or cartilage. Lola took in Antoine's erudite conversation until her eyelids started to flutter. Then, unable to absorb anything more and make sense of it, she asked where the couch was. She wanted to ask a favour of the psychoanalyst: for him to allow her to stretch out on this mythical piece of furniture.

"Before I met you I had no idea it was one of my fantasies," she explained.

Léger stood up and pointed to a blue-upholstered walnut-wood couch that matched the desk. Noticing a movement behind her, Lola turned and saw the Dalmatian yawning as it came over. She smoothed down her skirt, stretched out, then looked round and saw that Léger was sitting on an armchair behind her head. Sigmund settled down at her feet.

"Does he always do that?"

"Always. That means Sigmund is the only one who knows all my clients' secrets."

Lola found the energy to smile. She folded her hands across her stomach, took several deep breaths. She heard Léger cross his corduroy legs, once, then a second time. Then again, and many more times.

17

She awoke to the grey light of dawn filtering in through tall windows she did not recognise. It took Lola several seconds to realise she had spent the night on the psychoanalyst's couch.

She got up and managed to avoid knocking over the glass of water on the wooden floor. She walked towards the library. Psychoanalysis, psychiatry, psychology, sociology, several volumes of a medical encyclopedia, dictionaries of mythology, the Bible and the Koran, the meditations of the Dalai Lama, Vidal's pharmaceutical directory. On one wall, black-and-white photos of the Dalmatian, with parts of Doctor Léger's anatomy visible here and there. Could it be that Antoine only shared his life with his Dalmatian? The most striking photo showed Sigmund on an inflated lilo at the seaside, on guard next to a man lying down and only showing his shins and bare feet. There they were, feet again.

Lola searched the desk and eventually discovered what she had hoped to find: his client files. Lots of them, and arranged in alphabetical order. But Chloé Gardel wasn't under either G or C. Nothing about Khadidja Younis or Vanessa Ringer either. Did Doctor Léger see me coming in my big fat clogs? Lola wondered. She muttered a weary "Oh la la" before leaving the consulting room. And then going back into it. She searched again, looking for the name she thought she'd glimpsed a few seconds earlier.

Yes, there it was. The label read *Renée Jamin-Kantor*. The folder was crammed with sheets of paper covered with handwritten notes and dates. The bookseller had been seeing Léger for more than seven years. If Lola was reading correctly between the lines, Renée Jamin had indulged all her senses in a life replete with parties, artificial paradises, a plethora of partners. She occasionally asked herself metaphysical questions about this agitated existence. The first of these came after the departure of Patrick's biological father. Someone by the name of Pierre Norton who one fine day had decided to leave his wife and child, and from that day forth had given no further sign of life. Soon afterwards, Rodolphe came on the scene. He had played the father in the Addams family, and stepfather in the Kantor family. Lola closed the folder with the unpleasant sensation that she had been spying through a keyhole. Now I'm no longer an officer, the sewer rat aspect of the trade seems all the more depressing, she thought to herself. She put all the documents back in place and left the consulting room, for good this time.

The apartment seemed deserted. She hesitated, then started to look round its one-hundred-and-fifty square metres. One door ajar, leading to the bedroom. The double bed was unmade, someone had slept there alone. In the kitchen, Sigmund's bowl was empty, and the remains of a solo breakfast had been left in a sink filled with soapy water. The teapot stood in the middle of an imposing rustic dining table, its surface gouged with a thousand knife cuts, burned by hundreds of over-heated saucepans, thousands of family meals. Strange, for an apparently confirmed bachelor. Lola left.

Out in Rue du Faubourg-Saint-Denis, the tradesmen were opening up their shops. She greeted her favourite greengrocers and butcher.

The rain had ceased, daily life was returning to normal. That night while Lola was sleeping on a couch, the Seine had wisely stayed in its own bed. The remake of 1910 was not going to happen today.

A taxi pulled up outside Antoine Léger's building. The psychoanalyst climbed out, looking contented, a child in his arms and Sigmund on his heels. A pretty blonde woman, more or less Vanessa Ringer's age, also clambered out of the vehicle. Squinting as she usually did, Lola imagined that the young woman was returning from the underworld, where Léger had gone to rescue her. The taxi driver handed the blonde woman a suitcase. Lola stood rooted to the spot and then, realising she was standing in front of her hairdresser, decided to go in.

There was only one customer in *Jolie petite madame*, and young Dorothée was busy attending to her. Lola said hello to Jonathan and explained she didn't have an appointment.

"Tell me something I don't know, sweetheart. You never book an appointment. Or yes you do, once a year, before going to see your son in Singapore. But it's not the season for that. Come on, sit down. What can we do for you?"

"You can give me a cut and a blow dry. But I don't want to leave here with a birdcage on my head. Moderation, Jonathan."

"Moderation is my middle name, Lola."

And so Lola was able to take the neighbourhood's temperature regarding Vanessa Ringer's death. Nearly everyone was talking about it. Everyone knew she had been thrown out by her parents, who were fundamentalist Catholics. They had turfed her out because of her relationship with a young guy from the Maghreb. Vanessa had found refuge with Chloé and her mother. Until Lucette died in a car crash. After that, Khadidja, another schoolfriend, had moved in with the two girls, and together the three of them helped each other cope with the high Parisian rents, and the highs and lows of existence. At this point, Jonathan had paused, scissors in mid-air, expecting a quotation. But Lola was too engrossed in her thoughts to have any wish to scan her inner anthology. Noticing that Jonathan was disappointed, she made a great effort and, for lack of anything better, summoned the shade of Léon Bloy to *Jolie petite madame.*

"*My existence is a sad landscape where it always rains.*"

"It won't be once I've finished with you, sweetheart. There's nothing better than a good haircut to set your head to rights."

"Is that you or Vidal Sassoon, Jonathan?"

Lola left *Jolie petite madame* with a blue rinse in her grey hair. Jonathan was a meticulous craftsman who was proud of his profession, and although her hair did look like a birdcage, Lola was not worried because she knew the damp air would soon undermine her capillary high-rise. In Rue des Vinaigriers, the *Le Concombre masqué* bookshop was painted in a cucumber green, which did not surprise her. The shop window was full of comic books, but also had room for the third dimension, displaying a vast array of plastic statuettes of comic characters, superheroes, extra-terrestrials and monsters. There were also photos of the people who had created them. Lola noticed an Asian woman with long hair in the style of Yoko Ono in her John Lennon days. The caption declared that this was Rinko Yamada-Duchamp, immortalised fifteen years earlier. Sitting at a table inside the bookshop, she was signing her books. Beside her, in a leather skirt and a T-shirt showing some Hindu god or other, stood a little woman with a beaming smile and long, wavy hair the colour of *marron glacé.* The same small figure could be seen gradually ageing as the photos of the featured artists progressed through time. Lola failed to recognise any of them.

Renée Kantor was advising a customer who swore only by science fiction. She was around fifty, discreetly elegant in a way that matched the season: harmonious beige and brown with a splash of colour from a bright silk scarf. The woman in the photographs. Like Lola, she wore her hair cut short and had toned her clothes down, but unlike the ex-policewoman, she had not put on any weight at all.

Lola searched among the racks, listening to the two women's conversation. She would never have imagined comic book art to be so flourishing. People obviously had a tremendous desire for new ideas. Renée Kantor knew her business, and reeled off the biographies of several authors without hesitation. Her unrelenting charm won over the client, who left with three books and a free catalogue.

"If you need any assistance . . ."

"I've been hearing about the work of Rinko Yamada."

"Oh yes, she's marvellous. Look, all her books are here, in alphabetical order. That woman was a genius."

"Was?"

"Unfortunately."

"Did you know her?"

"We were friends. She lived in the neighbourhood. It's a dreadful story. Rinko was murdered. She and Maxime Duchamp were a perfect couple. Almost too perfect. They never found the killer. Rinko was attacked when she was alone in her studio, on Rue des Deux-Gares. It seems Maxime found her body on his return from a reporting trip to Romania."

Lola studied Renée Kantor's face. This woman remembered a twelve-year-old murder as if it were yesterday. She was still smiling, but her eyes had taken on a shade of grey, "*Otaku* is a cult graphic novel. I can recommend that if you don't know where to start. But I warn you, it's violent. And it comes in fifteen volumes."

"Are there any mutilations in it?"

"Er . . . among other things."

"Whet my appetite."

"I beg your pardon?"

"Tell me a bit of the story."

"It all starts with a schoolgirl who sells her image to make money. She'll live to regret it."

"Why?"

"If I tell you any more, it'll give the plot away. It's constructed like a thriller."

"No, go ahead. I like to know what I'm getting into."

"A collector decides to chop her into bits and parcel them up. Then he sends the parcels to other young girls who have posed for the same company."

"That sounds about as perverse as it gets. I'll take the first volume."

"An excellent choice. Shall I gift-wrap it?"

"No, don't bother, it's for me."

Lola paid, and took the receipt, but not the book, which Renée Kantor kept tight hold of. The two women stared at each other over the copy of *Otaku*.

"You're not really into comic books, are you?"

"Don't worry, I'm not into confrontation either."

"I know who you are. Lola Jost, retired police commissaire. And you're investigating the Ringer affair. My husband had the pleasure of a visit from you. He warned me."

"If only you turned out to be more co-operative than him."

Renée Kantor released the book – along with another of those smiles, of which she seemed to have a limitless supply.

"For your information, I'm delighted by what's happening. Well . . . obviously I'm not pleased at Vanessa Ringer's death. But . . . Oh, why hide it? I always thought Maxime Duchamp had killed Rinko."

"Why did you think that, Madame Kantor?"

"Because beneath the image of the perfect couple, there was something else. Rinko was unhappy with him."

"Did she tell you that?"

"He was always away somewhere or other. Rushing from one war to the next. She grew tired of waiting and being afraid for him."

"Tired?"

"Rinko sought comfort with someone else, and Maxime couldn't bear it."

"Who was it?"

"I don't know."

"But you were friends . . ."

"Perhaps he was married. Rinko wasn't one to create a scandal. And despite what you say, she wasn't perverse. She was a very sensitive artist who could pick up on and retransmit the cruelty of her time, but that didn't mean she accepted—"

"Did you go the police?"

"No."

"Why?"

"I had no proof. Maxime was officially away on a trip, but return flights can be changed. Anyway, if he's done it again with Vanessa Ringer . . ."

"This time you would go to the police?"

"Everybody knows Maxime Duchamp is in the police's sights. No point shooting at the ambulance. And I've no more proof today than I had yesterday."

Her smile had turned into a grimace. Her bitterness was hard to take, because for Lola it turned Maxime's face sour. Lola would have liked to ask her if she had something against him for other reasons. Had she tried to live out one of the "experiences" she seemed to relish so much with him? Had he refused her advances? But this hardly seemed tactful, so instead she asked, "So you see similarities between the two murders?"

"Both of them were strangled. There was no sexual violence. Although . . ."

"Although?"

"He had tied her . . . to the bars of the bed with stockings."

"Tied her?"

"By the ankles."

"Why only the ankles? Normally in bondage the victim is tied by all four limbs or by the wrists . . ."

"What can I say? It's a sick world. Utterly sick."

"Could I see your son Patrick?"

"Patrick is up in the flat. There weren't many customers this afternoon."

"Your husband told me he works with you."

"Unfortunately, my son isn't very enthusiastic about studying. He worked with Rodolphe at the Star Panorama for a while; now it's the bookshop. Actually, Patrick spends most of his time in front of his computer. The apartment is just upstairs. It's practical – perhaps a bit too practical."

Renée Kantor stared at Lola, on the lookout for a reaction. Lola was pondering absent-mindedly how curious it was that some middle-aged people still needed other people's approval. Renée Kantor gestured to her to follow. They left the shop through the back door, and came out into the foyer of the apartment building.

18

The apartment was done up in boho-chic style. Too many rugs, too many pot plants, bunches of dried flowers, an abundance of mismatched furniture that must have required frequent trips to junk shops to amass, and even a faint odour of patchouli. Lola had not smelt that for a good thirty years. Among the original illustrations on the walls was one by Rinko Yamada-Duchamp. Lola stopped to look at it. The uniformed schoolgirl was posing in the photographer's studio. It was the opening of *Otaku*. At the gates of Hell.

"There's someone who is about to sell her image to the devil."

"Goodness, you certainly seem to have given the matter a lot of thought. Perhaps it's true what they say about you."

"What do they say about me?"

"That you're not an ordinary police officer."

"Obviously. I'm not a police officer anymore."

"You're a friend of Maxime's, aren't you?"

"That's right."

"Are you doing this for him?"

"Right again."

"So, when it comes down to it, you're doing this out of friendship. Me too. In short, our intentions are pure, but we're not on the same side."

"Well said."

"Don't hold it against me for being rather short with you. I'm not really like that. But what you said upset me."

"I didn't mean to. I'm sorry."

"Listen . . . before you go and see Patrick, before you go dragging up the death of that poor girl, I have to roll myself a joint."

Lola followed the bookseller into her kitchen. A collection of blue porcelain jars decorated a dresser; their contents were not simply flour and sugar. Renée nimbly rolled a perfect, cone-shaped joint and offered it to Lola.

"Not for me, thanks."

"Really?"

"No, but I'd gladly settle for a glass of red."

"Do you mind if I call you Lola? Would you like a Côtes-du-Rhone or a Madiran?"

"Madiran sounds good to me."

Lola savoured her wine and let Renée ramble on wherever the wind took her.

"Did you notice, Lola? In *Otaku* there are young schoolgirls."

"More than a few."

"Don't you think that Rinko foresaw what was going to happen, Lola?"

"What do you mean?"

"With Maxime and Khadidja, years later. In other words, now. She's so young. And he's nearly forty."

"Khadidja isn't a schoolgirl anymore."

"But she was at school not so long ago, like Patrick. Or like Vanessa and Chloé."

"Were they at the same school?"

"Yes, the Lycée Beaumarchais on Rue Lafayette. You know something, Lola . . . I wish I had the gift of time travel. Forwards, backwards, forwards, backwards. That way Rinko and I could run into each other sometimes. But I'm not gifted at anything."

"No, don't say that . . ."

"Rinko was a great lady."

Lola let Renée wander some more. She poured herself another glass of Madiran, then got up to rummage in the cupboards for something to snack on. She came across some olives, which she poured into a bowl. The two women picked at them, until Renée returned to the subject of Patrick, her only son.

"His lack of purpose could be my fault. Rodolphe and I didn't keep enough of an eye on his education. But with *perhaps* and *if only*, you're bound to be embarking on a long, long, long, long journey."

"As long as that?"

"Patrick spends the whole day in front of his computer. I'm not even allowed to tidy up his room. It's his domain. From time to time he tries to justify himself, saying he wants to become a webmaster or I don't know what. His generation live a virtual life. Perhaps ours went too far, but at least we were alive, don't you think, Lola?"

"I've no idea, I'm older than you."

"The seventies were different. We wanted to party, enjoy ourselves, push the boundaries. Don't you agree, Lola?"

"My memories of the psychedelic years are hazy."

"Now it's all about banning porn on T.V., banning smoking, A.I.D.S. here, fundamentalism there, increasing violence, individualism, intolerance, the death of politics everywhere. We live in troubled but boring times."

Lola listened to more nostalgia for pot and three-dimensional orgasms. The Madiran was good, but she didn't have all day.

"O.K., so can we see Patrick now?"

"Oh yes, I'm sorry, Lola. I needed to talk. You know, Rodolphe is a workaholic. When he's not at the cinema, he attends lectures, conferences and seminars on the maestros of horror. It's no fun living with someone who only gets excited by work, if you see what I mean."

"Yes, my ex-husband is like that. Except that he got his excitement in more traditional ways: from other women."

"That's perfectly understandable. I'm sorry, but how can one even think of sleeping with the same person all one's life? Of course, I'm not referring to you."

"You can refer to who you like, I'm not thin-skinned."

"But what do you make of a man who's only interested in gore, Lola? There are horrors enough all around us. And nowadays they seem to be multiplying: the future is completely black. Why add to them?"

"You knew what Rodolphe's interests were the day you married him, didn't you?"

"I was a single mother with a seven-year-old child. If that hadn't been the case, I don't think I would have married anyone. And then to me, Rodolphe was the director of a cinema. In the broadest sense."

"In short, you thought he had more varied tastes."

"You understand me so well, Lola. Apart from that tense moment in the bookshop when I pretended not to want to give you *Otaku*, well, apart from that I've only had good vibes from you. And I can feel them now. You're not an aggressive person, and it feels good to have met you."

"How about we go and check out Patrick's vibes?"

"Never at a loss for words, are you, Lola?"

In a bedroom plastered with posters advertising horror films and video games, a boy slightly younger than Vanessa was glued to his laptop.

A red army was exterminating a green army on a futuristic battlefield. Yet again the eternal struggle between green and red – Ingrid would be pleased. With two clicks of his mouse, Patrick Kantor paused his game and stood up to shake the hand held out to him. He was the same height as his mother, but that was where the likeness ended. His fair hair, straggly beard and smooth cheeks gave him the look of a gentle fawn. His eyes betrayed a hint of annoyance. At being disturbed in the midst of a decisive battle?

"It's about Vanessa Ringer."

"And who are you?"

"Lola Jost. I'm investigating on behalf of the family."

"She's investigating out of friendship," Renée said with a giggle. "Go on, tell him you're doing this out of friendship, Lola! For Maxime Duchamp. You see, Patrick, Lola is great, but she's not perfect. Nobody is perfect. That would be such a drag."

"Do you think you could leave the two of us alone for a moment, Madame Kantor?" Lola asked.

"Oh, O.K., I'll go back to the kitchen. It's not a problem. No problem at all. I know how to keep busy."

Patrick followed his mother's facetious exit indifferently, then said in a calm voice:

"Vanessa's parents are religious freaks. They threw her out when they learned she was seeing Farid."

"Farid what?"

"Farid Younis."

"I sense you're going to explain a link with Khadidja."

"Farid is her twin brother."

"Where can he be found?"

"I've no idea."

"That's a shame."

"Farid dropped out of circulation a long time ago. They say he's turned to crime."

"Who is 'they'?"

"The pupils from Lycée Beaumarchais at the time."

"Had he and Vanessa broken up?"

"I think so, but I didn't follow it much. I wasn't Vanessa's confidant. She was just a friend. When I'd had enough of working in my dad's cinema, I suggested she take the job. She seemed pleased, but I knew it wasn't going to last. Deep down, Vanessa dreamed of being useful. The influence of her Catholic upbringing. Love thy neighbour, and all that. Of course, when it's really a case of rolling your sleeves up to help others, I can understand. It's a lot more worthwhile than all that religious claptrap."

"Did she have another boyfriend after Farid?"

"How should I know?"

"You can sense that kind of thing."

"Well then, I'd say Vanessa seemed to be on her own. But I couldn't swear to it."

The boy had the same intonation as his mother, and was equally outspoken. In a corner of the room, the abandoned computer was softly playing repetitive martial music. Kantor kept glancing towards it: he was desperate to get back to his game, and didn't bother to hide the fact. Taking a cue from the warlike music, Lola asked:

"Do you know if she had any enemies?"

"No."

"Are you sure?"

"As sure as I can be. Vanessa's world was very restricted. Her two girlfriends, her work at the shelter. Who could she have upset?"

*

After Lola had left, Renée Kantor listened to "Kind of Blue" by Miles Davis in her kitchen, twice in a row. Then Patti Smith five times. She joined in the chorus at the top of her voice.

Then she went back to see her son. Floating in clouds of Miles, Patti, and some excellent grass she had bought in Belleville, she stared for a moment at his silhouette. Highlighted by the flickering colours from the screen, Patrick looked a study in concentration. At first she had tried to tear him away from his machine. Then when she had realised that video games were his generation's passion, she had given up. From time to time, Patrick came to lend a hand in the bookshop, and he was always polite with the customers. It had helped him keep one foot in reality. And besides, reality wasn't that great, so why insist?

Thanks to the grass, the anger she felt towards Maxime Duchamp had subsided. It was an elastic anger anyway, one that came and went, bounced back again. Strange, after all these years.

"Who was that fat old woman? A nosy granny?" the boy asked, still staring at the screen.

Renée saw that a red nuclear reactor was about to be blown up by missile strikes from the Greens.

"Madame Lola Jost, retired police commissaire. But she isn't that ugly, or that old. I expect she was quite a looker in her day. Not exactly beautiful, but something more than that. Like Marlene Dietrich or Jeanne Moreau. Women who are too much, if you get what I mean. Women who can't be pigeon-holed. They're free, they elude us the whole time, get it?"

But Patrick didn't get it or didn't want to. He was too busy system-atically destroying all the Reds with the help of futuristic aircraft. Renée imagined herself piloting one of those planes. May the force be with you, O Renée! She stared at her son's elegant profile for a moment, and added, "Madame Lola Jost is a legend in the neighbourhood. Perhaps she's bored. Yes, it could be that. You're probably right, Patrick. Besides, you're often right, son. You just need to learn to be a bit more tolerant."

"I'm no sneak, but I could have told that legend of yours a thing or two."

"What kind of things?"

"Oh, nothing."

"Patrick, you've said it now . . . come on, out with it!"

"Vanessa was in love with Maxime."

"You're kidding."

"No, I'm serious. And as you can imagine, she wasn't going to confide her secret to Khadidja. So the only person left was little Patrick Kantor, the agony uncle. Yes, believe me, I was her confidant."

"Don't tell me Maxime slept with Vanessa."

"So it seems."

"That bastard had to have all the women! It's crazy!"

"Don't upset yourself, maman, it didn't last. And with her Catholic education, Vanessa felt guilty all the time because of Khadidja. Yet she suffered because she loved Maxime. Do you get some idea of the mess she was in?"

"But why didn't you say anything, Patrick?"

"Who to?"

"The police, for example."

"Me, blab to the police? Never. I can't stand them."

"Nor can I. I didn't pelt the riot police in 1968 only to eat out of their hand now . . . but that's no defence. There are times when we have no choice."

"You do as you like, but I didn't say a word. You're not going to get me to kowtow to a cop."

19

After all her years as a detective, Lola thought she had come across every nuance of blood, which she understood to have a limited palette. That was before she discovered Santo Gadejo, a Chilean whose imagination was full to overflowing with spattered brains, dismemberments and all-out carnage leading to the final Armageddon. "Crazy Dolls" was a riot of blood and cries of terror, but also sex and cries of joy. An evil, sex-mad genius had created an army of murderous dolls in his laboratory, and used them willy-nilly to satisfy a desire that see-sawed between Eros and Thanatos. It was the most tedious film Lola had ever had to watch, and her eyelids were struggling heroically against the weight of gravity.

As far as Ingrid was concerned, this first evening at Star Panorama was already buzzing with excitement. She suspected it might grow even more dramatic: she was hoping Spieler would appear at any moment (Elisabeth had promised to alert them if he did) and also that someone in the audience would start behaving strangely. For the moment though, the faithful were on their best behaviour. Most of them looked like students, and hung out in groups. Given Señor Gadejo's bloody fantasies, it was easy to appreciate the need for a companion who could offer a shoulder, a hand or a sympathetic, alive and reassuring thigh.

Ingrid had placed the box of popcorn on the arm-rest between their seats. Whenever the evil genius launched an attack, her right hand gripped Lola's left thigh, while her body juddered as though an electric current were running through it. There was something appealing about this adolescent reaction. The more she got to know her, the more Lola appreciated the Yank's freshness and spontaneity.

The most beautiful and deadly of the dolls had a sweet, luminous Madonna smile on her unmoving face. She slashed a porno actress across the throat with a sabre – after flaying her alive – and then took her place on a film set. She removed her black cape to reveal a splendid, articulated body, with a battery inserted in her back, and wielded her no less splendid samurai sword to systematically dismember the whole film crew. Each time she chopped off a limb, a nose, an ear or even an entire head, the green light of her battery flashed on and off, and from some obscure part of her body came a short recorded sentence, spoken in a little girl's voice: "My name is Bella and I'm hungry." After this particular massacre, the pace of the film slackened. Bella was sitting on the bed, dripping with blood, sabre in hand. Close-up of her plastic face and her expressionless glass eyes. But the fixed, angelic smile was still there.

Lola took her hat off to the actress and waited to see what came next. Bella was wiping her sword on the decapitated script-girl's skirt when the door opened. In came the hero, an investigative journalist who was also a martial arts expert. He was determined to vanquish the creature, despite all her ultra-erotic attempts to seduce him. Bella's murderous adventure came to an end beneath a falling row of lights that emitted a shower of sparks on impact. In a Christ-like pose, the dismembered doll repeated over and over: "My name is Bella and I'm hungry . . . My name is Bella and I'm hungry . . . My name is Bella and I'm hungry . . . My name is Bella and . . ."

Lola was thinking about Rinko Yamada-Duchamp's dolls. The collection of lifelike effigies of young girls that had inspired the manga artist. She regretted not having asked Maxime to show her the dolls. The action in "Crazy Dolls" slowed once more: the hero was returning to his bare loft to gather his strength before facing the inevitable ruthless counter-attack. Lola closed her eyes, and fell asleep.

She was walking alone on a quay by the Seine. The rising waters lapped around her shoes. She came to a bridge covered in lichen which floated like windswept hair. She was wearing a long grey coat and Ingrid's Russian hat. She wished her American friend were walking beside her as she approached a big bridge with the letter K on it. Behind her was the bridge marked N for Napoleon, but she did not know this K bridge. There was no K bridge in Paris. Lola knew perfectly well she was dreaming.

All of a sudden she saw Vanessa Ringer. In a black cornet and white cassock, the young woman was tied to one of the columns of the bridge. Her body was enormous: as big as the Zouave soldier sculpted on the other bridge. The water had reached her ankles. "Tell me who killed you, my girl!" Lola roared. But Vanessa couldn't hear her. Lola moved forwards under the arch. Her footsteps echoed as she shouted at the dripping walls: "My name is Lola and I want to go home . . . My name is Lola . . ." On the horizon, a red dot blinked on and off. Lola continued her advance. The dot was none other than Grousset's cap. A Phrygian cap or the kind worn by the Smurfs? Jean-Pascal Grousset had lost a good twenty centimetres in height and was pushing the handles of a wheelbarrow full of something red.

The quay was cluttered with wheelbarrows. They were piled up against each other. Some of them had tipped over and spilled their bloody loads.

"It's Toussaint Kidjo," Grousset said, looking distraught. "He's been chopped into pieces. I don't know what to do with all the bits, the wheelbarrows are jammed solid, you have to come, Madame Jost . . ."

Grousset flung himself impatiently on Lola. He only came up to her chest, and his little clenched fists were hammering at her ribs . . .

"Lola, wake up! You said we were going to leave before the end of 'Crazy Dolls' to get a look at the audience! Lola! Wake up, Lola!"

"What's going on?" Lola muttered, staring at the screen.

"In the film?"

"In everything."

"In the film, the bad guy created a doll that looked like the journalist's fiancée. But she's so perfect you can't tell the difference. And in the real world, nothing. Spieler hasn't come, and the audience have been good as gold."

The two women took up position at the exit and surveyed the crowd coming out of the Star Panorama.

"Nothing," Lola admitted.

"Absolutely nothing," Ingrid echoed her.

"Come on, let's go home. We'll come back tomorrow. Be patient, we'll get him, this Spieler."

"I'm sure we will, but I can't tomorrow. I've got an appointment."

"Are you by any chance leading a double life, Ingrid Diesel?"

"Do you think we're on a bus heading for Oklahoma City?"

They walked in silence as far as Rue du Faubourg-Saint-Denis, then Ingrid offered Lola the promised massage, guaranteeing it would help her sleep. The light over the entrance to her building revealed Tonio the tramp. He opened one eye, and when he saw Lola exclaimed, "My Good Samaritan! I was hoping you'd come!"

"What is it, Tonio?"

"I found loads of newspapers in the dustbins. They talked about the little blonde girl who lived here and who's dead now. Well, I know something, and it's only you I'm only telling it to, my St Bernard. That's Tonio for you. He has his likes and dislikes. And he likes your kind old head."

Lola knelt down beside Tonio. He was making the moment last: he waited for her to light the cigarette and stick it between his lips, then light herself another. Ingrid went to get three Mexican beers, handed them round, then sat on a step.

"I saw the beautiful Vanessa in Passage Brady one night. She was arguing with the restaurant owner."

"When was that?" Ingrid asked.

"Sshh! Don't interrupt him!" Lola said.

"Yeah, keep quiet, you blonde gazelle. I'm coming to that. It wasn't in summer: it was raining the whole time. It was already autumn, my lovely. And on nights like that I sleep in Passage Brady, because it's covered. Anyway, they woke me up with their arguing. There you are. I was sure it'd interest you."

"Of course it does, but I'd like to know what they were arguing about."

"I've no idea anymore."

"Oh, no! You build up my hopes, then pour water on them!"

"To be honest my dear, I wasn't really listening."

"Was it a lovers' tiff?" Lola insisted, glancing at Ingrid, whose face was as unmoving as Bella the evil doll's.

"How should I know? All I can say is, the girl wasn't happy."

"What about him?"

"He was talking calmly, but she didn't want to know. He was holding her by the sleeve. And the lovely Vanessa didn't seem to like what she was hearing. That's all. Don't give me the third degree, that's all I have to tell you, but I'm only telling you."

Ingrid and Lola finished their beers sitting on the orange sofa. Lola was smoking, staring into space. Ingrid seemed transfixed by her lava lamp. She no longer felt like massaging Lola, and Lola no longer felt like relaxing.

"The skies are darkening," Lola said eventually. Today I learned from Renée Kantor, the wife of—"

"The owner of the Star Panorama, I know. I may look out of it, but I hear you loud and clear. Go on, Lola."

"I learned that things weren't going that well between Rinko and Maxime. He was never there; she had taken a lover."

"Fuck!"

"As you say. And that's not all. Rinko Yamada-Duchamp was found with her ankles tied to the bars of the marital bed. Even Grousset is bound to make the connection between bound ankles and chopped-off feet. It's raining evidence, Ingrid."

"No, that can't be."

"Yes, there's a smell of floodwater. The threat is rising like a river. Before we know it, the water will have reached the Zouave's moustaches, and he'll sneeze."

"What's the matter with you, Lola? Are you hallucinating, or what? Is it the lack of sleep?"

"Don't get so worked up, please. The waters are rising, the sky is growing darker and darker, but there is one white cloud on the horizon."

"Will you tell me what the fuck you're talking about?"

"Do you remember that Maxime and Khadidja were quarrelling, he reproached her for having hidden the fact that she had a brother from him?"

"Yes, of course."

"That brother, Farid Younis, went round with Vanessa Ringer at school. He was expelled quite early on. Apparently, he went to the bad."

"In what way? Drug dealing?"

"I don't know. But that's not the point."

They relapsed into thoughtful silence, until Lola asked:

"D'you know what's the greatest advantage of not being on the force anymore?"

"Not having to lift the lid on all the miseries of the world?"

"Exactly the opposite, Ingrid. Not having to keep to official hours to lift those covers. I'm free to go and ask awkward questions at any time of the day or night. She looked down at her watch, and added, "At one in the morning, for example."

"Are we going to Maxime's?"

"No, to your neighbours'."

Ingrid could not conceal her surprise, nor the disappointment she felt when her neighbours' door opened and there was Maxime. All he had on was a pair of jeans, and his face was that of a man who has left a bed where he was not exactly sleeping. In the background they heard Khadidja's voice, still struggling with a maelstrom of emotions.

"Who is it, Maxime?"

"Oh, good evening. What a surprise."

"Maxime, who is it?"

"Ingrid and Lola."

"Oh, but they've got a nerve! What is this?"

"I must say, she's not entirely wrong," Maxime said, with a rueful smile. Khadidja's head appeared in the doorway, her body pressed up against Maxime. She was wearing a salmon-pink baby-doll nightie with cream lace trimmings that showed off her little golden face, her golden shoulders, her golden breasts.

"O.K., I'm going to bed," Ingrid said.

"Fine by me," Lola said, wincing. I'll tell you all about it in the morning, sweetheart, she thought to herself.

★

The strains of Fatboy Slim swelled like a tidal wave. Headphones on, Ingrid was running quickly and powerfully, aware of every muscle in her body. And Maxime was running alongside her. It was as if they were escaping together towards a boundless other world. They were keeping the same pace. One day, he had let slip how much he admired her for being able to run as far and as fast as a man. She had taken that as a huge compliment. From time to time she glanced across at him, enjoying the profile of his concentrated face, his muscular body, his skin gleaming with sweat. Occasionally, he turned towards her and smiled. They were as one in their exertions, in the delicious surge of adrenalin, the carefree, primitive spirit. They were on the same wavelength.

Ingrid opened her eyes. Onto a view of her waiting room. For a moment, stretched out on her floor, thanks to the memories the music brought back, she had relived the beloved scene. A training session with Maxime in the Supra Gym on Rue des Petites-Écuries where they had first met. A slice of happiness that would stay forever in her memory. She closed her eyes again, let herself slide back into her dream, rewound, reinvented the memory until her eyelids burned. Alone in the changing rooms. The door opened. Maxime came towards her, silently, studying her with a lingering gaze. Then he took her in his arms and gave her a voluptuous kiss. His arms held her to him, held her tight . . .

Ingrid took off her headphones, stood up, and looked down from the window on Passage du Désir. By the lamplight she saw that Tonio had returned to his cardboard bed. She went to get another Corona and drank it. She put her headphones back on and danced to Fatboy Slim. When she had worked up a sweat, she lay down again on the floor.

"I swear I'll get you out of this, Maxime," she said aloud to her orange ceiling light. "And whether you love me or not doesn't matter. The main thing is that you exist in this world. That's what makes it beautiful."

She soon had enough of this day-dreaming. At first she thought of sending an e-mail to Steve, then her thoughts turned to Lola. Her watch showed two thirty-five in the morning. The ex-commissaire must have finished her questioning by now and gone home; would she be asleep yet? She was exhausted to the point of rambling on about flooding rivers, a Zouave catching a cold, personal problems turning into a public threat. Ingrid hesitated and then, unable to contain herself any longer, dialled Lola's number. The gruff voice had obviously been roused from sleep, but it softened as soon as Lola recognised who was calling. And this token of friendship warmed Ingrid's heart.

"What did Maxime say?"

"That he had quarrelled with Vanessa over her attitude towards Khadidja. Maxime accused her of stifling Khadidja, of draining her energy with her need to be mothered the whole time. In fact, Vanessa used to have supper in the kitchen at *Belles* almost every night."

"Did Maxime seem sincere?"

"Yes, and besides, Khadidja backed up his story. But . . . you know, Ingrid . . ."

"Yes?"

"I like Maxime a lot, but I don't know him that well. Our affinity is based on what isn't said, on shared silences. They're valuable of course, but I can't guarantee how genuine they are. In short, we have to decide whether we believe in Maxime or not."

"Lola, if necessary, I'm ready to lie on his behalf. I'll say he stayed longer with me that morning."

"So you envisage the possibility of his guilt?"

"No, Lola, I envisage the possibility of a judicial error."

"Hold on, that's a very important nuance. Tell me: do you think it's possible Maxime could be guilty?"

"No."

"Good. I'm glad we're in agreement on that score."

"You're welcome."

"Anyway, Grousset wouldn't believe you. And your testimony is only likely to make things worse. The best way of helping Maxime is to finish what we started. And to clear a path where my colleagues won't venture. But to do that we'll need a proper machete, to wade through a slimy swamp, and to not be scared of leeches."

"Is there a path to be cleared towards Farid Younis?"

"Khadidja claims not to have seen her brother for years. They had a bust-up."

"Perhaps the police have a file on him?"

"Before I questioned Khadidja, I asked Barthélemy to take a look. He hasn't found anything yet. Which isn't a good sign. Barthélemy is always happy to dig around. Especially if it gets up Grousset's nose."

"So that's another needle we have to search for in the swamp, Lola."

"First we find, then we search."

"What does that mean?"

"That can mean lots of things. In this case, it means we can't afford any mistakes."

The two women wished each other a good night without much conviction. Ingrid rummaged in her wardrobe and found her favourite sleeping-bag, the one she had taken with her on her treks in Colorado. With it under her arm, she slipped out of her apartment and covered Tonio with it as discreetly as she could; then she got back into bed. She lay there a long time, her eyes wide open in the darkness.

20

The next two days sped by. Ingrid and Lola spent their late afternoons and evenings at Star Panorama trying to locate Spieler. For his part, Lieutenant Barthélemy still hadn't had any success in tracing Farid. His last known address was his parents' home in Rue de l'Aqueduc. They had heard nothing from their son in years.

On the third night, Ingrid went with Lola as far as the cinema, before once more leaving her in the lurch. She managed to fob off Rodolphe Kantor, who wanted to know when Dylan Klapesch was coming. As time went by, Lola was becoming increasingly convinced that Ingrid Diesel wasn't nearly as innocent as she looked. She still had no idea who the Yank spent her mysterious nights with. Spieler had still not deigned to sign up for the cult of Santo Gadejo, so Lola went home sniffing the night air. It smelt of carbon monoxide, the exhalations of the Canal Saint-Martin, and of the square alongside the church where the infuriating, invisible Spieler had been seen talking to Vanessa.

As she reached Rue Château d'Eau, her mobile rang. Ingrid's voice was struggling against loud background noise. She asked Lola to join her on the corner of Rue Pigalle and Rue de Douai. She had discovered an informer who was willing to sell some of the most recent events in Farid Younis's life. The meeting point was the Calypso cabaret. The open sesame for the doorman was "Lola Jost has an appointment with Gabriella Tiger". Then Ingrid said her battery was running low, and soon all Lola could hear was the noise of the street.

With the aid of half a litre of coffee, Lola quenched her desire to sleep, then left her apartment. What was falling from the sky could not be exactly called rain. It was slow and very penetrating. In other words, the clouds were offering Parisians an authentic Breton mizzle. Lola regretted not having worn the pair of plastic boots she had bought at Cap Fréhel thirty years earlier. For a night out at a cabaret, a pair of walking shoes was more appropriate. She walked a good distance before finding a taxi, a threatened species in Paris, especially at night.

The façade of the Calypso was in tune with the weather. Streams of liquid rose and fell behind plates of glass in an endless movement that chimed with the flashing neon signs advertising their wares across the front wall: CABARET, STRIPTEASE, NUITS DE PARIS. Muffled music seeped out onto the pavement outside. On a poster, a creature with flaming red hair was undoing the zip of her sheath dress; the photographer had captured the sinuous gesture at the level of the thirteenth vertebra. The artiste's face was invisible, but apparently she was known as "Gabriella Tiger, the fiery temptress".

What kind of adventure had Ingrid Diesel got caught up in? wondered Lola as the doorman cast his sepulchral eye over her. Marie-Thérèse Jost, a.k.a. Lola, buttoned up to the neck in her severe raincoat, her hair the bedraggled remains of the blue-tinged bird-cage thanks to the vagaries of the weather, her swollen feet in wet flat shoes, did not exactly look like one of the jet-set.

"Lola Jost has an appointment with Gabriella Tiger."

She felt as though she had just given the feeblest password of her whole career, but as promised these few words had a magic effect, and the doorman let her pass without another word.

Before reaching the belly of the Calypso, Lola went down a long, purple-lined corridor. She found herself in a mauve and yellow room full of men in dark suits and a handful of women in slinky dresses. Tourists in the know, fashionistas and members of the criminal fraternity of whom Lola recognised at least two specimens. She was surprised to spot Maxime, sitting alone at a table, nursing a cocktail. Two statuesque blondes dressed only in thongs and plexiglass shoes were writhing to the sound of Madonna on a see-through stage in the form of a crucifix. Maxime, handsome as an unkept promise, was following their every move.

"Lola!"

"Maxime," she replied, slowly unbuttoning her raincoat.

"I'm relieved to see you. I've been sitting with this gin-fizz for an hour now. Apparently the idea is to buy a table dance by stuffing notes in a girl's garter, but I can't see myself doing that."

"Table dancing? What's that?"

"The dancer leaves the stage at your request and comes to the customer's table, wrapping herself round that steel pole you see there. It's an American import."

"Speaking of which, where's Ingrid?"

Maxime explained that Ingrid had begged him to come an hour earlier, to say he had an appointment with Gabriella Tiger, but had still not put in an appearance. He was waiting patiently for the Calypso's main attraction: the star turn from the Fiery Temptress.

"A full strip," he announced.

"Nice," Lola commented, looking at the menu.

She quickly got into the swing of things, ordering herself a gin-fizz at the price of a litre of champagne. The champagne itself was the price of a kilo of caviar, and so on. A relentless food chain.

Where was Ingrid? What link was there between Farid Younis and the Calypso? Who was the mysterious informer? The regulars were shouting: "Ga-bri-el-la! Ga-bri-el-la!" and stamping their feet under the tables. The din pitilessly drowned out Madonna: it was time for the Fiery Temptress to set her public alight.

Everything went dark. Then a curtain of flame exploded at the back of the stage, and the voice of the black American singer Lina pinned the audience to their seats.

Gabriella appeared, moulded in a red sheath dress, her long fiery-red tresses cascading down over her shoulders. Tall, muscular, with proud, superb breasts, generous hips, thoroughbred legs.

"Wow," breathed Maxime.

The striptease began. Classic, no table dancing, no steel pole. The real thing. An atavistic affair. Nobody uttered a word, or so much as blinked. The fiery temptress peeled off her dress, her stockings, her thong; all she kept were her shoes. Then she started to undulate, bend, sinuously, insinuatingly. To surrender, hesitate, give way. Relinquishing. Generous. The flames burning at the rear of the stage made her body glisten. A body with an amazing tattoo descending from neck to buttocks, showing a geisha frolicking with a joyful carp. The poster outside had been retouched. The tattooed stripper's concept was subtle: she didn't take absolutely everything off. Her camouflaged body allowed her to retain her mystique. Naked but not nude.

"Wow," Maxime whispered again, just before everything was plunged back into darkness.

A silence as dense as a black hole, then the light came back, and with it torrents of applause. All that was left on stage was a few wisps of smoke.

"None of that leaves us any clearer about Ingrid's whereabouts," Lola said.

"What a magnifi—"

"Mademoiselle Tiger is expecting you in her dressing room," one of the waiters informed them.

Maxime stood up hurriedly. As she followed him across the room, Lola could not help thinking of Mercury's winged feet.

She was sitting in front of her mirror, her body wrapped in a mauve dressing gown with "Calypso" embroidered on it in a silver rainbow. She was smoothing down her incandescent tresses. As soon as the waiter left, she took off her wig.

"Ingrid!" Maxime exclaimed, almost choking.

Lola sighed loudly, lit a cigarette, and sat on the nearest seat she could find, a fake zebra-skin sofa.

"I'll explain about Gabriella Tiger later, but Farid Younis is easier."

"I'll bet," Lola said.

"Enrique works at the Calypso. He knows the Paris underworld," Ingrid explained, removing her false eyelashes. "The big fish, the little sprats. Everyone. Enrique is a veritable address book. I've been pestering him night after night to find out about Farid Younis. And tonight, bingo!"

"Put on your navy-blue sailor's jersey and your Peruvian hat, my fiery temptress. We're going to have a few words with your address book."

"You'll have to go without me. I don't want the boss here to see me talking to Enrique in your company. I don't want to lose my job."

"It's weird, but I for some reason I thought you were a masseuse. I must have got the wrong end of the stick."

21

Enrique, the affable doorman who had let Lola in, was waiting at the intersection of Rue Pigalle and Rue de Douai. His face was as expressive as a cold cut of lamb, but his eyes had a life of their own, on the lookout for any opportunity. Lola gave him two hundred euros to learn that Farid Younis had been seen in the Cité des Fleurs estate in Saint-Denis. That's all she could get out of him, apart from a brief description of Khadidja's brother: good-looking, tricky, average height, very often dressed in black.

Ingrid emerged suddenly from the stage door. Despite the drizzle, she walked with her two friends towards Faubourg-Saint-Denis. Lola was content just to listen while Maxime and Ingrid held a lengthy discussion, marching along in step. Maxime kept turning towards Ingrid, and couldn't stop smiling at her. Wow!

"Why go against your own nature? I have a tendency towards exhibitionism. Besides, I love dancing, and I know I'm good at it. I learned in Bali."

"I knew it reminded me of something."

"The thing is, when I dance for those men, I know I'm giving them pleasure, and that makes me happy too. At the same time, it stays chaste. I work on the principle that you shouldn't waste your talents."

"And you're right."

"With the wig and the make-up, I'm a different person. If I hadn't invited you to my dressing room, a fiery temptress was all you'd have seen."

"Yes, we certainly saw her," Lola cut in, fed up with all this billing and cooing. "Enough of justifying yourself, Ingrid. We accept that you're a striptease artist. That's just fine. And no-one's insisting you say three Our Fathers and two Hail Marys as an act of contrition, young lady . . . Go in peace, Gabriella Ingrid Tiger Diesel. And try not to catch a cold."

"Have you been doing it for long?" Maxime said, undaunted.

"A few years."

"I thought your show was poetic."

"It's exactly that! That's the whole idea. I only work two nights a week, because it's an art."

"Is it well-paid art?" Lola asked, struggling to control herself.

"Not too bad."

"It struck me that for a masseuse working from home you didn't exactly put yourself out to find clients," Lola added.

"Perhaps, but it's at the Calypso that I met Dylan Klapesch."

"I thought he only liked horror."

"Dylan is making a film called 'Gore Cabaret'. He interviewed all the dancers and is fond of me. Don't forget, he's agreed to come and do something at the Star Panorama. But he didn't say what exactly. Rodolphe Kantor had better beware."

"Rodolphe Kantor isn't my chief concern. But I appreciate people who keep their promises, Ingrid. So well done for Klapesch. And bravo for your striptease while I'm about it. You're talented. Your show stays in the mind long after you leave the stage."

"It does?"

"Yes, it does."

"You can say that again," Maxime said.

The three of them carried on chatting in the dark, still Brittany-inspired, cityscape of Rue du Faubourg-Saint-Denis. Eventually they had to part. Ingrid and Lola left Maxime at Passage Brady, then walked on in silence for the few steps separating them from Passage du Désir. Lola asked Ingrid to offer her a drink.

"I agree to Mexico, but don't you have anything more warming than beer?"

"How about tequila?"

"That's exactly what I was hoping you'd say. Tequila for me, Gabriella."

Ingrid poured the drinks, and Lola downed hers in two gulps. Ingrid did the same. Lola asked for a top-up.

"If you have something to say, spit it out," Ingrid said. "No need to get drunk for that."

"I merely wanted to congratulate you. You killed two birds with one stone, my girl. Hats off to you."

"What?"

"You didn't need me at the Calypso to make Enrique talk. And you certainly didn't need Maxime."

"Cops always work in pairs, don't they? Enrique co-operated because he took you two for detectives. He doesn't give out information to everyone."

"Maxime looks nothing like one, as you well know."

"True, he looks more like a sailor," Ingrid admitted. "A coastguard perhaps. Aren't they police?"

"Let me finish, will you? Four nice crisp fifty-euro notes would have got you the same result."

"D'you think so?" asked Ingrid, with an innocent smile.

"So you've been going to the Calypso every time you've vanished?"

"I can't hide anything from you anymore, Lola."

"Admit you wanted to seduce Maxime. He could never have imagined a Gabriella Tiger, a geisha, and a pond-full of fish hiding under your airman's jacket and faded jeans. Never."

"Gabriella Tiger is only one side of me, Lola."

"And a very attractive side. *Some make an art of seduction, others a glory out of being seduced,* as Esprit Fléchier used to say."

"I'm not sure it's a question of seduction."

"You don't say! What is it then?"

"I have an obsession."

"Which particular one?"

"Leave me alone, Lola. Can't you see I'm tired?"

"Ingrid, you talk all the time, but you never say anything serious. Tonight's the moment. Talk, Ingrid, *t-a-l-k.* And give me some more of that firewater."

"I'm afraid the human race is coming to an end."

"That's your obsession?"

"Yeah."

"Is this because of 9/11?"

"No. It's the cyber revolution."

"What's that, for heaven's sake?"

"I'm afraid that one day human beings will become obsolete. That they'll be wiped off the face of the Earth and replaced by robots or cyborgs. Mankind has always dreamed of immortality. We've almost achieved it, but at the cost losing all sense of who we are. We only have to give up on ourselves, and we'll become perfect. No more suffering, no more racism, no more wars over religion or territory. No more sex, no more child-bearing, no more sleep, hunger or thirst, no more seduction, no more repulsion, no more death and no more life. There will be nothing left apart from the glorious future of the

DOMINIQUE SYLVAIN - 154

conquest of space. We will finally and definitively become immortal, and we'll be caught like rats in a trap."

"Wow, as Maxime would say."

"That's the reason I use my body to dance. And that's why I massage other people's bodies. Because our bodies are all we have. Once our flesh rots or is eaten away, we no longer exist. It's all over."

"I don't get the impression that it's imminent."

"Science is evolving exponentially, Lola. If it doesn't affect us today, if it only happens in thirty or forty years, what does that alter? I'm thinking of us as a species."

"You're a rather excitable young woman, Ingrid. But that doesn't bother me. In fact, I'm beginning to like it."

"You're only saying that because the tequila is making your head spin."

"You're wrong there. I speak my mind. In fact, I'd say I find us both admirable. We're prepared to fight for love and friendship. Even if those feelings are nothing more than the product of chemical processes in our mutant chimpanzee brains."

"What are you trying to say, Lola? That Maxime is worth fighting for? Because he's the salt of the earth?"

"Precisely, my girl. The salt you forgot to serve with the tequila."

22

"*From the depths I call out to you, O Lord. Lord, hear my voice; let your ears be attentive to my voice in supplication! If you, O Lord, mark iniquities, who, Lord, can stand?*"

The priest closed his missal, paused for a moment, and then declared, "We are here to say farewell to Vanessa, whom we are delivering into the hands of the Lord, and whom we shall meet again in the Kingdom of Heaven."

Jean-Luc imagined God's hands: big, strong, gnarled; he couldn't help glancing down at his own huge paws. He was the tallest person in Belleville cemetery, but with so many people swarming round the grave, there was no risk of being spotted by the police, who were keeping a discreet distance. He had put on his skipper's cap, tied a scarf round his neck, and was wearing his reefer jacket. A promise had been made to Farid to bury a text in Arabic as close as possible to Vanessa's grave. A farewell to the beloved. For once, Farid had taken some trouble: he had gone to see an old man at the mosque on Rue du Faubourg-Saint-Denis to ask him to write it for him. Farid could more or less speak the language of his ancestors, but did not write it. Jean-Luc had opened the folded piece of paper to admire the calligraphy. He really had to get Farid to go to sea with him. The Mediterranean would teach him to be a man.

Farid also wanted Jean-Luc to keep his eyes and ears open. For him to spot a guilty face, a misplaced smile. Anything to add fuel to his desire for vengeance. Jean-Luc was content. Farid loved his Siamese twin Noah, but for more delicate matters he turned to his pal Jean-Luc.

So far he had not detected anything out-of-place on the mourners' faces. They all looked suitably distraught. Their long, sombre faces stood out all the more distinctly against the clear blue sky. It was nine in the morning, and the sun was repainting the headstones with orange brushstrokes. And making the priest's purple and silver stole sparkle. It was cruelly beautiful.

Most of the mourners were young. For such a solitary soul, Vanessa Ringer seemed to have known a lot of people. Among the handful of adults, a couple who looked not only sad but embittered; they must be the parents. The father was stiff as a post, and the mother seemed about to dissolve in tears. *Stabat mater dolorosa* . . . Jean-Luc recalled a few snatches of Latin; as a choirboy he had been to dozens of burials.

There was also a fat old woman dressed in a raincoat buttoned up to the neck. Possibly an aunt. It was the kind of coat Bogart wore in old films, except that it looked much better on him. Yet she did not look particularly gaga – she was studying the crowd with owlish eyes. Next to her stood a blonde who was like something out of a Scandinavian yoghurt advert. Not bad, except she had no make-up on and was wearing a man's jacket. From time to time, she leant towards Auntie and whispered in her ear. They looked a bit like Beauty and the Beast.

And then of course, there were Chloé and Khadidja. Chloé had brought her cello. Jean-Luc remembered seeing it in her bedroom the day he had put the wind up her. So there was going to be a little homage to the dead girl. A good idea, a brave act. How was she going to avoid playing wrong notes at the edge of the hole where her dead friend's coffin was about to disappear? Black coat and bell-bottoms, with the white collar of her blouse poking out, her face all pale, puffy-eyed, Chloé was the perfect brave kid.

Khadidja was something else. Done up to the nines. Figure-hugging suit, fur toque, dark glasses, clutching three white roses to her chest. Beside her was a guy who was good-looking but older than she was, though not much taller. He must be the boyfriend Farid couldn't stand. The guy who would never marry his sister because she was an Arab. Or because that kind of guy never married anyone. Who knows? He had his arm round Khadidja. The strong arm of a guy who might not marry but who is a great comfort. He was staring straight ahead of him, at the buildings on Rue du Télégraphe.

"*My soul waits for the Lord, I trust in the Lord, and my soul trusts in His word.*"

The priest fell silent, there was a slight ripple in the crowd as Chloé stepped forward, followed by a choirboy carrying a chair for her. She took her time sitting down, tuning her instrument, and then raised the bow. Jean-Luc had never heard the music before: it was a very beautiful piece, very sad, very mathematical. After his initial astonishment, he concentrated on Chloé, trying to read her. In the glorious golden glow he saw a pure white unicorn appear. Her mane and tail bristled, shooting out sparks. The cello's steel spike was the animal's silvery horn. Its face was that of Chloé, without the puffiness and the rivulets of tears. She was completely pure. Her silken robe shone in the milky sunlight.

Then everything went dark, and Jean-Luc came out of his trance. The sky had turned grey. The closer it came to winter, the more mornings seemed like dusk. He sensed a shiver run through the crowd; they had taken the change as a sign from above, and sadness encroached still further. But then a boy with the face of a shepherd, blond curls peeping out from under a woollen cap and a goatee to match, had an idea. He raised his arm; he was holding a lit cigarette lighter in his hand. His gesture spread among the mourners, and soon dozens of tiny lights were flickering at the end of upright arms. As if this were a fucking rock concert, Jean-Luc thought. Vanessa's old man, who probably had never heard of Woodstock, looked all round him, apoplectic.

Lieutenant Jérôme Barthélemy had got to the bottom of this huge gathering at Vanessa Ringer's funeral. Renée Kantor had proudly explained that her son had managed to alert all the former pupils from Lycée Beaumarchais over the internet. It was he who had had the spontaneous idea of the lighter. A thoroughly modern paradox: in life, Vanessa Ringer had been a solitary person, not particularly funny, not excessively warm. She could count her friends in less than three seconds. In death, thanks to the magic of our hyper-communicative world, the young girl was playing her exit scene to a full house. Everyone wanted to say goodbye to her. The lighters flicked on. The faces oozed nostalgia. Wouldn't it have been better to have all these dummies around when she needed them? Barthélemy glanced round at the boss, to see if she felt the same way.

In the meantime, he was glad he'd been able to warn her about the Gnome's intentions. Grousset was on the warpath. There was bound to be trouble. The day before, off her own bat, Renée Kantor had come to make a statement at Rue Louis-Blanc, and her surprise visit had electrified the Gnome. She had portrayed Vanessa Ringer as Maxime Duchamp's mistress. She hadn't pulled any punches, directly accusing the restaurant owner. When she had declared, "He used to be an adventurer, someone who's been everywhere and done everything. He's not afraid of blood or violence. And besides, a cook, even if he has come to it late, knows all about cutting up carcasses, doesn't he, commissaire?" the Garden Gnome had given her his undivided attention. When she had gone on to stress the similarities with the Rinko Yamada affair, Grousset's delight became almost orgasmic. His ecstasy had quickly given way to a hysterical outburst when Renée let slip about the visit Lola Jost had paid her.

"We have to talk, Madame Jost."

"Why not, Grousset? But are you sure a cemetery is the ideal place?"

"Quite so. What business do you have here?"

"As you can see, I'm paying homage to a young girl from my neighbourhood."

"Rather a forced homage, Madame Jost. Don't try to lead me by the nose. I know you're treading on my toes."

"You need to be more careful with your metaphors, Grousset. Your body's flying off in all directions."

"You're questioning witnesses when you're no longer entitled to do so. You're interfering in a police investigation that is none of your business. That's a very serious matter."

"Do you think so, doctor?"

"Don't try to be cute with me, Madame Jost! Anyone can see what's going on: your friendship with Maxime Duchamp is leading you into dangerous waters. You've lost control. You've been seen running about all over the neighbourhood."

"Do you really think I look like a free electron, Commissaire Grousset? Thanks, I take that as a compliment."

"I don't want to see you trampling all over *my* investigation anymore. Is that clear? If you persist, I can guarantee it will be mentioned in high circles. And since your reputation is all you have left . . ."

"Yours suits you so well. Time goes by, yet it remains unblemished . . ."

"Keep your sarcasm to yourself. It's the lowest form of wit. And by the way, I'm arresting Maxime Duchamp right here, right now."

The Gnome's anger had about as much effect on Lola as bird droppings on the Rock of Gibraltar. Her eternal raincoat converted into a mantle of scorn, fists stuffed in her pockets, chin and mouth held high, the boss withered Jean-Pascal Grousset with her Medusa-stare, shrinking and shrinking him until, utterly routed, he plonked his pipe in his mouth and fled. He made for the police car where two uniforms were waiting to arrest Maxime Duchamp. Barthélemy had no special sympathy towards the restaurant owner, but felt a twinge of compassion for Lola. Despite all her best efforts, the owner of *Belles* was in a tight spot. The lieutenant gave a melancholy smile to Lola and her athletic sidekick, then hurried off, head down, in the Garden Gnome's slipstream.

Jean-Luc was pleased with himself. Unseen and unrecognised, mission accomplished. The shepherd boy had hit on the bright idea of throwing his lighter into the grave, and his gesture was like a powder trail. All the youngsters copied him. Jean-Luc had done the same, surreptitiously adding Farid's ode to his loved one. Now he was sitting opposite Chloé in a café on Rue du Télégraphe.

Chloé was still flustered from all the commotion at the cemetery. The moment when the police had taken away the boyfriend, and Khadidja with him, screaming blue murder. Unlike her man, who had stayed very calm, and followed the officers with a resigned smile on his face. Chloé explained that his name was Maxime Duchamp, and that he ran the only French restaurant in Passage Brady. Before that, he had been a war photographer. Jean-Luc was impressed. Those kinds of guys were either completely bonkers or had the balls of an elephant.

While she ranted on about the police, telling him the story yet again as if he had not seen it all for himself, Chloé kept glancing at him as if seeking his approval. She didn't seem afraid of him anymore.

He was beginning to find her face quite pleasant; her freckles accentuated her air of innocence. He got her talking about music, and let her mention composers he had never even heard of. This girl knew her stuff, and was as passionate about music as he was about the sea. Jean-Luc began to toy with the idea of taking Chloé on board *The Dark Angel* as well. She was determined and humble enough to make a good crew member. Besides, someone who knew how to tell a story was a godsend on long voyages. The drawback was sharing with Farid. Yet another reason for lancing the boil.

"You know a lot about Farid, Chloé."

"Me? No, I don't. We've known each other since school, but he wasn't exactly an easy student. And then you saw the beating he gave Khadidja. All the more reason why I don't particularly like him. Apart from that, nothing special."

"Chloé, don't imagine that just because I have the body of a brute, I have the mind of one too."

"I never said you were a brute."

"Don't go all defensive on me. I'm much more open than you think."

"No problem."

"You can tell me anything you like about Farid. Whatever he's done, he'll still be my friend, because loyalty runs in my blood. Besides, he's staying with me at the moment."

"That's kind of you."

"I'm sure he has a disreputable past. Noah says Farid arrived on the estate one fine day out of nowhere. Farid loves to do what he wants when he wants. He hasn't even got a driving licence. That's why Noah or me have to ferry him around everywhere. I've always thought he behaved like a refugee. But not a political refugee, if you follow me?"

"More or less. I think Farid keeps a low profile like any self-respecting crook."

"It's not just that. My house in Saint-Denis is a perfect hiding-place. It's a stone-built detached house, very respectable, never any noise after ten o'clock at night. With a base camp like that, who'd want to pick a fight with Farid? No-one, believe me. Tell me what you know about him, Chloé."

"A lot less than you: you're his friend."

"You're wrong not to trust me. But we hardly know each other, so that's normal. Of course, I've done time. And I'm a thief. But I steal for my dream. A boat. A sixty-footer that's waiting for me in Palma de Mallorca. Unlike Farid, I believe in something."

"That's easily said."

"Not as easily as all that. No-one else knows what I've just told you. When I was fifteen, I decided to take rather than to beg. I'm an anarchist, Chloé. I *am* political. The world's a mess, especially for people like you and me. We're born without any inheritance, and we have to choose whether to live our dreams or not. Wouldn't you like to play your cello on the deck of a yacht while the sun sets on a turquoise sea?"

23

Full, round, beautiful as a boy-king's marble, the moon shone with all its diamond brilliance. For the boss of the Star Panorama this exactly chimed with the atmosphere at the cinema, because tonight marked the close of the Santo Gadejo festival, with a screening of several incandescent works, including "Pyromania" for starters. The customers were crowding the pavement outside. Ingrid and Lola were waiting in the foyer, basking in Rodolphe Kantor's beaming approval. Overjoyed at having finally received the call from Dylan Klapesch, he had welcomed them like royalty. The film director had agreed to give a talk. He asked only for free drinks for him and a few friends. Ingrid was careful not to reveal that Klapesch's entourage was in fact a gang of drunks with outrageous habits.

Lola was explaining to Ingrid that the situation was far from brilliant. So far, Lieutenant Barthélemy's persistence had got him nowhere with the police files. The only address given for Farid Younis was Rue de l'Aqueduc, and his parents had no more news of him than on the previous police visit. Barthélemy had failed to work his magic in Saint-Denis as well. Either the Calypso bouncer's tip was wide of the mark and Younis had never set foot on the estates there, or the witnesses refused to co-operate with the forces of order. Or Farid was a slippery eel with an impenetrable alias.

However, it was the excess that the ex-commissaire concentrated on.

"The excess, Lola?"

"Yes, my young apprentice. The evidence pointing to Maxime in the Ringer affair stacks up with incredible generosity. It's quite simple: all the clues point to Maxime Duchamp, like the sacred rivers to the legendary delta."

"Where is this legendary delta of yours? And what on earth are the sacred rivers?"

"Mere products of my imagination, my girl. I'm warming to my subject. In fact, I'm trying to recapitulate. Action is all very well, but it's high time we had a pause for reflection."

So Lola sifted methodically through all the evidence piling up in the cupboard marked "suspicious". The whole jumble of certainties, probabilities, suppositions, false realities. Maxime, the war photographer, sets up home in Paris with his Japanese wife, a creator of graphic novels. He is often away on reporting trips. People around them whisper about disagreements. The artist is strangled to death, her ankles tied to the bars of the marital bed. She leaves behind her a work as dark as it is mysterious: a cult manga book dealing with the abuses of advanced capitalist society, the perversity of immature adolescents, and the cutting up of venal schoolgirls. Rinko Yamada's murder is never solved. Twelve years later, the still-attractive Maxime, reborn as a chef, finds himself embroiled in a similar situation. And there are schoolgirls again. Real ones, this time. Khadidja, Chloé and Vanessa, three girls without roots who form a surrogate family and stick together in the face of adversity. One of them is strangled. Her killer, who knows the three girls' habits well, adds a symbolic dimension by mutilating her *post mortem* with a meat cleaver, and signing his crime with a Bratz doll with detachable feet in effigy of his victim.

The affair becomes even more complex when rumours hint that Maxime Duchamp was Vanessa Ringer's lover.

The same Duchamp who is now engaged to Khadidja, with whom he has a stormy relationship. The same Duchamp who was near the scene at the time of the murder. The same Duchamp who has keys to the apartment on Passage du Désir.

"Duchamp, here, Duchamp there, there's too much of him, and therefore it doesn't fit. That's what we have to focus on. Because you know, Ingrid, contrary to what certain over-excitable film-makers would have us believe, intelligent murderers are an extremely rare species. In reality, murderers are usually stupid."

"What about serial killers?"

"Doubly stupid. Otherwise, why get into trouble up to your neck and risk winding up in prison for next-to-nothing? Rather than taking advantage of the relative, but real, joys of existence? Because in cases like that, crime doesn't pay. No, believe me, the only intelligent criminals I've ever come across are the hold-up merchants. They have a clear motive. It's a four-letter word: L-O-O-T. Their activity requires a sense of strategy as well as impeccable organisation."

Ingrid had plenty of time to reflect on Lola's theories. Besides four massacres carried out with a flame-thrower, the slow death in close-up of a crew of firemen, and the apocalyptic demise of the entire staff of a hospital engulfed by a river of molten lava, all orchestrated by a crazy, scarred *deus ex machina* seeking revenge for fifteen failed skin grafts, absolutely nothing happened during the screening of "Pyromania". The employees of the Star Panorama behaved as normal, and nobody came to tap the two women on the shoulder to announce that Spieler had arrived.

Afraid that the copious "Pyromania" was merely the starter for an even more indigestible main course, Ingrid and Lola left the auditorium before the end of the film, and went in search of Elisabeth. The red-headed usherette was having a cigarette out on the pavement, staring idly at the small garden next to Saint-Laurent church.

"Spieler never turned up; I'm sorry."

"Not as sorry as we are, my girl. I thought he was hooked on the work of that other psychopath."

"Perhaps he knows Gadejo's films backwards."

"He plays them through in his mind, and that's enough," Lola said. "I can understand that. Fifty-two deaths a minute must leave their mark on the cerebellum."

"But I do know where he lives. Rue Dieu. Right above a Lebanese restaurant."

"Why didn't you say so straight off?"

"I couldn't."

"And in Rue Dieu! That's not hard to remember!"

"Are you all fucking nuts in this country, or what?" Ingrid cried.

"Two days ago, I ran into Spieler. I followed him home, but he saw me. I managed to get out of it by making up some excuse, but if he's the one who killed Vanessa, I don't want him to know I gave him away. His real name is Benjamin Noblet."

"That's understandable, my girl," Lola said magnanimously. "Everyone has the right to be scared."

"Fucking nuts!"

Oriental aromas swirled cruelly round the stairwell, making Lola's taste-buds swoon. She was running on empty, deprived of the delights served up at *Belles de jour comme de nuit.* All she had eaten for dinner was a meagre helping of pasta and a banana. This did not stop her from opening Monsieur Benjamin Noblet's door with a flourish, thanks to her credit card. Breaking into a stranger's apartment did nothing to assuage her appetite, and she was seriously considering raiding the fridge for an acceptable snack. Ingrid was in a very different mood. Lola sensed she was ready to knock Benjamin Spieler flat with a karate kick if need be.

They searched the modest studio for cleavers, women's shoes, Bratz dolls, or any evidence that Noblet was an obsessive. Apart from several film cameras, lighting equipment and a fabulous D.V.D. collection, the dwelling revealed no penchant for fetishism. The D.V.D.s also showed eclectic tastes: among the horror films, there were box sets of Chaplin, Melville, Orson Welles and David Lynch. Lola went so far as to empty the waste-bin onto the tiled floor of the kitchenette. After sifting through an uninspiring, trivial reality, she washed her hands, then opened the fridge and the freezer. With Ingrid leaning over her shoulder, she was able to determine the absence of any frozen human feet. She pulled out some ham, Comté cheese, pickled gherkins and beer to have a picnic on the kitchen table. She was even intending to make coffee.

It's crazy the amount of time you spend waiting around "in the police force", thought Ingrid. She had grown used to the darkness. Sitting cross-legged on her jacket, she was listening intently for any noise inside the building. All she could see was the silhouette of Lola, her hunger finally satisfied. It was so late that despite the caffeine Ingrid sensed her mind playing tricks on her. She had not slept much recently, either because she was so wrapped up in the manhunt with Lola, or because she was too worried about Maxime. She tried to take deep breaths and stretched out to relax her numbed muscles. All she could hear was Lola's slightly laboured breathing.

"You know, Ingrid, this reminds me of some of my stake-outs with Toussaint."

"Your former partner?"

"Yes, before Barthélemy. Toussaint Kidjo, a good kid. Whenever we were on a stake-out, Toussaint used to hum. Old hits by Otis Redding, Curtis Mayfield, Burt Bacharach. He had an amazing repertoire. And a fine voice, the little jerk. Good-looking, too. Praline-coloured skin, thanks to a father born in Yaoundé and a mother from Brittany. Blond streaks in his curly hair, hazel eyes. He was always in a good mood, and you know how rare that is. The other thing he had in common with you is that he inspired me."

Ingrid allowed Lola to let it all out. For some time now she had been waiting for her to unburden herself, to tell her all about Toussaint, killed on duty before he reached thirty. Ingrid knew from Maxime that Lola still felt responsible for his death. A gruesome end. A beheading. In fact, Ingrid knew more about it than Lola imagined. Rightly or wrongly, Kidjo's demise had led the ex-commissaire to quit her old life, her responsibilities, her position, her team, a profession she loved. Even now, it was obvious how much she loved it. This fucking job.

"You see, Ingrid, I'm not one of your solitary hunters. I never scent the quarry so well as when I'm working with someone. My neurons only function when I can talk things over. That's how I am. That's why I'm monopolising you instead of allowing you to wiggle your backside for late-night Paris."

"I'll show them tomorrow. Don't worry."

"I'm not worried, I've understood you're a methodical girl, serious about everything you do. Nice and curvy, but with your head screwed on straight. And I like the contrast, my girl, I like it."

"Someone's just come into the building, Lola."

"O.K., get ready. If it's our Benjamin, we'll nab him."

"I thought we were going nick him."

"Poor little innocent. Do you really think you can fit police vocabulary onto a postage stamp?"

Someone Ingrid and Lola hoped was Benjamin Noblet had just placed a key in the lock and was opening the front door to the flat. Time stood still. And came rushing back at the speed of the steps that same someone took to chase his shadow down the staircase. Ingrid leapt after him.

The stocky silhouette sped along Rue Dieu towards the Saint-Louis hospital. Ingrid sprinted after him, all the years she had spent on the treadmill giving her the speed of a trained athlete. The fugitive hesitated over crossing the bridge. His body froze in the bright moonlight. Shorter than Ingrid, he had brown hair and looked quite young. He set off again to his left, along the canal. Ingrid chased after him without a second thought. She could feel the anger rising in her, driving her on. I'll get you, fucking bastard! I'll get you! she promised as she tasted her own blood in her throat and the sharp night air burned her lungs.

The two of them raced along the deserted quay. Then all at once the fugitive had had enough. He came to a sudden halt. Bent double, hands on his knees, blowing like a seal. Ingrid caught a glimpse of his face in the lamplight. Not a glimmer of fear: he had just realised his pursuer was a mere woman. His body spoke for him: he was going to stand and face her. Built like a little fighting bull, he couldn't run any further, but he could do damage. The voice of Elisabeth the red-headed usherette seemed to rise from the drab waters of the canal, muffled words inside Ingrid's head. *But if he's the one who killed Vanessa . . . if he's the one . . . Vanessa . . . if he's the one.*

Ingrid suddenly wondered whether he had a blade. She had seen a big, strong man die from a knife-wound in a Chicago street, stabbed by a crazy kid weighing fifty kilos soaking wet. She couldn't count on Lola's wheezing pursuit. The cavalry would never arrive in time. Did Lola have a jinx on her? Did all her partners end up paying with their lives? Ingrid shouted out: that was all she could do.

"Police! Don't move!"

A sly smile came over the face of the stocky figure in front of her, then he laughed openly.

"So they employ Yanks now, do they?"

Ingrid thought hard of Maxime's eyes, Maxime's body, the salt of the earth – one could fight for him, yes, one could. She clenched her stomach muscles, flexed her shoulders, and stood as straight as she could, stretching out her long giraffe neck. The youngster had slipped his hand inside his jacket pocket, and kept it there. They sized each other up. Then he took a step backwards, spun on his heel, and ran off again. Shit, this guy can't make his mind up! But for me, it's now or never! Ingrid flung herself at him, grabbed him by the shoulders, using her weight to bring him down, and collapsed on top of him. He groaned, swore at her. She held him as tight as she could, grinding his kidneys with her knees.

"We nick him, nab him, grab him. What else, Lola? Hurry up, Lola! What the fuck are you doing, lady?"

The man wrenched one hand free, punched her on the side of the head. Pain rocketed through her skull. Their bodies next to the canal. He grabbed her by the neck and squeezed. She went limp for a moment in order to aim for his flesh, his neck. Sank her teeth in. He reached for one of her ears and pulled. I want to keep my fucking ears! With all her remaining strength, Ingrid wrestled their two bodies into the canal. The sting of the icy, stinking water. He got hold of her jersey, she grasped his jacket collar, their legs bicycling.

"YOU WON'T GET ME LIKE YOU DID VANESSA, YOU BITCH!"

"What are you talking about?"

"You killed her, didn't you? But you don't scare me."

A slap from the little bull missed its target. Ingrid responded with one that was more accurate.

"I was going to ask you the same question, you asshole!"

He stopped punching, so Ingrid did the same:

"I've got a suggestion. Let's save ourselves from drowning, and then we can talk."

"O.K., but let go of me!"

They scrambled back up onto the quayside. Ingrid was the first out of the water. She watched him struggle for a couple of seconds: he looked frozen stiff, so she held out her hand and hauled him up. They collapsed against each other, and fell on their backs, staring up at the stars. There were a few that night, twinkling feebly.

"You're as strong as a mare, you madwoman!"

"The same goes for you, Noblet. Because I hope to God you are Benjamin Noblet?"

"What's left of him. I can't move, you would-be Wonderwoman!"

"We discuss how we feel later on, Cassius Clay. Why did you think I killed Vanessa?"

"I thought you were a lesbian. With that hair, and the way you look . . ."

"Lesbian or not, what's the connection?"

"As Vanessa didn't seem to be interested in men, I thought she must be gay. When I realised you were a woman, I thought you were out for a lover's revenge. I saw myself coming runner-up in a 'crime-of-passion victim' competition. You're not a lesbian?"

"Not that I know of."

They fell silent, allowing their breathing to return to normal. Then

Noblet sat up and said, teeth chattering, "There's a big, fat old lady leaning over the parapet staring at us. I think we ought to get out of here before the police arrive. The real police."

"Don't worry. The big fat lady *is* police. Retired, it's true, but . . . Well, it's a long story. Let's go to your place and have a hot toddy. I notice you had some rum."

"And gherkins and coffee. It was when I smelt them that I realised you were waiting for me at my place. I'd love to hear why you rifled through my cupboards so thoroughly, Wonderwoman."

"No way!"

"What d'you mean, no way?"

"Not until you've answered our questions, Cassius."

24

Noblet's studio was not equipped with a hairdryer, and so Ingrid had pulled her Peruvian hat down to cover her ears. But the washing-machine did have a spin-dryer, and clothes were tumbling gently round behind the porthole. Swathed in a strange dressing gown, with her feet in a basin of hot water she was sharing with Noblet, Ingrid was warming her hands on the porcelain mug of grog stiffened with a large shot of rum by Lola. Although the boss was in no danger of hypothermia, she was furnished with the same drink and followed the interrogation without a word, for once allowing Ingrid to lead the dance (once doesn't make a habit).

"So in your view, Vanessa was a lesbian?"

"I saw two options. Either she was gay, or she'd given up on sex. In fact, I thought she had something of the nun about her. Not the bride of Jesus type, more in the style of Mother Teresa. She had an all-consuming need to devote herself to something. But I bet the lady from Calcutta had more human warmth than Vanessa."

Ingrid stared dubiously at Noblet while their toes did their best to share their restricted shared space equably.

"I know what you're thinking. And no, I'm not some frustrated Lothario bad-mouthing a girl just because she snubbed him."

"Even so, I bet she *did* snub you."

"Vanessa was pretty. I tried. She blew me off. I got the message; I didn't make a song and dance of it. Besides, frigid girls always get their way with me. They turn me off. Anyway, all I wanted was to get her to do a screen test for a film I'm making with some friends. I'm a student at a film school."

"A gore film, naturally."

"A film that plays with the conventions of the genre. It's not the same thing."

"Whatever. Why choose Vanessa?"

"I don't much like professional actresses. And an usherette from a gore cinema is by definition someone who has seen a bellyful of twisted screenplays."

Ingrid wasn't bad as an interrogator. She posed some questions several times, trying unsucessfully to lead Noblet to contradict himself. She got him to revisit his meeting with Vanessa, pushed him to talk about his likes and dislikes with a skill a criminal psychologist would have envied. But the two women had to accept the evidence. The Spieler was not trying his spiel on them, and Monsieur Noblet was rather likeable. When Ingrid examined him closely, now that his brown hair was dry and curling round his unshaven face, she had to admit he looked interesting.

By about three in the morning, they decided it was time to leave. Ingrid put her still damp jeans and pullover back on – she refused point blank to borrow anything from Noblet – then slipped on her airman's jacket. When they were out in the street, Lola finally spoke up, and said they were going to *Belles*.

The alarm only rang for a few seconds. As soon as they had broken in, Lola rushed behind the bar and switched it off. Then they established their battle plan: Lola in the cellar and pantry, Ingrid in the apartment.

"What are we looking for, Lola?"

"Anything that might incriminate Maxime. Rinko's dolls, for example. When Grousset comes to search the place, he'll find everything neat and tidy."

"So this is an emergency?"

"You said it. Draw the curtains and use your torch, understood?"

"No problem, boss."

Lola found herself once more beneath the fine arched ceiling of the cellar running the whole length of the restaurant, with the familiar smell of beaten earth and the aroma of wine. An image of the last time she had been here with Maxime, tasting his latest discoveries straight from the barrel, flashed into her mind. Before she began her search, nostalgia led her to serve herself a glass from his own special reserve. Then she looked through each rack in turn, knelt down to peer beneath the barrels, tested the floor for any hidden hatch. Serving herself another glass of the unpretentious chateau wine that could be relied on in even the most unlikely circumstances, she began to study the bottles one by one. Italian, French, Spanish; Maxime was obviously looking for a certain idea of Latinity in his wine. Lola did not really know what she was expecting to find, but went at it with a will. Now and then she imagined the spirit of Toussaint beside her, humming while hard at work.

It seemed that even though he was dead, Toussaint Kidjo had more vitality in him than Vanessa Ringer had ever shown. It was as if she were already dead before she was killed. Vanessa, described by Benjamin Noblet as a kind of nun without human warmth. By the manager of the Star Panorama as someone who never made her mind up, who could not be trusted. And by that sneak Renée Kantor as a sad, abandoned girl in love. On the other hand, to Constantin the street kid, she was the only one who knew how to comfort him. To her girlfriends, she was a serious, straightforward sort. And to Guillaume Fogel she was a brave little soldier. A portrait with light and shade, but nothing out of the ordinary. A few essential pieces were missing from the Vanessa jigsaw.

Hands on hips, stationed in the exact centre of the main arch, her body flooded by the yellow light from the ceiling bulb, Lola slowly turned full circle. Then she looked up at the ceiling to see if any bricks were sticking out. But it was all carefully whitewashed, and appeared not to conceal any secret hiding-place. Just a normal cellar, giving off an agreeable smell of the soil and its robust pleasures. She began a painstaking examination of the adjoining pantry. Plump hams were curing as they hung from the ceiling, adding their perfume to that of apples. Lola inspected the stocks of rice, oil, spices, condiments, cordials. Everything was meticulously labelled and lined up. Each label was in Maxime's handwriting. The mysterious, painstaking Maxime. Lola switched off the light and went back up to the restaurant.

She had sent Ingrid to the apartment because she could not bring herself to search her friend's drawers, poke around in his linen, open his medicine cabinet. Ingrid though had accepted the task without a protest. Lola could hear her coming and going on the floor above. With that almost animal energy of hers, she was sure to be making a thorough job of it.

Lola sat at the bar until her eyes became accustomed to the gloom. The contours of the restaurant slowly emerged, accompanied by images of its owner. He was greeting customers, coming over to her, sitting at her table, pouring her a glass of wine, smiling at her. The room was filled with his voice, fragments of his recipes, the secrets of his cooking, revealed only to his closest friends. His memories. His family in Le Quercy, gathered together the day they killed the pig. All of which would be used, from trotters and tail to ears. And the stories from his roving-journalist days, the photographs snatched from the heart of the storm. His addiction until he went cold turkey in 1991. All these stories, told without show by a man who had lived several lives.

Lola grimaced and got down from her stool. Her desperate search for Ingrid earlier that night, the breathless, frightening discovery of the big giraffe thrashing around in the canal, had left her exhausted. The dank cold of the streets had seeped into her bones, her shoulders were a tight knot, the flu lurking in her body was back on the warpath.

As she climbed the stairs, Lola listened to the silence. It was deep, soft and warm like the intimate life of a man, the life she was peering into despite herself, uneasy about this obscene snooping around. Oh Maxime, my friend, there's no dirty work I wouldn't do for you! She pictured him at the Rue Louis-Blanc police station, and hoped he was asleep. She was sure Barthélemy would have found him an individual cell and made sure he got a good blanket.

No sound came from the apartment. Lola called out: "Ingrid! Ingrid!" keeping her voice as low as possible, but the Yank made no reply.

Lola found her in the bedroom, stretched out on the bed. She had removed her jacket and boots. She wasn't moving, and with half her face lit by the bedside lamp, it looked as if she were asleep.

Lola caught sight of the doll lying between her breasts.

"INGRID! OH! INGRID!"

The tall blonde woman opened her eyes.

"I lay down . . . to sniff his odour. It's crazy how good a man's skin can smell."

Lola thought her voice sounded strange. Even so, she sighed with relief as she sat on the duvet: she had feared Ingrid was dead. Twice on the same night was hard to take. Mechanically, she felt for Ingrid's forearm: it was warm. She took deep breaths. If I lie down on this bed, she told herself, I'll never get up again. She felt the force of gravity weighing on her shoulders, like a depraved bird pecking at her neck, leaving it to the lack of sleep to gnaw at her eye-sockets.

Ingrid waved the doll glumly. It was wearing a navy-blue and white uniform, with lace ankle socks. Its creator had given it a face with wide, innocent eyes.

"I've found two friends of hers. Both in pretty boxes, with a photo of a schoolgirl on top."

"Don't tell me they're replicas of Khadidja, Chloé and Vanessa."

"No, don't worry, they're Japanese," Ingrid replied dolefully.

"What's so sad about that? Isn't it a relief?"

"What depressed me was what I found in the wardrobe next to the dolls."

"What's that?"

"A duvet."

"Ingrid, you can tell me Mother Goose tales some other time. Quick, get to the point, or I'm going to fall asleep like a log."

"Just a minute, I'm coming to that. Maxime is a tidy man, he doesn't like a mess."

"That much is obvious."

"You're sitting on his winter duvet."

"Yes, this one is nice and fluffy."

"In the wardrobe I found an empty duvet cover, marked *Winter Duvet*, and a full one marked *Summer Duvet*. I took out the summer one. It's there by the side of the bed. Touch it and see."

Lola looked at her blankly, then stretched her arm out and did as her companion asked.

"*Bougre de coquinasse!* What's that, Ingrid?"

"Banknotes, Lola. Bundles and bundles and bundles of banknotes."

25

Elbows propped on the bar of *Belles*, Lola was lost in her meandering thoughts. Ingrid was talking to her, but she didn't respond. The Yank wanted to deal with the most pressing task: hiding the money in Passage du Désir. A canvas bag they had found in Maxime's wardrobe was at their feet. In it was all the loot they had found stashed in the summer duvet.

"Lola! Wake up! Are you listening to me or not?"

"Of course, my girl, I can do two things at once. You're right. Let's get out of here and hide the money at your place."

When they got there, Ingrid saw the green light flashing on her answering machine. She went into the kitchen, made some coffee, poured some for Lola, then began to count the money.

"Lola, there's about five hundred thousand euros here."

"Is that all?"

Ingrid freed the messages trapped in her machine. They were all from Rodolphe Kantor. Each more desperate than the last. The most recent was from just an hour earlier.

The voice of the manager of the Star Panorama echoed round Ingrid Diesel's waiting room, and faded out with these words: "Get me out of this right now, or I'll hold you responsible for the wrecking of my establishment!"

"That's all we need," Lola said, raising eyes and hands to heaven.

"I'll have to go there," Ingrid said.

"I'll come with you."

"Are you sure?"

"Going to sleep is like taking a train, my girl. If you miss one, you simply wait and catch the next one."

"What if after all this we forget how to go to sleep?"

Rodolphe Kantor was wearing an ordinary suit. His hair was not slicked back, his eyes were haggard, and he had removed the false moustache.

"Six rows of seats destroyed, one of the red curtains torn to shreds, the bar drunk dry. I hope you're going to find the magic words to make them get out of here. Because if not, in two minutes' time I'm calling the police and giving them your name."

"Why didn't you start by doing that?" Lola asked.

"Because in spite of everything, and as far as possible, I want to stay on good terms with Dylan Klapesch. He is a star, after all."

His words were interrupted by the crash of breaking glass, together with a drunken cry somewhere between happiness and rage. After that all they could hear was the singer from the Red Hot Chili Peppers. His imperious voice was inciting people to get rid of their T.V.s. *Throw away your television, Time to make this clean decision.* The bass guitar was booming away. The lead guitar solo responded harshly. Ingrid explained they were Dylan Klapesch's favourite group. The cinema owner ran his trembling fingers through his hair.

"I've got an idea," Ingrid said.

"Thank God for that!" Kantor groaned.

"You're a specialist in disguise. You must have a sexy dress and wig somewhere."

"Wait . . . er, yes. The ones my wife left here. We organised a big fancy-dress party last summer, and Renée came as the mother from the Addams family."

"Find them for me, put on 'Don't Forget Me' from the Chili Peppers C.D., and leave the rest to me."

"Are you sure about this, Ingrid?"

"Don't worry, Lola. Sometimes it's better to capture the imagination than anything else."

The two women entered the auditorium. It was a Berezina of seats, a Trafalgar of velvet, a Dien Bien Phu of bottles. The air reeked of cigar smoke. The music made the walls vibrate. Klapesch's entourage were dancing in frantic clusters. The director himself was seated on the edge of the stage, avidly embracing a pretty dark-haired girl. Ingrid took off her jacket and her Peruvian hat, handing them to Lola for safe-keeping.

Lola and Kantor looked on as she sauntered down the main aisle and headed for Klapesch; under her arm, the dress and wig looked like a captive animal, mane blowing in the wind. Ingrid hugged the film-maker and embarked on lengthy negotiations with him. After that, she climbed up on stage and disappeared behind the tattered curtain.

The film director harangued his horde. After much talk silenced by the frenetic energy of the Californian rock group, Dylan Klapesch's friends sat down one by one. The music stopped, started again, jumped, as Kantor searched the C.D. for the right track. The lights slowly dimmed, a melancholy guitar intro filled the auditorium, and then the singer began.

The curtain fell back to reveal a cone of light, in the centre of which stood a tall sorceress with flowing black hair and pale skin. She stretched her long arms up to an imaginary sky.

Her shiny dark satin gloves reached so high up her arms that only her shoulders were left bare. Her multicoloured dress hid everything, and ended in a threatening tail. At first there was nothing but the undulating dance of the arms. One after the other, in a torment measured by a thousand years of black magic, the gloves slowly rose up twin marble-like columns. She taunted her public, whirling them round then flinging them into the darkness as an offering. The invisible audience was completely silent. Then it was the hips' turn to sway to the steady rhythm of Anthony Kiedis's voice. She pulled back the fold of her dress, and a leg appeared. The foot was naked, so slender without the guile of shoes. Without the trickery of high heels, she became Esmeralda from *The Hunchback of Notre Dame*.

Brilliant! Lola thought. Who could ever have imagined a striptease artist performing shoe-less.

One side of the door opened and Rodolphe Kantor slipped in

beside her, a broad smile on his face. On stage, the dress slowly evaporated, before flying off into the audience like a flock of demented crows. The flowing hair only hid the dangerous orbs of her breasts for a second. Then Esmeralda turned, revealing the back and buttocks of an Amazon, ran towards the edge of the light, came back with a chair, and began a caressing dance around it. She took hold of the chair back, lifted it in a movement that sketched in an infinity of smooth, taut muscles, then smashed it on the floor until all that was left were two small fragments of wood. She quickly turned them into a pair of horns.

Then she vanished, to thunderous applause and shouts of joy.

"Your young friend isn't an eccentric anymore," Kantor struggled to say. "She's positively baroque."

"*Smooth icy skin on a slender frame, Neck opened on a tender breast . . .*" Lola murmured.

"I couldn't agree with you more, Madame Jost."

"Not so fast, Kantor. I haven't finished my quotation . . . *Under eyelashes like blue-black willows, The almond of her eyes launched stars.*"[*]

"A promise made to Ingrid Diesel is a promise we keep, lads! We're outta here!" Dylan Klapesch shouted to his cohorts.

"Like magic!" Kantor crowed.

[*]   Xiaoxiao Sheng, *Flower in a Golden Phial.*

26

She had put her Peruvian hat and her jacket back on, and was eating butter croissants that left a shiny film on her fingers. Now and then she smiled and drank a mouthful of coffee, as comfortable as Lola in their shared silence. Joseph, the owner of the bar on Rue Fidélité, was talking in a low voice to two regulars.

She's amazing, that Ingrid Diesel! Lola thought. With her eyes, she told her how much she had admired her presence of mind, that there weren't many women like her on this earth, that she was as crazy as she was generous. But only with her eyes, because it was a tranquil morning, that had only recently taken over from dawn. There was a spell around their heads and above the city, which would last until alarm clocks sounded and the masses headed off to work. Perhaps Lola could tell her one day, casually, when they were talking on the phone. Much easier to confess to people how much you appreciate them when they aren't sitting opposite you.

They could hear the news bulletin on the radio loud and clear. The strike at Lycée Alexandre Dumas in Créteil was continuing. The teachers were refusing to give lessons after the return of a pupil who had been expelled by the disciplinary committee. The little daddy's boy had hired a lawyer. An oil spill was threatening the French coasts, and anger among the oyster farmers was growing. So too were the threats of war against Iraq. A gang of five robbers had broken into an auction house in Paris and escaped with a haul of eight million euros in less than fifteen minutes. Twenty-nine people had been killed in a working-class area of Tel-Aviv. The attack had followed the death of three Palestinians the day before.

Bang goes the early morning magic, Lola sighed as she ordered another two coffees from Joseph. Through the window she could see a few rare pedestrians walking past, well wrapped up. One of them was wearing a hoodie that made him look like a terrorist, or rather a bank robber. Lola stopped stirring her coffee and stared at Ingrid, who, her cheeks stuffed with croissant, looked at her inquisitively.

"The day of Vanessa's death, just after Barthélemy's visit . . . on the news they announced a robbery at a bureau de change on the Champs-Elysées. Three hooded men, in a dawn raid."

"What a bloody Sunday!"

"They stole a million and a half euros. If you divide that by three . . ."

"You get five hundred thousand euros," Ingrid finished for her, beaming. "Lola, you're a genius!"

"Not so fast, Ingrid. It's only a supposition."

"'Supposition' is such an ugly word. There are others I don't much like either: 'omission', 'commission', 'purification'. Don't ask me why. Then there are 'intermission', 'infraction', 'injection'."

"Obviously, we can't take the idea of Maxime, Chloé and Khadidja smashing their way into a bureau de change with sledgehammers seriously."

"Or Vanessa, Chloé and Khadidja. Can you see three girls doing that?"

"They'd all need to be built like you, Ingrid, but that's not the case."

"As you say, Lola."

"At any rate, that stack of money provides us with a great motive. Just imagine that for some reason or another the loot was stowed at the girls' place after the hold-up."

"We found it at Maxime's. But why mutilate Vanessa if this is only a question of money? Strangling her would have been enough."

"Exactly. That confirms my theory: the idea was to point the finger at Maxime. And to play down the true motive by replacing it with passion."

"That makes sense, Lola."

"Vanessa was an idealist. Think about it. Shortly after the hold-up, one of the robbers decides to use her apartment to stash the loot. Vanessa refuses, and threatens to go to the police. The robber kills her. Now, who might know their apartment well enough to think it was a good place to hide the money? Who but someone close to them? Someone who had *turned to crime*?"

"Farid Younis."

"Got it in one."

"But there's one thing that doesn't fit in all this, Lola."

"What's that?"

"The fact that we found the money in *Belles*. It doesn't work."

"I know. But then again, there could be an answer. One that would explain why Chloé and Khadidja have only been telling us what suits them from the start. The two of them are there when a quarrel breaks out between Vanessa and Farid. Vanessa dies. Khadidja, who has it in for her because of Maxime, decides to help her brother. They disguise the murder as something premeditated. Chloé, who can be easily influenced, promises to keep quiet. Khadidja or Farid, or both of them together, hide the money at Maxime's."

"That's a risky idea, since all the suspicions were bound to converge on Maxime some day or other."

"Khadidja is a very smart girl, who knows the inside of Maxime's apartment like the back of her hand, Ingrid. Hiding the money in a carefully re-sewn duvet is clever. Way beyond the skills of certain bloodless bloodhounds I've worked with over the years."

"So how do you explain that an amateur like me found it so easily?"

"Because of your open-mindedness, Ingrid. Your complete lack of preconceptions. Your incredible spontaneity, even if I find it a little trying."

"What d'you mean?"

"You're in love with Maxime. Even when you're searching his apartment, you think of things that would never occur to one of my lot. The smell of his skin, the bed, the sheets he has slept in. You don't censor yourself, you let your mind wander, you free-associate. The body leads you to the bed. The bed leads you to the duvet. And the duvet to the banknotes."

"And the banknotes to Saint-Denis. On the trail of Farid Younis."

"You took the words right out of my mouth, Ingrid."

27

Khadidja strode briskly out of the police station. There was no time to lose. Grousset was keeping Chloé there: he knew she was the weak link. As soon as he had finished interrogating her, he would search *Belles*. As she walked, Khadidja was willing her friend to hold out, to defend Maxime tooth and nail. That bastard, the little Napoleon, liked putting people down. She had seen the pleasure in his eyes when he had thrown the affair between Maxime and Vanessa in her face. "Malicious gossip," she had replied as coolly as possible. Better die than show him how much she was hurting.

Maxime and Vanessa. Khadidja would never have dreamed it. She had always thought she was the only one. Rushing to get rid of the evidence that would finish him off, for the first time Khadidja thought about leaving him. Of living without Maxime.

The deliveries entrance, the kitchens, the apartment. The duvet stowed away at the top of the wardrobe. She unzipped the cover, felt inside, and her blood froze. Someone had taken the money.

Her head swam. Then she regained control, forced herself to think. Not even Chloé knew exactly where in the apartment she had hidden it. The police couldn't have searched so quickly and already left. Everything would be upside down.

Could Maxime . . . Khadidja felt as though a rusty needle were piercing the top of her skull. If he had found it, what had he imagined? That she had killed Vanessa out of jealousy, and stowed the hoard in his place to make him look guilty in the eyes of the police?

There were other possible scenarios. One more horrendous than the rest: Maxime killing Vanessa and leaving the money Farid had brought behind in her flat, knowing that neither she nor Chloé would have any other option but to lie to the police. Realising he was going to be arrested, had Maxime recovered the money and then hidden it somewhere safe? But he was only a suspect, the police had nothing concrete on him.

Maxime, waiting for the affair to die down before disappearing with the loot.

Khadidja felt as if her chest was being crushed in a vice. How could you share so much with a man and not know him at all? But no, she could not see him as a murderer. Sure, he had slept with Vanessa, but he was no killer. Maxime wasn't Farid.

She stayed for a while in the bedroom, staring into space. Then she went down to the restaurant. Farid and Jean-Luc were sitting at the bar. She was taken aback, but not frightened, because she saw a glimmer of hope: perhaps Farid had only come for his money. He soon disabused her.

"Was it your guy who killed her?"

"Whether I answer or not, you won't believe me."

"I've always listened to you, Khadidja. Always. Well then? He killed her and took the dough, is that it?"

"Maxime never killed anyone."

"And yet they say he murdered his wife. At least, that's what Jean-Luc has been hearing round the neighbourhood."

"If Jean-Luc wants to behave like a concierge, that's his look-out."

"I'll show you what kind of concierge I am, you bitch!"

"You don't scare me, you big brute."

"Your sister is worse than badly brought-up, Farid. She's plain stupid."

Khadidja stared at them defiantly. The giant looked riled. Farid had that air of an imperturbable madman about him. So calm he appeared half dead. She took a deep breath and said, slowly but clearly, "If you kill Maxime, Farid, you're going to have to get rid of me too. Because otherwise I'll hand you over to the police. I'll tell them about now. I'll tell them about the past. There'll be nothing to stop me anymore. You'll be dead in my heart forever. So think carefully."

"Does that guy really mean so much to you? When he's killed your best friend?"

"That's not the point."

"So what is the fucking point?"

"It's violence, Farid. The violence you take everywhere with you. Without that violence, Vanessa would still be alive. And with you. Because she cared for you. So much so that she never replaced you. She had given up on men. She lived like a phantom."

"You're talking nonsense. She was just as beautiful and lively—"

"You destroyed her, the way you destroy everything around you, because all you know is hate."

"You're spinning me a line to save your man. What are you talking about anyway?"

"I'm telling you the truth. There's not a single one of your pals who has the balls to say it. And to show you I'm not lying, it wasn't Maxime who took the money, it was me. And I stashed it in the restaurant without anyone else knowing. When I wanted to get it, it was gone."

"Magnificent," Farid said, applauding.

He had recovered his super-cool tone. His elegant irony, the stylish nonchalance that matched the clothes he bought with the money from the robberies. The money he did not know what to do with. His life was pointless after Vanessa's death. Khadidja was surprised to find herself feeling an ounce of pity for her brother. And for herself. Neither of them would ever be lucky in love. She was sure now that it wasn't Farid who had searched the apartment. It wasn't him who had found the money.

But Farid was talking again. He had to, if only to show she hadn't wounded his masculine pride. He had to have the last word. She wasn't afraid, she was ready. She had already made her mind up: if Farid touched Maxime, she would turn him in to the police. Now though she knew she was going to pay for speaking out. Farid got down from his stool. Khadidja didn't move.

"Where's the loot? You and your man took it, didn't you?"

"I've got nothing more to say. I've told you the truth."

"You're lying."

"I don't know a thing. And I couldn't care less. I've never been as interested in money as you. The old saying is true: money can't buy happiness. You ought to know that."

She could not stifle a howl when he grabbed her hair. As he forced her to the floor, she kicked out at him, hitting his knee. Farid didn't let go. He slapped her with his free hand. When she punched back at him, he closed his fists and hit her in the stomach and chest. She began to scream. He pushed her flat, put his hands round her neck. She struggled, but he was in a rage. An immense rage. Much stronger than hers. He started to squeeze. She plunged her nails into his flesh, scratched as hard as she could. But she could feel her strength ebbing away as her fear mounted. She was caught in a trap; her throat was on fire, her lungs about to implode. Unbearable pain. She could not cry out anymore. Soon her brother's face started to blur. He disappeared in a fog punctuated by jagged red veins. The pain seemed to be easing . . . Bizarrely, she thought of the paradise for believers her mother would tell her about as a child . . .

28

"Hello, Peter, it's great to have a friend like you I can count on! I've just been released by the police. It was tough . . ."

Chloé was surprised to see letters appear on her screen. It took her a few seconds to realise she was communicating live online with Peter. She was so pleased she didn't bother to calculate what time it must be in Tokyo.

"Hi Magdalena, the death of your friend is a terrible drama, but everything that happens to you interests me. I'm hopelessly fucking selfish. An emotional vampire. I hope you forgive me. So what did they want from you?"

"You're forgiven. They wanted me to turn in my boss. The commissaire reckons he was the murderer. But if he thinks I'll be a witness for the prosecution, he's got a surprise in store. My flatmate and I – we're not giving in. That kind of solidarity helps you live."

"I understand you. And admire you. What's happened to your friend's brother in all this – the hold-up guy? He's the one they should be questioning."

"He swears it's not him, and wants to get his revenge on the killer. In the meantime, he's holed up in Saint-Denis!"

"The police have got plenty of informers on the estates. They'll soon find him."

Chloé searched for the right words. It wasn't easy to explain Farid and his complicated network, his crazy friends . . .

"The clever thing is that he's not on the estate anymore. He's staying with a friend."

Chloé stopped typing and waited a few moments. She liked the idea of building up the tension, of keeping Peter Pan in suspense. He couldn't resist for long.

"Don't tell me his friend is a crook too!"
"Of course! A giant who claims he's an anarchist. Strange for a guy who lives like a bourgeois in a stone-built villa. He's a real character."
"Yes, I like the sound of him. Tell me more, Magdalena."

Jean-Luc's visions never let him down. Farid Younis truly was a dark angel. A powerful, sad man who was already dead inside. A man driven mad by jealousy. There was a big bone of contention between Chloé, Khadidja and Farid. A quarrel related to Farid's passion for Vanessa. She had loved him. Until the moment he committed an act of violence. An act she couldn't accept. So then, sick at heart, she had driven him out of her life.

They were driving towards Belleville cemetery. Farid had put his gloves back on; his hands were resting quietly on his lap, as though nothing had happened.

Jean-Luc did not interrupt his silence. He put on an American rap C.D. he'd bought especially for days like these when he was acting as Farid's driver. Eminem. He didn't much like the music, but that didn't matter. Perhaps it would grow on him. He parked on Rue du Télégraphe and they both got out of the Volkswagen. Jean-Luc was expecting to be told to return to Saint-Denis, but no. The two men exchanged glances. Pale-faced, eyes shining, Farid headed towards the cemetery. Jean-Luc followed, amazed at being allowed to do so. For a long while, they stood by the grave. Then Farid said two short sentences in Arabic, took off one of his rings, and slipped it inside a marble vase. He turned to Jean-Luc, who asked, "What did you say to her?"

"I asked for her forgiveness."

"What was the ring for?"

"I asked her to be my wife, in death."

Jean-Luc nodded: "I've got a proposition for you."

"Go on, I'm listening."

"We draw a line under that money. We do one last hold-up. We pool our savings and buy a boat. And we clear out of here on it. Nobody will ever find us, I promise you. The sea is the only balm for a broken heart. I swear to you it's true, brother."

Farid's face betrayed no emotion. The drizzle left tiny pearls of damp in his black locks.

"O.K., we leave. But on one condition."

"What's that?"

"First we kill Duchamp."

29

She was sitting in the café window, and could see her reflection super-imposed on the façade of the police station and the pavements of Rue Louis-Blanc, still glistening from the most recent rain. She had been waiting a long time for Maxime. Finally, he came out. It was past ten o'clock. She waved to him, tapped on the glass. He caught sight of her. His smile made her suffer: he looked so happy to see her. He came in, ordered a coffee from the waiter, walked towards her. Khadidja let him kiss her. His face looked drawn, but she sensed he was calm on the inside.

"You mustn't go back to *Belles*. He mustn't find you."

"Who are you talking about?"

"My brother."

"Oh, yes, the invisible man."

"He's looking for you. He wants to kill you. Because of Vanessa. He thinks you did it."

He knew what was coming next. He could see it in her face. As usual, he advanced towards the danger.

"Nothing happened between me and Vanessa," he said evenly. "You have to believe me."

"Why would the witnesses lie? And after all, she could have loved you . . . it's not hard."

She said to herself: what's hard is stopping. She said to herself: how am I going to live without seeing your face? She stood up and handed him a key. The Excelsior, a hotel in Rue Saint-Martin where she had rented a room for him.

"Promise me you'll go there. Promise me you'll hide until the police have finally finished with you. And that after that you'll leave France."

"I'm not a coward, Khadidja. I've been in tighter situations than this in my time."

"I know you're not scared, but Farid is deranged."

"Your brother doesn't frighten me."

"You don't know what you're talking about."

Without thinking, she touched the scarf concealing her bruised neck. She couldn't take her eyes off his face: Maxime, I don't know you. Why have you told me so little about your past? Who are you?

"Leave Passage du Désir and come and live in Passage Brady. In other words, marry me, Khadidja. That's what you want, isn't it? So let's do it. You only have to move three hundred metres."

And he was grinning. She felt so tender towards him. At the same time, she wanted to slap him. He should have said this before. A long time before. It was too late now. She imagined herself at an audition ready to say her lines back to a partner, prepared to give her all. All she had to do was concentrate. And say the words. The ones she had found time to rehearse a hundred times inside her head.

"I took all my things while you were being held. There's none of my stuff in *Belles* any more. Believe me, it's better this way for everyone. I don't love you anymore, Maxime. That's why it's over. For that reason alone."

Calmly, she laid the key beside her empty coffee cup and forced herself to stand, avoiding his eyes. As soon as she was in the street, she started to run, without looking back.

Maxime called for the bill and drank his coffee. *I don't love you anymore, Maxime. That's why it's over. For that reason alone.* It sounded like a line from a T.V. soap opera. He found it touching. Like the time when she had made such a scene explaining she was going on a sex-workers' march. He had let her talk, wind herself up. Then he had smiled at her. Khadidja had taken it as a mocking smile. He had been obliged to explain that far from mocking her, he intended to go on the march as well.

Khadidja was as tough as tempered steel; he was her only weakness. He was well aware of this, and found the situation very erotic. I don't love you anymore, Maxime. Pull the other one. He paid the bill, took the hotel key, and stood up. He had never run after a woman.

There's always a first time. At last all those years of sweating like a pig on the treadmill were going to be useful for something other than staying fit. Maxime sprinted off down Rue Louis-Blanc. Khadidja wasn't far ahead: there was no way that she could match his antelope strides in her high-heeled boots. He caught up with her in Rue du Faubourg-Saint-Martin.

He stood there while she shouted at him, flinging every possible accusation in his face, not giving a damn about the passers-by staring at them, mostly in amusement. He took her by the wrists, pushed her lithe body up against an old carriage doorway, but still had to struggle for a moment to get what he wanted. The last time he had passionately kissed a girl in the street had been at secondary school. Still holding Khadidja close, Maxime took out his mobile to call Chloé at the restaurant and tell her to call the regulars one by one: due to exceptional circumstances, *Belles* would be closed that night. Without any further explanation, he took Khadidja by the hand and dragged her towards Rue Saint-Martin. He was thrilled at the idea of spending the day making love to her in a hotel. At the Excelsior he would repeat in every way imaginable that nothing had happened between him and Vanessa. And this time, she would believe him.

30

Ingrid and Lola had reached Saint-Denis very early, only to discover that the Cité des Fleurs estate was a vast labyrinth. It was eleven o'clock already, and they had got nowhere. They had explored the eastern half, and were now starting on the west. The lift in Block 8 was out of order. They were having a hard time reaching the sixth floor by the stairs, particularly Lola. To Ingrid it sounded as though a huge sick bird had nested in her colleague's thorax.

"Time for a rest!" Lola declared. She sat down on a step and wiped her glasses with the hem of her dress, a grey and mauve number that Ingrid found as distressing as her red dressing gown. But hey, each to their own. "I'm beginning to wonder if your informer wasn't selling us a pup."

"Well anyway, Grousset has released Maxime. We've got all the time we need."

"That's what you say! He's let him go because he has no concrete proof. But the Gnome is a sly, stubborn creature. He'll be back. His trump card is Chloé and Khadidja. Those two girls have been hiding something right from the start. Grousset will eventually worm it out of them. Chloé is vulnerable, and as for Khadidja, she's had the stuffing knocked out of her by what happened between Vanessa and Maxime. Believe me, my girl: we don't have our whole lives in front of us. Especially me; as you can see, I'm shattered."

"You should take up sport and stop smoking."

"Gently does it, young lady: keep your Californian advice to yourself. My body is like my old Twingo, it's still going, and doesn't ask anything of anyone."

"As you like, Lola."

"That really would be the limit! Can you see me running on one of those ridiculous conveyor belt things? A Valkyrie who's strayed onto the set of 'Modern Times'. Unbelievable!"

"I always wondered why you were so scared of modernity in France."

"I always wondered why you were so scared of thinking in America! O.K., shall we go?"

An hour later, and they were still at square one. Nobody knew Farid Younis. At least no-one who was willing to open their door to them.

When they reached the eleventh floor, Ingrid and Lola came face to face with a lift repairman and the seventy-year-old who was keeping him company.

"Good morning, ladies!" the old man said. "Eleven floors on foot! You must be tired."

"Good morning to you! More than tired," Lola said. "Dead beat."

"I feel fine," Ingrid said. "Do you know a young man called Farid Younis?"

"Good morning, miss, my name is Hopel, Sébastien Hopel."

"Good morning. Mine's Diesel."

"Pardon?"

"Ingrid Diesel."

"That's original and very pretty."

"As for me, I go by the name of Lola Jost. Younis is about average height, quite good-looking, usually wears black. If you can help at all . . ."

"My neighbour was a bit like that. Always smartly dressed. I never knew what he did for a living. He came back home at very strange hours . . ."

"*Was* . . . ? What happened to him?"

"An overdose problem. He took some substances, then barricaded himself in. His friend was banging on his door. In the end, he came back with the firemen. Or rather, one fireman who broke the door down. With a sledgehammer."

"A sledgehammer? Not an axe?"

"That's right, but it worked just as well. The door was out for the count. As you can see, the owner still hasn't repaired it. And yet I called the caretaker. They're all as useless as each other, aren't they?"

"What did this friend and the fireman do then?" Ingrid wanted to know.

"The friend and the fireman took my neighbour away wrapped in a blanket."

"Do you know the friend?" asked Lola.

"No. He was yelling 'Open up! Open up! It's Noah here!' at the top of his voice. So it's quite likely his name was Noah."

"Had you ever seen him before?"

"I think I've run into him on the estate."

"Can you describe him for us?"

"A young fellow. I don't remember him very well."

"And yet you've got an excellent memory," Lola said.

"I didn't pay much attention to him. I was more interested in the fireman."

"Why was that?"

"He was a sort of giant, and looked as if he was in disguise. He was wearing a red jacket all right, but his helmet was odd."

"How d'you mean, odd?" Ingrid asked impatiently.

"Oh, it's probably not important . . ."

"I'm sure it is," Lola insisted, looking daggers at Ingrid. "Every detail is important."

"Well, his helmet . . ."

"Yes, his helmet, Monsieur Hopel. His helmet. Try to remember, it's important," Lola said gently.

"I remember it well. His helmet smelt of paint. And it looked more like a biker's helmet than a fireman's. Their helmets are spectacular. At the time, I said to myself: this fireman hasn't seen too many fires. Ladies, excuse me, but . . ."

"Yes?" Lola asked.

"I don't suppose you're the police . . . any more than that young man was a fireman."

"We've never said we were. I'm a retired commissaire. Here's my old I.D. card."

"Oh yes, I can see it's you. You have the look of a cop. This is the first time I've ever met a female commissaire. I'm honoured."

"I'm investigating the murder of a young woman in the 10th arrondissement in Paris. She was strangled, mutilated. It was in all the papers."

"I saw it on the telly. A real shame. Such a beautiful girl. Have you been hired by the family?"

"More or less."

"I know where that Noah lives."

Ingrid, Lola and Hopel turned as one to stare at the repairman. He was around forty, with a crew-cut, and had a smirk on his face.

"I'd never dare ask for cash from the cops, but it must be all right if you're private, mustn't it?"

"In theory it's possible," Lola said. "But I need something concrete. An address."

"I'm not selling anything that isn't concrete. I come here every time this old crock of a lift gives out. Two young men who must be brothers live three floors higher up. They're called Noah and Menahem. Names you remember. Noah for the tennis player. And for Menahem Begin, the Nobel Peace Prize-winner: that stays in your mind."

"Can you describe them?"

"Noah has blue eyes and black hair. He's small, and apart from that, pretty ordinary-looking. The younger brother is something else. A handsome guy. Tall and thin, with chestnut hair down to his shoulders. Small round glasses. This winter he's been going around in a long, grey overcoat."

"As for myself, my services come free of charge," Hopel said sniffily. "I like to be useful."

"I like to help people too!" the lift repairman protested. "But I've got three kids."

"Maybe, but you're not wearing a wedding ring," Hopel insisted.

"That's never stopped anyone having kids."

"Gentlemen, we'll leave you to your debate about civic duty, with our thanks. Needless to say, you've never set eyes on us," Lola said, paying the technician with what to Ingrid looked like a rather graceful gesture.

They walked with a spring in their step back down the eleven flights of stairs, then sat in the Twingo. They toasted their success with two cups of coffee from Lola's thermos.

"You almost messed that up because you were so impulsive," Lola remarked with a smile.

"If I hadn't made a move, we'd still be there now, boss."

"And another thing: try to remember to say hello before you dive in head first, Ingrid."

"I don't know what it is with you French and politeness. You're always so quick to point it out to people when they don't say hello or thank you. But that doesn't stop you being rude to tourists and anti-social with everyone else."

"The difference between here and the United States is that over there, anyone who is rude or anti-social doesn't get very far. In general, he ends up with a bullet in his guts."

"All the same, for Latins you're not very warm."

"We need time. You want everything to go so fast. For people to clap you on the back two seconds after you've met. You're too impatient, Ingrid."

"Talking of which: we're not going to spend the night in the Twingo, are we?"

"If need be. In any case, we're going to wait for Menahem to show his face."

"What if he's shipped out with his big brother, Farid Younis and the bogus fireman?"

"Patience, my dear. Patience. There are sandwiches and blankets in the car. It's a remarkable vehicle which, despite appearances, is very comfortable to sleep in. At least, if we take turns. I've even got an alarm clock in the glove compartment."

"I don't believe it! This is a fucking nightmare! You could've told me we were going to sleep here."

"Need I remind you that for once it was you who wanted to come along? Anyway, I had no idea what was going to happen. And while you're at it, stop spraying us with your swear-words."

"If you'd warned me, I'd have brought my portable electric tooth-brush. I can't bear not brushing my teeth."

"What! A globetrotter like you?"

"So what? I brush my teeth three times a day."

"Go to the chemist's and buy yourself a brush."

"No! I only use electric toothbrushes."

"You're in a bad mood because you didn't get enough sleep. It's at moments like these that you really see what people are worth. We ought always to take new recruits camping up in the mountains before giving them a permanent job."

"What?"

"To see how they respond when the going gets tough."

"What the fuck are you talking about? We're in Saint-Denis! And all I'm concerned about is my dental hygiene. As for the rest, I don't mind eating beans for a month, sleeping on the ground, walking twelve hours non-stop with a backpack filled with stones and—"

"We're in Saint-Denis and it's Christmas in November."

"Now what?"

"Look who's just come out of Block 8? Wearing glasses, and a long grey overcoat. Hallelujah! It's him."

"Menahem. Oh, fuck!"

"You bring me luck, Ingrid Diesel. You inspire me."

"You wouldn't think so. You spend your time tearing strips off me."

"Clumsy attempts at affection, my dear."

As the day wore on, Ingrid and Lola's enthusiasm wilted. They followed Menahem, who was driving a red Mini, only to find themselves outside the Université Paris VIII. The young man re-emerged several hours later, went straight home, and spent the night there. No visitor matching the description of Farid, Noah or the giant fireman crossed the threshold of the block. Ingrid decided to go and buy herself a primitive manual toothbrush at the corner pharmacy, whose flashing green sign stained the night sky.

31

The next day, Menahem did not go to the university. He swept Ingrid and Lola along in his slipstream as he made numerous trips back and forth between Paris and the suburbs. In the late afternoon, the youth had stolen a grey Opel in Courbevoie. The car belonged to a man who had left his key in the ignition while he waited at the school gate for his kids to emerge. Menahem had carefully parked his Mini before driving off in the Opel. He had then parked the stolen vehicle on Avenue Franklin-Roosevelt in the 8th arrondissement, and had hailed a taxi back to Courbevoie, where he picked up his car. Now, at ten minutes past midnight, the little red car was entering Levallois-Perret. It slowed down as it passed a nightclub. Parked cars. Small groups of young people chatting. Lola was still following him with great expertise, keeping a discreet distance between the Twingo and the Mini. Ingrid was impressed by her skill.

"You really know your business, don't you?"

"Whatever."

"I wasn't being ironic, Lola, I was admiring you."

"What I admire is the fact you spent two nights in this car without moaning."

"A night and a half. And I already explained that the only thing I was concerned about was my dental hygiene."

Lola parked in a driveway.

"What are you doing?"

"I'm parking, you ninny. Didn't you see him stop?"

"No! Do you think he's going to steal another car?"

"I don't think he's going to bother. He's locking his Mini. And here he comes up the street. Wonderful!"

"You're enjoying this, aren't you?"

"It reminds me of the good old days. Here we go!"

Lola pulled out again. Ahead of her, a metallic-grey 4×4 was speeding off. Ingrid again admired the smooth ride all the way back to Saint-Denis. Menahem did not turn off towards Paris and Avenue Franklin-Roosevelt, or head back to the Cité des Fleurs. Instead he aimed for a residential neighbourhood in Saint-Denis, where a few detached houses had survived. He parked on Rue de Quinsonnas and rang the doorbell at a stone villa. Lola quickly pulled into another driveway.

The light above the front door came on. A huge guy in dark clothes came out. He had a shaved head and a slightly Mephistophelian goatee. He smiled at Menahem, said a few words. Then a short, dark-haired man appeared. Menahem gave him a hug. The giant went back inside, leaving the small guy and Menahem to a brief but animated discussion.

"Don't move, but keep your eyes peeled. I'll be right back."

"Where are you going, Lola?"

"To play the part of the intrepid lady returning home early in the morning. That's all."

Lola walked determinedly up the pavement. The night was icy cold, so she turned up her collar as she walked in front of the villa. She had enough time to register a scene that was not without interest. Menahem had handed some keys to the small guy, who did not close his hand around them but stood waiting. A brief order from the midget, and Menahem shrugged his shoulders and dropped another set of keys into the outstretched hand. Lola turned down the first street to walk round the block.

When she returned to the Twingo, Ingrid explained that after Menahem had left, the little guy had driven a Beetle out of the drive and parked it in a reserved space in front of the house. Then he had driven the 4×4 down into the garage.

"Menahem has just given him two sets of keys," Lola said. "He didn't want to hand over the second lot. I get the feeling our jigsaw puzzle is taking shape. That's always a satisfying moment."

"I would've thought the most satisfying moment was when the last piece was in place."

"No, with the last piece it's more like a post-coital glow."

"Really? Perhaps I should take up the hobby."

"Why do you think someone would steal two cars in the space of a few hours, park one somewhere in Paris, then deliver the other to Saint-Denis? Especially to a guy who already owns a Volkswagen?"

"Another question: why does Menahem hand over the key for one car, and yet seem reluctant to give him the other?"

"Let's have some more coffee, my dear, that'll help us think."

"The thermos is empty, Lola."

"I have another one."

"Of course, I should have known."

"Two keys, two cars, Ingrid. Menahem came to deliver both of them to the same person. But one of them is parked on Avenue Franklin-Roosevelt. That fellow must be Noah. He was the only one who hugged Menahem. The other guy has to be the giant Sébastien Hopel described to us."

"The bogus fireman. The one who took Farid Younis away wrapped in a blanket."

"That's right. And if Farid Younis, Noah Whatsit and the phoney fireman are the ones who did the hold-up at the bureau de change on the Champs—"

"The two cars are the tools of their trade."

"A 4×4 to ram into the front window. An Opel for the getaway. They operate at dawn, when Paris is still coming round. And when the bureaux de change have discreetly filled up with nice fresh euros."

"All of which means there's going to be a hold-up on Avenue Franklin-Roosevelt, Lola."

"Excellent reasoning, Ingrid. I'll call Barthélemy."

"Brilliant idea."

*

"Where's Menahem?"

"My little brother isn't doing the driving, man."

"What's this crap?"

"Yo, Farid! You know I respect you, man! But Menahem is my flesh and blood."

"You're just shit-scared, Noah. That's what it is."

"Man!"

"Shit-scared, I tell you."

"On my mother's life. Menahem is the only one in our family who's any good at studying. There's no way he's gonna get hurt."

"So he could run the risk before, but not this time! What d'you mean?"

"I'm not happy about this job, man."

"First I've heard."

"We haven't done our homework."

"What?"

"Checking things out. You usually set things up better."

"A bureau de change five hundred metres from the last one, Noah. Who would imagine that?"

"I'm talking about checking things out, man!"

"We ram-raid it like all the others. Nobody moves. Because they know that the first one to lift a finger is a dead man. We get out of there. And that's that. You just need to want it enough, Noah. It's a question of having the balls."

Jean-Luc had switched on C.N.N. and was watching the sport while he listened to Farid and Noah argue. This was the first time Noah had been unhappy about a job. More than that, it was the first time he had ever gone against Farid. Noah was different from Farid in one respect. Noah had a sense of family. He would never have near strangled his sister, stopping just in time as her face turned blue, with her gasping for air like a fish out of water. Farid had this incredible violence inside him: that's how he was. Jean-Luc had chosen Farid. Such as he was.

The sea would change him. The sea had changed many men. And if not, then nothing ever could. But it was worth trying. It was worth crashing straight into a brick wall one more time.

Jean-Luc felt the same fear as before. No different. This time he had taken the pills before the symptoms emerged. Even so, his stomach was churning, but it was alright. The main thing was to concentrate, to visualise Farid on the deck of *The Dark Angel*, leaving the past behind.

Obviously, with Menahem out of the equation, Noah would have to be the driver and the lookout man. There would only be two of them doing the raid, running more of a risk. But Farid was so wound up since Vanessa's death, the hatred spilling out of him, that he alone would be worth two men in the heat of the action. Besides, they had no choice now. Noah had instructed Menahem to park the Opel near the bureau de change on Avenue Franklin-Roosevelt. Getting the kid to follow the 4×4 like the last time was out of the question.

Jean-Luc couldn't back out now. He and Farid had made a pact. They'd do the raid, Noah would go back and stash the loot in the villa, and while he was doing that, Farid and him would go to Passage Brady to waste the restaurateur. Jean-Luc thought that was a shame. He would really have liked to read that guy before finishing him off. Even the name of his restaurant made him want to know more. *Belles de jour comme de nuit*. What was it supposed to mean? That the guy loved girls too much, that his restaurant was a homage to all those he had known?

A restaurateur. What a weird idea after the excitement of war and a life of freedom, to want to bury yourself in a business, to take on responsibilities, worries. Jean-Luc had seen men like that in every port. Men with quiet gestures who had risked their lives in the heart of storms. Men with eyes washed pale by sea spray. Men who have befriended fear. Who respect it and are respected in return.

It wasn't going to be easy to kill someone who had befriended fear.

"Damn it! No reply from Barthélemy."

"I imagine he's lucky enough to get some sleep from time to time."

"It's no joking matter, Ingrid. Barthélemy always answers the phone. Especially when it's me calling."

"Perhaps he's on a stake-out somewhere where the sound of a phone could ruin everything."

"That's exactly what worries me."

"Call Grousset. Garden Gnome or not, he's still a cop. And our aim is to prevent a hold-up."

"No, our aim is to save Maxime. It always has been."

"Even if it's Grousset who does it by arresting Vanessa's murderer, the main thing is that Maxime is saved. So we agree. Call Grousset. Call the fucking bastard now."

Lola stared hard at Ingrid. The American tilted her head slightly and grinned. Then she mimicked someone dialling a number. Lola took the mobile out of her pocket once more, and did what duty and Ingrid were expecting of her.

"Fate is against us. The Gnome doesn't reply either."

"Do you think Grousset is with Barthélemy?"

"It's possible. We're stuck, my girl. O.K., that's enough joking, I'm calling the 10th arrondissement station."

Lola gave her details as a former colleague to the desk sergeant on duty. He promised to pass the message on to the Anti-Gang Squad. Twenty minutes later, the garage at the stone villa opened, revealing a 4×4 with three men inside. The giant was in the front passenger seat, wearing a black balaclava.

At last the garage door opened. A 4×4 came out of the villa, with three ram-raiders on board. He felt as ready as possible. The arrival on the scene of Lola Jost and her colleague did not upset him. He was on a motorbike. He let Jost slip in behind the 4×4, pulled out and followed them at a distance.

Finding the house had not posed any great problem. There were hardly any stone villas left in Saint-Denis. You could count the streets where they survived on the fingers of one hand, and Mickey Mouse's hand at that. From then on, it had been plain sailing. Finding Farid Younis's lair hadn't taken long.

A guy who lives like a bourgeois in a stone-built villa. Said villa was in Rue de Quinsonnas. A pretty house with white shutters, tall, narrow windows, with geraniums on their sills and above them red and blue decorative arches. A charming low red-brick wall. A similarly smart wrought iron gate. Thank you Magdalena, alias Chloé Gardel. Thanks for your splendid naivety. Anyone can pretend to be living in Tokyo if he takes the trouble, you know.

And because he was the quickest, the most flexible, he was going to win. He was born small, and therefore light. Faced with determination, and above all a strategy, physical strength was unimportant. He could turn everything to his advantage: false trapdoors, Trojan horses, all the tricks. If you can't kill your enemy with your own hands, use someone else's.

If, as he supposed, Farid Younis and his accomplices were setting off on another hold-up, there was only one thing to do. Carry on tailing them, ring the right number at the right moment, and wait.

For the first time in his life, Peter Pan intended to tip off the police. And he was sure Farid Younis would not let himself be caught by the Anti-Gang Squad. Farid Younis would choose death. A death that had been waiting for him on a street corner for three long years. A pretty young girl, with long blonde hair, blue eyes, and pale, icy skin.

32

The grey Opel was where Menahem had said it would be, opposite a pizzeria. Noah pulled up parallel to it, engine running, got out of the 4×4, climbed into the Opel, turned on the ignition. Jean-Luc moved over into the driving seat of the 4×4, and Farid came to sit alongside him. Farid picked up the two Kalashnikovs. They waited for Noah to pull out into Avenue Franklin-Roosevelt. The bureau de change was a hundred metres further up, next to a luxury menswear boutique. Ahead of them was the big Champs-Elysées roundabout. Completely empty.

Jean-Luc glanced in the rear mirror. The façade of Saint-Philippe-du-Roule was lit up, with the same banner displayed. Jesus is still there to listen to you, what a shame you've nothing to say to him, he suddenly thought, as images of the mass flooded back into his mind. The swinging censer, the hymns they sang at the tops of their voices.

He drove the images away, and turned towards Farid, who was smiling at him. His black eyes galvanised Jean-Luc.

Another quick glance in the rear mirror. There was a car pulled up at the lights. And a biker parking his motorbike on the pavement. Jean-Luc waited for the lights to turn green. Three youths in an old banger with a Paris number plate. They chugged away towards the roundabout. Further on, Noah was waiting outside the bureau de change. His side lights were two red dots glowing in the darkness.

"Are we going, Jean-Luc, or what?"

"There's a biker in that phone box."

They waited a few moments longer. The biker came out, got on his bike, started the engine, and headed off towards the roundabout.

"*Ciao* to the biker," Farid said. "Get going."

His impatience ruffled Jean-Luc. But then Farid made the gesture, the same one he had made with Noah, the gesture that Jean-Luc dreamed of. Farid rolled the ski-mask down over Jean-Luc's face before doing the same to his own:

"Here we go, brother."

Jean-Luc started the engine, accelerated into the avenue. The bureau de change was fifty, twenty metres away.

A car came hurtling towards them. At top speed. Headlights full on. Up a one-way street.

"THE FEDS!"

Farid picked up his Kalashnikov, passed Jean-Luc his. They started firing. Deafening noise; glass everywhere. Jean-Luc hit reverse, accelerated backwards. Farid smashed the rest of the windscreen with the rifle-butt, firing, firing, firing. A voice bawling through a megaphone. Noise, the stench of burning rubber. Jean-Luc sped backwards towards the church. The banner looked like a fucking shroud. An image of the Holy Shroud flashed through his mind. The shroud with the face of Christ on it. He imagined his face and Farid's imprinted forever on the shroud he was speeding towards, his foot to the floor. They had to get away along Rue la Boétie, escape from the shroud, head for the sea, right now. Another car came out of nowhere at full tilt.

"BEHIND US!" Jean-Luc screamed.

Farid fired again. The back window shattered. Jean-Luc turned the car, accelerated towards a hail of bullets. A groan from Farid. Jean-Luc saw his body slump against the side door. The 4×4 hurtled into a bakery window, which smashed to smithereens.

Glass everywhere, blood. Not mine, thought Jean-Luc. He stretched out a hand towards the motionless Farid, felt his shoulder, felt the wool of his black ski-mask. He tore it off, shouting his name, on the verge of passing out.

"My brother is dead. My angel. Someone betrayed us."

Jean-Luc had lost all fear. A pig was bawling into a megaphone. Flashing lights whirled. Jean-Luc grabbed the Kalashnikov, struggled out of the 4×4, retreated towards the bakery, emptying his magazine at them. Bullets whistled around him. He forced a door open, smashed his fist into the face of a baker, ran out into the hallway of a building. A stairwell, a window – he smashed it with the butt of his rifle, jumped down into a yard. An interior garden, with stunted palms. Sirens wailing in the early morning. Another building. A building with lit-up windows, transparent. Offices one on top of another. Jean-Luc climbed in through a ground-floor window. Another alarm went off, rivalling the police sirens.

Dozens of screens, computers, thousands of sheets of paper. A maze of offices. Possibly a bank. Jean-Luc sprinted across the room, unlocked a window, jumped. He ran along Rue du Faubourg-Saint-Honoré. The police would soon cordon off the area. He saw a shape lying on the ground. A tramp sleeping on an air vent. Jean-Luc swung the butt of his rifle at the sleeping form, slamming into it again and again. Then he stretched out alongside the dead body and waited. For the area to empty of police, for the crowds to start to surge towards the metro, so that he could mingle with them and go and wreak vengeance. Because he knew who had killed his angel.

Eyes tight shut beneath the stinking blanket, Jean-Luc concentrated. To see who he really was. The creature that had lain dormant within him for years had just awakened and displayed its power. He concentrated as hard as he could, eyes closed, heart closed, shutting out the dead body next to him, refusing to give it an identity. And soon, he saw.

A magnificent werewolf, its yellow eyes shining.

33

Khadidja was sobbing on a kitchen chair. Chloé was bent over her, stroking her hair. Lola was smoking a cigarette, leaning back against the sink. Ingrid was gazing sympathetically at Khadidja. In her mind's eye, she could see yet again the big guy bleeding on a Chicago street. He was Sharon Dougherty's brother. And Sharon Dougherty had been Ingrid's best friend as a teenager. Ingrid had never forgotten the oceans of tears Sharon had wept. Possibly his death had been what had aroused in Ingrid the desire to comfort others. She wasn't interested in medicine or psychoanalysis, so she had chosen to become a masseuse. She had travelled to the four corners of the earth searching out ancestral recipes for easing pain. Now here she was, in a kitchen, a big giraffe standing helplessly by while a young woman cried her heart out over her brother. Her brother had been no angel. All the same: a brother was a brother, especially if he was a twin.

Young Chloé, though, was not crying. In fact, once she had got over the initial shock, she looked relieved to hear Lola's news. Farid Younis, shot by the Anti-Gang Squad in the 8th arrondissement while attempting a smash-and-grab raid on a bureau de change. His accomplice, Noah Zakri, had been arrested. The third robber, Jean-Luc Cachart, the man who had been driving the 4×4 alongside Farid, had got away.

It was Khadidja who opened the door to the two women. While Lola was describing what had happened, they could hear Chloé playing her cello. Ingrid thought she played well. Dumpy, timid, quiet as a mouse, but an excellent musician. After a while, the music had stopped, and Chloé had appeared in the kitchen doorway, still holding her instrument and bow. She listened to Lola repeat her story without reacting. It was as if, after Vanessa's death, nothing more terrible could happen to her. Apart from Khadidja's death, of course. Because Ingrid could tell there was an unbreakable bond between the two girls. Lola agreed with her. She went so far as to talk of a pact between them, with all the ambiguity that word entailed.

Ingrid was beginning to know her Lola. The ex-commissaire was going to take advantage of the situation and Khadidja's momentary weakness to go on the attack, to blow open the door to the girls' secrets. Once a cop, always a cop. Especially as they didn't have all day. It wouldn't be long before Grousset arrived. He would interrogate Khadidja and her flatmate about the death of a delinquent brother. This new development would open up new possibilities for the diminutive commissaire. He would see there were other suspects besides Maxime. In the meantime, Lola had no intention of letting up. They had made giant strides in Saint-Denis. There was no way she would allow things to slow down in Passage du Désir.

"Ingrid and I found a lot of money hidden in a duvet at Maxime's. It's time to talk, Khadidja."

Unfortunately, at that very moment the front doorbell rang.

"Damn! That must be Grousset," Lola said. "I can guarantee you're not going to have an easy time with him, Khadidja. Why don't you make an effort? What have you got to lose?"

"I'll get it," Chloé said, walking out of the kitchen.

"Police!"

Chloé was so sure it would be Grousset that her brain was trying to superimpose what she had just heard onto her memory of the little pipe-smoking policeman's voice. At the same time, deep down inside, she could not allow her musician's ear to spoil the perfect scenario being played out: Farid's death, and the relief this brought. Until that morning, Chloé had never imagined to what extent his disappearance had cleared the horizon. Despite Khadidja's grief. The only dark shadow on scene.

She opened the door confidently, then stood paralysed just long enough to allow Jean-Luc to push his way into the apartment with his rifle. His face had an icy, crazed look. He raised a finger to his lips and signalled to Chloé to step back. She took only one step: he's going to kill everyone . . . he's going to kill Khadidja . . . I may as well die now . . . that'll give her the time to get away . . . perhaps. But Jean-Luc forced her ahead of him, and silently closed the door behind them. Chloé could hear a little voice inside her head: *Strange, I was sure he was going to shoot.*

All the women in the kitchen turned their heads towards the giant, who was now training his gun on Khadidja.

"YOU GAVE US AWAY TO THE PIGS, YOU BITCH!"

"If you only knew how fed up I am with your violence, Jean-Luc. Stealing, fighting, killing: that's all you know how to do. And you, you great stupid arsehole, you could never imagine I might be different."

"You threatened Farid in front of me because he had decided to kill your man. You wanted to save his skin. Have the guts to say it. I WANT YOU TO SAY IT!"

"It's not Khadidja who informed on her brother."

Chloé saw Jean-Luc's features harden, then he turned towards Lola. She was very calm, both her hands still resting on the sink. Chloé felt a surge of admiration for this obstinate woman who only wanted to get at the truth and was not afraid of standing up for herself. As for Ingrid Diesel, she was special too. Calm and collected, she confronted this madman as though trying to X-ray his mind.

"Who are you, fatso?"

"A neighbour."

"You should never have poked your nose into your neighbours' business."

"What are you going to do: shoot us all?"

"You know something? You're really getting on my nerves, you great mammoth!"

Chloé scanned the kitchen in search of a knife, or anything else that might save them. They were only women. And Madame Lola no longer carried a weapon since leaving the police. We've had it, Chloé told herself. A madman is threatening us with a gun. There's nothing we can do. The only thing in the kitchen, on the stove near Ingrid, was a pressure cooker full of vegetable and bacon stew.

"You burst in here like a lunatic, you threaten us with a gun, and you expect us to be quiet!"

This time it was Ingrid who spoke. The two women were trying to play for time. They were probably just as frightened, but they kept their fear under control, prevented it from turning into panic. Imperceptibly, they were working on him together.

"Eh you, you big gawk, shut it!"

Chloé felt renewed hope. After all, if Jean-Luc had wanted to kill Khadidja, he would have done so by now. Without asking any questions. He was simply deranged with pain because he had lost his best friend. He had been nice to her in recent days. He'd even suggested she join him on his boat.

"It's not Khadidja," she dared whisper. "She would never have betrayed her own brother."

"It's not you I want to hear, roly-poly. It's your bitch of a friend."

Chloé took the blow on the chin. Accepted defeat. Jean-Luc was too far gone. No-one could reach him now. No more the political idealist, no more the long-distance yachtsman. The giant was nothing more than a killer: in fact, perhaps he was the one who had butchered Vanessa. She could sense fear grip her throat.

"O.K., if you're so sure it's me, if that's what you want to believe, shoot me and get it over with, you retard."

Khadidja's voice was expressionless. She spoke with her last reserves of energy. She had no more tears: she had used them all up on Farid. To Chloé it felt as though her throat, her lungs, her stomach were shrivelling. She remembered the pills Doctor Léger had given her. She could feel her anguish welling up . . .

Jean-Luc did something none of them expected. He hurled himself at Khadidja, brandishing his rifle-butt, and screaming at her. Khadidja collapsed from a blow to her right shoulder.

"HE'S RUN OUT OF AMMUNITION!" Lola shouted. "JUMP HIM, INGRID!"

Jean-Luc was whirling the rifle above his head, ready to strike again. Chloé seized her cello and charged, the steel spike raised. When she pierced his left kidney, Jean-Luc howled like a madman. Ingrid took advantage to finish him off with the pressure cooker.

Lieutenant Barthélemy was pleased as punch. Not only had Lola Jost foiled a raid on a bureau de change by raising the alarm, but on top of that, she had helped them arrest Jean-Luc Cachart, the only one of the ram-raiders to have escaped the Anti-Gang Squad. The Garden Gnome had taken delivery of this parcel, neatly gift-wrapped. The said Cachart, who had unwisely come to settle his account with Khadidja Younis, had run into the boss herself. That had been his undoing. The big brute had ended up concussed by a pressure cooker, his kidney perforated by a cello spike. He was still recovering in hospital.

Lola was unique for the way she always emerged triumphant from the worst possible situations. That woman was a godsend, although to her enemies she was a disaster. Lola was Grousset's own personal nemesis, and would remain so until the end of time.

With breathtaking finesse, the boss had given all her information to the Gnome. Placing herself above the fray, she had, like an aristo-crat of the detective world, passed on the fruits of her investigation to the man she most despised. Grousset was officially in charge of the Ringer case, and Lola was keen to demonstrate that she respected the law. Her only mistress, except perhaps for her free will. Oh, it had been exquisite. So exquisite you felt like climbing the curtains, getting out the decorations and the poppers, blowing whistles, throwing rose petals while you danced, peeing in policemen's caps.

The balance-sheet was looking positive: the doubts surrounding Maxime Duchamp were dissipating. He was lucky to have the boss protecting him! The Gnome had allowed him to go home. From now on, the police were focusing on Cachart and Zakri, Farid Younis's accomplices. Farid had been Vanessa Ringer's boyfriend before she broke it off, terrified by his violent side. Younis had never accepted this break-up. He had kept a key to the apartment in Passage du Désir. Grousset was counting on Cachart and Zakri to reveal the exact circumstances of Vanessa Ringer's death. For the moment, Cachart was saying nothing. Police questions slid off him as he lay ravaged in the white hospital bed. Had he lost the plot forever, knocked sense-less by the Valkyrie duo of the boss and the incredible Ingrid Diesel?

That left Noah Zakri. He was a different kettle of fish. A charac-ter with a hefty police record. He had come into contact with Cachart in Fleury prison. And presented Cachart to his best friend, the young Farid Younis. Younis and Zakri had met on the Cité des Fleurs estate in Saint-Denis. The place where Younis had washed up after leaving behind his parents and Rue de l'Aqueduc in the 10th arrondissement. About three years earlier.

The only dampener was that the boss seemed to really enjoy her retirement. Barthélemy was forced to admit it: there was little chance she would reinstal herself in Rue Louis-Blanc. Obviously, circum-stances had shown that nothing was forever. There were few situations in life when every door was double-locked. Lola Jost's remained ajar. The lieutenant could keep her informed under the G.G.'s nose, ask her for a helping paw if need be. The boss loved her profession. Barthélemy and her would still have occasion to meet. In fact, on that score, the lieutenant was dying to go and ask her something. About one detail in particular that was still bothering him.

34

Ingrid and Lola were seated at their usual table at the back of the restaurant. They had both just finished the day's special. Lola had washed it down with a Bergerac. Ingrid had made short work of the stew, but held back on the wine. *Belles* was packed. Not only had all the regulars turned up, but the restaurant had attracted a few English tourists, delighted if somewhat overwhelmed by the assault on their taste buds. Maxime was in the kitchen, Chloé and the new waitress Catherine, a big, solid woman of around thirty, were doing their best to cope with the demand.

"I wouldn't want to be in the Gnome's shoes. What I like is the field work. Having your muzzle to the ground, following a trail, pouncing on your quarry at the right moment. Sport, in other words."

"Yes, I'd noticed," Ingrid said, forcing a smile.

"Even so, you can't just go out and enjoy yourself and delegate the rest of the job. The two go hand-in-hand. Are you following?"

"Yes, no problem."

For several days now, Lola thought Ingrid had a vacant look about her. Was it decompression? Resurfacing to the prosaic world? Whatever the reason, Ingrid seemed absent, and replied only with brief polite replies to the questions one was kind enough to ask her. It was odd.

"I'm beginning to see interrogation as a science," Lola ploughed on, undeterred. "Some of my colleagues have a way of making their clients talk. Others have more difficulty. In my case, when faced with a criminal, I was often more tempted to slap him round the face than ask him questions. Do you get my point?"

"Yeah, yeah, I think I see it."

"Since we've brought Farid Younis into the equation, everything in the Ringer case has taken on another aspect. Maxime has escaped from Grousset's clutches. Even he has realised that in Jean-Luc Cachart and Noah Zakri he's dealing with very different characters. That leaves Chloé and Khadidja. It's more than obvious that those two are hiding something. As recently as last night, when you were stirring things up at the Calypso, I was questioning Khadidja at her place. As silent as the grave."

"Really?"

"As you heard. You'd think that after being saved by the cavalry – in this instance, Lola Jost and Ingrid Diesel – the least she could do is let something slip. But not a peep. *Nada*."

"That's annoying."

Lola studied Ingrid for a long while. Her blank look, lack of energy, her apathy. She swallowed another mouthful of wine:

"Have you caught the flu, my dear?"

"No. This morning, before we met here at *Belles*, I went for a long walk in Paris. Everything was bathed in a magnificent wintry light."

"It's still autumn, Ingrid."

"Winter's arrived early. At a certain moment, the sun was an orange ball perched on the top of trees with their ashen-coloured bark. The tall balconies of the nineteenth-century blocks were bathed in a golden glow. The passers-by scurried along, and there were a lot fewer people in the streets than usual. I walked as far as Parc Monceau, then came back along Faubourg-Saint-Denis. I knew that after this expedition, I'd find him the same as ever. Maxime the meticulous. Focused on his work whatever may be going on around him. I sat in his kitchen and we talked. And believe me, Lola, that's happiness. Moments like those."

"So it's the pleasure of cornering Maxime by his ovens that's turned you into this giant ectoplasmic cucumber?"

"This morning I experienced a moment of sheer beauty."

"Listen, Ingrid . . ."

"Go on."

"You've built yourself a world you stroll through at your athletic, elegant pace. You go for your little walk every day, smiling beatifically at the angels. Shall I tell you what you're actually doing, young lady?"

"You're going to tell me, whether I like it or not."

"You're dreaming your life away instead of living it. If it weren't Maxime, it would be someone else. And I think that's a real waste."

"It's our right to dream. Your Brillat-Savarin said that wine is the food of the soul. Apparently you agree, judging by the way you knock it back. For me, it's day-dreaming."

"Oh, now you're being pig-headed! You'll be telling me next how scared you are of the cybernetic revolution. Live for the present! Tomorrow it will be dead and buried. And so will we! So here's to our primate bodies."

"You've got a priggish side to your nature, haven't you?"

"And you have your pretentious one. It makes for a great contrast. I've got a suggestion for you."

"You're going to harangue me while we have dessert?"

"Not at all. I don't like desserts. You should know that by now."

"What then?"

"We go to your place, and you give me the massage you promised ages ago. Since you won't look after your own body properly, you can take care of mine."

"You shouldn't have a massage after such a humungous meal."

"It wasn't a humungous meal. It was a normal, well-earned one. Let's go for a humungous constitutional. Have another look at your picture postcard Paris to check it really exists. After that, back to your place, and you give me a massage."

"You really are a bitch, you know that?"

She was wearing nothing more than a bath towel and was letting Ingrid work her magic. The long-awaited massage. The warrior's repose. But the wait had been worth it! By Jove, how good Ingrid's pummelling felt! Now I'll massage your shoulders, now I'll stretch your vertebrae one by one, now I'll knead your flesh, the fat, blood, lymph, I'll energise your old carcass, roll you out like dough, break you in pieces and put you back together renewed. Wow, what a treat! Massage ought to be a compulsory subject at school. It would be like grooming for chimpanzees, a social bonding ritual. Everyone would make each other feel so good they'd be much less inclined to harm one another. Oh, what a gift from the gods, what a victory over grey, dreary everyday reality!

Diesel performed her massage exactly as she did her stripteases: with total dedication.

The doorbell rang.

"Don't move! I'll get it," Ingrid said.

"Don't worry, you're not getting rid of me that easily. Have you got another client?"

"No."

Ingrid returned with the news: it was Lieutenant Barthélemy. He had taken a seat on the pink sofa, and was leafing through a women's magazine.

"Botheration! Finish me first."

"But I still need a good half-hour, Lola."

"Barthélemy can wait. Today I'm the Queen of Sheba."

Barthélemy waited. It was a pink, fresh Lola wrapped in an XXL bathrobe who sat down opposite him in Ingrid Diesel's psychedelic waiting room.

"So, what can I do for you, my lad? Is the Gnome up to his usual tricks?"

"Not a bit of it, boss! Since you gave him the two armed robbers on a plate, the Gnome's in nirvana. He's floating on his own little cloud and leaving us all in blessed peace. No, there's something else bothering me. A small detail, and yet . . ."

"Spit it out, lad. As you can see, I'm extremely relaxed. I want to stay that way for a good while. Don't stir my impatience. It's curled up by the fireside, and it's happy there."

"Boss, do you remember the day when you rang the duty sergeant at the 10th arrondissement, who then alerted the Anti-Gang Squad?"

"As if it were yesterday."

"Well, the Anti-Gang people took another call. Minutes after yours. Just before the attempted raid. A witness who didn't leave his name. A young man's voice."

Lola froze. Diesel and Barthélemy stared at her.

"*Carambouillasse!*" she finally managed to say.

"What?" Ingrid said.

"It can't have been a witness who happened to be on the spot and did his civic duty by calling the police. As you say, it was only an 'attempted' raid."

"Exactly," Barthélemy said, "because the raiders were caught right at the start."

"Are you sure it was a young man?"

"Yes, I'm positive. I made the sergeant go over his story twenty times. The poor guy, he was getting sick of it."

"We have to have a tempest under our skulls, right now."

"Can't you say *brainstorming* like any normal person, Ingrid?"

"I thought you French people hated *franglais*."

"I don't know about anyone else, but I couldn't give a damn. It's not by imposing restrictions that we'll save our language. It's by making it live. It's like an investigation: if you're blinkered about it, you get nowhere. You have to let things come to you, let the wave take you, let the slope launch you. Come on, let's think big."

"Alright," Barthélemy said, a broad smile on his face. "Everything suggests you weren't the only ones who discovered where the three robbers had their hideout."

"Everything suggests Jean-Luc Cachart was right when he said Farid Younis had been grassed up," Lola interrupted him. "The important distinction is that hitherto Ingrid and I were convinced we were those dastardly informers. Isn't that so, Ingrid?"

"Yes, that's right, Lola. What if it was Menahem?"

"Who's he?"

"Noah's younger brother," Lola replied. "The one who supplied the getaway cars and acted as driver. No, I can't see why Menahem would have wanted to rat on his brother. A brother who pays for his studies. Studies that interest Menahem, because we know he attends classes regularly. No, no. Come on, think hard."

"That's a bit difficult, because two names keep flashing up. The first: Maxime Duchamp. He had every reason to want to get rid of Farid before he got rid of him. Second: Khadidja Younis. She had to choose between her twin brother and her lover."

"If I said 'Think hard' I was hoping to avoid that kind of facile conclusion, my lad," Lola retorted imperiously. "Open your mind to all possibilities."

Some time went by, with Barthélemy and Ingrid going over what they knew, while Lola looked on impassively, nodding her head now and then, and offering only the occasional vague "why not", "interesting", "not bad". She was like a rotund, inscrutable Taoist monk, sitting bolt upright on the orange sofa. After a while, Barthélemy said he had to get back to the station. The Gnome would be growing impatient.

Ingrid saw him out, then came back to sit opposite Lola.

"I thought he was never going to leave," Lola said.

"So all that was an act to persuade him to leave?"

"Precisely. Barthélemy soon gets a headache when you ask him to think in the abstract. He prefers concrete questions. I knew I'd wear him down."

"Why remove him from the scene?"

"To receive our visitor in peace."

"What visitor?"

"I had a call yesterday from Guillaume Fogel. He'll be here in a few minutes."

"It's strange, Lola, this feeling I get that my apartment has turned into your office."

Guillaume Fogel hesitated for a moment between the pink and the orange. Eventually he chose the pink sofa, probably so that he could sit facing Lola, whom he suspected of being in charge of the improbable duo.

"Constantin went back to Romania. Before he left, he insisted on speaking to me. He told me that Vanessa didn't just have a diary to confide her problems to. She had a friend, the person who had recommended she keep the famous journal."

"So that's the missing link. The kid had forgotten to tell us the most important detail."

"He hadn't forgotten. Constantin said he didn't see why that friend would have wanted to harm Vanessa. But since the police still haven't found her murderer, he wanted to tell me absolutely everything he knew. To make a clean breast of it. So as not to feel any remorse."

"And you really believe children have such a complex view of reality, Fogel?"

"Pardon?"

"I'll tell you how it really happened: Constantin told you straight off about the journal and the friend. But you gave me an abridged translation. You left out the friend. Possibly because you don't like playing the informer. It's probably second nature in your job. I could tell we had to drag things out of you. Besides which, if it were only about Constantin, you'd have told me all this on the phone. You came because you felt spineless for having twisted a kid's testimony. Well, am I right?"

"You're a woman to be feared, Madame Jost."

"Not really. But for the moment I'm necessary, because you came here seeking my absolution. Very well, I grant it. In any event, I've never known an investigation where everything led in a straight line to the truth. You take one step forward, then two steps back. People talk, people stay silent, people get their memories mixed up, people lie. No, I'm not a woman to be feared, Fogel. Perhaps I'm just clear-headed."

The shelter director did not stay long after that. Almost as soon as he had made his exit, Lola dressed in a hurry and told Ingrid to put on her airman's jacket and her weird hat. Bemused by all these discussions and machinations, the Yank did as she was told, and rushed after Lola without even asking where they were going.

35

They were sitting side by side in a corridor waiting for a door to open. The door was marked: ALAIN MIREPOIX, HEAD SUPERVISOR. They could hear a man's voice giving a dressing-down to someone who was having a hard time.

"Look, Ingrid, we no longer say 'Head of Discipline'. That probably sounded too much like a cop."

"Oh, yes, I've noticed that you're becoming very scared of words in France."

The door opened to reveal a tall, stern-looking man and a livid teenager. The man waited for the boy to return to his classroom before turning his sharp gaze on the two women.

"Mesdames, did you have an appointment?"

"No, Monsieur Mirepoix, but this won't take long," Lola said, standing up and demonstrating as much authority as avoirdupois.

Lola Jost, head supervisor of putting your foot in it, Ingrid thought, stepping into the room without being asked. She took one of the chairs facing the desk, and when Mirepoix sat down, she offered an innocent smile to counter his angry glare.

The supervisor quickly recovered his composure. It took a few moments to clear up a misunderstanding: Ingrid and Lola were not the parents of any pupils. When Lola explained she wanted to find out about three former students in the light of Vanessa Ringer's murder, Mirepoix almost choked. Ingrid realised Lola was going to tell a lie. Sure enough, she quickly pulled her police I.D. from her coat, and this proved a highly successful move. Mirepoix knew Commissaire Jost by reputation. From then on, the interrogation went as smooth as silk.

Mirepoix remembered the three girls well because they had often been sent to his office. Their inseparable trio was also a trio of poor students. Vanessa, Chloé and Khadidja were quiet girls who picked up average grades and took little part in the life of the class. He spoke of a falling-off. They had done quite well up to sixteen, especially Vanessa Ringer, who had received above-average grades, but as soon as they entered the sixth form, everything went to pieces. Their marks dropped, and the three girls seemed to lose interest in the school and in their futures. They did the bare minimum. Their parents gave up on them. The teachers grew weary of them.

"Chloé and Vanessa failed all their school-leaving exams. Khadidja left before taking them."

"What about her brother, Farid Younis?"

"A catastrophe, commissaire. Expelled by the discipline committee in the third year. Not only did Younis refuse to work, but he was aggressive. An uncontrollable student."

"I believe he went out with Vanessa Ringer."

"Yes, and I went so far as to warn Vanessa about the company she kept."

"How did she take that?"

"She just looked at me coquettishly."

"Vanessa, coquettish? But everyone has described her to us as a girl who had no interest in men."

"You're joking, aren't you? Vanessa Ringer had the reputation of being a flirt. She was one of the prettiest girls in the school, and she knew it. I could see how the boys behaved around her. She loved being the centre of attention. I quickly made her realise that fluttering her eyelids at me would get her nowhere."

"Apart from Farid Younis and the two other girls, did she hang around with any others?"

"No, I've told you, not with any other pupils . . ."

"Teachers then?"

"No, never."

"Monsieur Mirepoix, I can sense you're feeling less co-operative all of a sudden."

"Not at all, madame, I'm at your service."

"In that case, please answer me frankly. The investigation is stalled, and if it stays like that, the Ringer file will simply add to the pile of unsolved crimes. That would be unjust. A young girl of twenty, a social worker . . ."

"Yes, I read she had found a job in the Rue des Récollets shelter. I was astonished at such a commitment from her . . ."

"Let's get back to what you remember of her."

"It's an old story, and I don't really see what link it could have with your concerns now."

"Try anyway."

"We had a young class assistant, Grégoire Marsan. I often saw him chatting with Vanessa. Too often. I reminded him that an assistant should keep a distance between himself and the pupils. Everything went back to normal."

"Meaning?"

"Meaning that Marsan's relationship with Ringer cooled off. I make it a point never to let a problem fester."

"Where does this Grégoire Marsan live?"

"Unfortunately, he's dead. His body was pulled out of the canal. It was obvious he'd been attacked, and then thrown into the water. Three years ago, it must have been."

It took several seconds for this piece of information to sink in, and for Lola to ask if the girls' poor marks began around that time. Mirepoix thought about it, and said, "More or less. But I always assumed it was a coincidence, or the straw that broke the camel's back, if you prefer."

"Some straw," Ingrid said, despite Lola's scowl.

"The basic problem was that Vanessa, Khadidja and Chloé all had problems at home. I saw the parents – at least, the ones who took the trouble to come in – and found I was dealing with people who either could not cope with what was going on around them, or were too rigid to find solutions. Add to that the fact that the three of them lived increasingly cut off from the world, and you have a pretty clear picture of the situation."

Mirepoix gave Lola the address of Grégoire Marsan's parents. They still lived in Rue de Paradis. The two women left the school, and found themselves under a grey, stormy sky. It was windy too, with that kind of treacherous breeze that blew in from afar, from the Arctic Circle for example, and intended to freeze a few thousand noses and twice as many ears before it blew out again. For once though, Ingrid did not comment on the Parisian weather: she was still excited by their meeting with the head supervisor.

"I think we've put our finger on a big hare, Lola. An *enormous* hare. A mutant beast from outer space."

"The expression is to *start* a hare, Ingrid. And since you've mentioned it, don't forget the one in La Fontaine. The tortoise won that race. Wait and see before you cry victory!"

"Lola – you party-pooper!"

"Grousset may be slow, but he could have got there before us. And perhaps it's a false lead."

The mademoiselle tried to cool down a few degrees. But Lola knew what was going on in her great giraffe's mind: Ingrid was as enthusiastic about the investigation as a Santo Gadejo fan would be at the discovery of a previously unknown roll of film. Her splendid enthusiasm was enviable. And also very annoying, because it was catching. Lola was only too aware that her love of the job was resurfacing. She thought she had crushed it beneath the sole of her shoe, but it was still there, squirming, appealing. She had imagined herself doing jigsaw puzzles to the end of her days, to find peace in that impeccable Zen art, believing herself to be fully retired rather than in limbo; now what was to become of her? Once this affair had been concluded, she would have to take her head in her hands and think about the morrow. What was Lola Jost going to do with the fine days she had left? Especially as moving to Singapore was out of the question. Palm trees, humidity, and mosquitoes were fine for three weeks a year. Just about.

By the time Ingrid and Lola arrived at Paul and Elise Marsan's apartment it was almost seven in the evening. Elise was preparing dinner. Reminding parents of the death of their son was a burden they would have sooner avoided. Ingrid had never been through anything like this before, and had no idea how to behave. She decided to stay in the background. Her considerate companion became even more considerate. She explained that she also had a son and two granddaughters. The Marsans relaxed, and the two women learned that Grégoire would have been twenty-three the following April. He had been stabbed four times. Then thrown into the canal. The river police had pulled his body out of the Récollets lock. No witnesses had come forward. The police had put it down to a robbery that had turned ugly. Skilled at karate, Grégoire must have defended himself, and his ruthless attackers had stabbed him to death.

Then Lola asked the Marsans to tell her about Grégoire's friends. There wasn't much to learn. The young man was preparing for the entrance exams to a leading university at Lycée Chaptal, and working as a class assistant at Beaumarchais. This double timetable left him little time for friends. Or for holidays. He had been killed in July, when he had been planning to spend the whole summer swotting for his exams at home. Paul Marsan remembered the name of the police officer in charge of the investigation. Someone called Toussaint Kidjo. Nice enough, if a little inexperienced, it had seemed to him.

Ingrid and Lola went into the nearest café for a pick-me-up. The cold that had descended like a dirty grey blanket over the city seemed ever more determined to seep deep into the bones and destroy the Parisians' morale. Lola ordered a hot toddy, and Ingrid the same. They blew on their drinks, warmed their hands on the glasses. One had her Peruvian hat pulled down over her eyes, the other her coat collar pulled up over her frozen ears. Their feet were freezing in wet, flat-heeled shoes.

"Damn and blast. It happened in July. And in July I'm always in Singapore with my son. Toussaint took on the Marsan killing in my absence. If it had been a fortnight earlier, I would have had all the information up here," Lola said, tapping her right temple.

"Ask Barthélemy to go through the files for you."

"Barthélemy's going to get into trouble if he carries on playing this double game. He's risking suspension for me."

"Whoa! It's the exact opposite. You're offering him a priceless gift. You're giving him a lead . . . Oh, I get it . . ."

"Get what?"

"That's what you hate about this! If you dig into the Marsan affair and it links with the Ringer murder, we'll be pushed off the case. And that bothers you. At first, you didn't want to know, but now you're hooked, Lola!"

"Strange, these sudden flashes of intelligence you have. It must be my influence."

They changed cafés and drank a second toddy at *Compère Robert* in Rue Louis-Blanc. Lola knew the place like the back of her hand, and the owner too. The famous Robert, an intelligent man, was used to dealing with the constabulary. Picking up on Lola's warning wink, he gave her a restrained welcome.

"I swore I'd never set foot in there again," she murmured, nodding through the misted-up window towards the entrance to the police station on the far side of the street.

"Would you like me to go with you?"

"Are you kidding? That wouldn't exactly be discreet, would it? And don't look at me with those eyes."

"My eyes are my eyes."

"No they're not. This evening they're the eyes of a Breton spaniel. You'd accustomed me to something more interesting."

"Is this better?" Ingrid asked, yanking the hat down over her nose.

"Now you look like a Peruvian spaniel. That's even worse."

"Will you tell me one day what happened to Toussaint Kidjo?"

Ingrid took her hat off, tried to appear unconcerned, and waited. Lola's response was to get up and leave *Compère Robert*, with a mournful air. The Yank watched her cross Rue Louis-Blanc, come to a halt outside the police station entrance, light a cigarette and then stand there like an ancient oak tree waiting to be struck by lightning. Time seemed to slow down. To Ingrid, it seemed as if she was staring at the bulky figure for many minutes. Finally, the ex-commissaire tossed her cigarette butt into the gutter and went in. Ingrid could not suppress a slight grimace as the door closed behind her friend. She felt bad on her behalf.

When she reappeared, Lola looked more relaxed. Dropping a thick volume onto the table, she declared: "I made up a story that the desk sergeant swallowed whole. You see before you a retired policewoman who has rediscovered a taste for studying. As a law student, I came to recover my old Dalloz legal dictionary. As the Mata Hari of the Faubourg-Saint-Denis, I stuffed the Grégoire Marsan file under my coat. It's very uncomfortable."

"Bravo, Lola, I'm proud of you," Ingrid said enthusiastically, and meaning it.

"That doesn't surprise me, young lady. O.K., let's go to your place or mine to sift through all this paperwork."

"I can't. Tonight is one of my Calypso nights."

Lola's eyes narrowed, then she smiled. Intrigued, Ingrid returned her smile.

"Has it ever occurred to you to send him an invitation?"

"Him who, Lola?"

"The little jerk who nearly drowned you on Quai de Valmy."

"Benjamin Noblet?"

"That's the one. I'd forgotten his name. You hadn't, apparently."

"Why should I send him an invitation?"

"To intrigue him, of course. I could see he was a deep one, that kid. A film-maker, an intellectual, and so on."

"Lola!"

"Remember what I said, young lady: tomorrow, the present will be dead and buried. I haven't changed my mind."

36

Lola had put her red dressing gown on top of her flannelette nightie. The board with the unfinished puzzle on it was on the floor, waiting for happier days. Papers were strewn all over the kitchen table. Toussaint had not stinted on witness statements.

She poured herself another glass of her favourite vintage port, then went back to work. The kid had worked hard, if the labours of an ant were your kind of thing. Lola imagined him spending hours pounding the pavement. Because you had to go down many streets, climb many a staircase, introduce yourself many times to carry out the mammoth task of investigating the death of a class assistant. It was July. Everyone was on holiday, and yet Toussaint had taken it upon himself to question all the students from Lycée Beaumarchais who had stayed in Paris. As well as Marsan's classmates at Chaptal.

In August, all change. Kidjo had been called away to investigate a series of break-ins in the neighbourhood. So had I, Lola remembered. I was back from my holidays, and rejoined my foot-soldiers. The then Commissaire Grousset had taken over the Grégoire Marsan affair, had quickly undermined everything in his own inimitable way, and hastily archived the file.

Lola carefully read through all the witness statements Toussaint had taken. Then moved on to Grousset's. She rediscovered an excitement she thought she had lost: sticking your nose into bundles of paper trying to find a pearl. It was almost eleven when her persistence was rewarded. She read and reread the document in her hands. It contained a wonderful phrase: "Greg was my best friend, but I suppose that means nothing to you." That witness had been right: his declaration had meant nothing to Grousset.

Lola was sorry that tonight Ingrid was performing at Calypso: she was going to miss the climax. That would be frustrating, and she was sure the stubborn Yank would never let her hear the last of it. Lola was going to be alone at a crucial moment, and that was something she'd never liked. And so she called Barthélemy, then cursed his answering machine and its excuses. You nincompoop, what is this habit of never replying when you're needed? Lola left an offended message, hung up in disgust, then calmed down: "Well, if tonight's the night, so be it."

She opened a window and stuck an arm out to test the temperature. The Arctic wind had given way to a more cunning acolyte. A wind from the distant steppes which long ago had driven the invading tribes on from behind. O.K., if that's how it is, tonight I'm a one-woman Genghis Khan with my Mongol horde, she told herself, grabbing her only pair of trousers from the wardrobe: a pair of flannels she was hoping would go with an old pair of fur-lined boots. It was high time she got her winter coat out of its cover. Once she had climbed into all this gear, Lola tied a scarf round her head, and set off into the freezing night.

She walked along at a brisk pace, only slowing down when she reached Rue des Vinaigriers. The little plastic figurines were sleeping soundly in the window of *Le Concombre Masqué*. Lights were on in the

Kantors' apartment. And in Patrick's room. High above, the sky was in tumult. It was dark, unruly, torn with grey streaks and wild cotton-wool clouds swept along by the furious wind. A huge turmoil of aimless anger.

Rodolphe Kantor was attending to business at the Star Panorama, and so the Kantor clan was made up of only the mother, floating distractedly on clouds of cannabis and dreams of the seventies, and her son, busy with the subtle manoeuvres of mass destruction on his trusty computer.

Lola made out this was just a friendly visit. Dropping in on someone as stoned as Renée Kantor meant the late hour was no problem. For now, the bookseller was wavering between The Doors and Jefferson Airplane. Lola recommended "Riders on the Storm", which fitted in perfectly with the weather outside. Renée clapped her hands and invited Lola to listen with her. Throwing the living-room window open wide, she sniffed the stormy air, and suggested she and Lola look for the glow from the Eiffel Tower in the distance. Unflappable in her thick brown overcoat, Lola caught a ray of light and said how fantastic it was. Renée went to fetch a bottle of Madiran. She poured a glass for Lola, then started to dance, eyes closed, the remote control still in her hand. When "Riders on the Storm" came to an end, she pressed the remote to take it to the start again.

"I'll be back," Lola said.

She headed for Kantor junior's bedroom.

The only light came from the screen's glow, and so she switched on the main light. Patrick groaned: "What is it now, maman?" and turned round. A quiet astonishment he quickly stifled. He nodded briefly, acknowledging Lola's presence. Then returned to his game.

"You said one day: 'Greg was my best friend, but I don't suppose that means anything to you.' That was wrong, wasn't it, Patrick."

"I'll tell you once I've finally worked out what on earth you're talking about."

"Grégoire Marsan was a bit older than you and was an assistant at your school. He was your friend, your big brother, your father figure, because Rodolphe Kantor never quite measured up."

"I love it when cops dabble in psychology. It's always a hoot."

"In short, Marsan was very important to you. Unfortunately, he fell for a tease, the beautiful but inconsiderate Vanessa Ringer, who already had a boyfriend. A difficult lad by the name of Farid Younis. A violent sort who'd been expelled from the Lycée Beaumarchais. Younis wasn't happy that Marsan was courting Vanessa. He stabbed him four times and threw his body in a lock on Canal Saint-Martin."

"It's incredible all the stuff you know."

"You went to the police. You were received by Commissaire Grousset. You told him you suspected Farid Younis. Since Grousset wasn't convinced enough to arrest him there and then, Younis vanished into thin air. So you swore to take justice into your own hands. Even if it took years. Vanessa and her friends went on living in the 10th arrondissement. Deeply affected by Marsan's death, Vanessa was a shadow of her former self. But for Farid Younis, Vanessa was unforgettable."

"So are you, believe me!"

He sniggered, but underneath he was growing nervous. Lola moved closer to him, and went on: "She was so horrified by the violence that she had broken it off with him, but he hoped he could win her back. You waited, ready to pounce. But nothing happened. So you decided to force him to react, by killing his Vanessa."

A smile was still playing on the corners of his mouth, but she could see he was vulnerable. She came closer still.

"The problem was how to cast the suspicion onto someone else," she went on. "Maxime Duchamp made the ideal suspect. You invented a fling between him and Vanessa. You cleverly manipulated your mother so that she went and had her say to Grousset, by now a commissaire. Look at me when I'm talking."

He turned towards her. He was trying to control himself, but found it hard. She was encroaching on his space, and he didn't like it. His fist had tightened round his grey plastic mouse.

"You liquidated Farid Younis just as you liquidate your pixel soldiers. Without dirtying your hands, and without running any risks. I don't know how you managed to find out where he was hiding in Saint-Denis, but you did. You waited for Younis and his accomplices to launch a final raid, and you shopped them to the police. Clean, precise, impeccable. What do you say to all this, my boy?"

"That your imagination is as impressive as your girth, madame. Bravo."

"It's true that yours leaves a lot to be desired. You copied *Otaku*. That's where your idea of creating a murderer obsessed by schoolgirls comes from. Just like your mother, you've always been obsessed by Rinko Yamada-Duchamp's work. I'm sure you knew that Maxime has dolls inspired by the manga."

"You're really not bothered about how ridiculous you come across, are you? It would be glorious if it weren't so sad."

"The idea of a ritual killing wasn't bad. The police might label Maxime Duchamp as a crazy fetishist when they discovered Rinko's dolls at his place. No doubt that's why you slipped a Bratz doll with detachable feet in Vanessa's bedroom. And for those who still didn't get it, you chopped off her feet. Shame. It's your wish to be so precise that was your downfall, Patrick. You added too much. The police were overwhelmed with choice details. Real life never corresponds to a manga story or a video game, young man. Otherwise, we would know about it by now."

Kantor made as if to return to his game. He attempted to control his voice.

"Your fiction is not going to get any further than a script. You don't have a shred of proof."

"That's what you think!"

"Plus you're not even a cop anymore. What gives you the right to come here and harass me? Because that's what this is, and I could make a complaint."

"Who says I'm no longer a cop? In fact, I was never retired. My sabbatical year has just come to an end."

"Cop or not, you're seriously beginning to get on my nerves. You're way outside the legal hours for questioning."

Lola grabbed the mouse and tugged. Everything came away in her hand – the animal's tiny body and its long plastic tail. When Kantor sprang up, he had his fists clenched and was sweating with rage. The heels on Lola's pair of old fur-lined boots were quite high, so Patrick's head reached only slightly above her breasts. From being shut up so long in his room, Patrick had forgotten what a physical barrier certain people's bodies could be – Vanessa had been so slight a figure. Lola made as if to raise her arms to protect herself, like an elderly matron fending off a young whippersnapper, but he took her by surprise. He grasped the lapels of her coat and yanked them as hard as he could. Closing them around her gullet. It was a very unpleasant feeling. She slapped him. He made to return the blow, but she grabbed his wrist and twisted. He gave a piercing cry. Lola used the tail of the mouse to bind his hands. She was just finishing a fancy knot that she had learned at Cap Fréhel when the door burst open.

After her dance accompanying the ghost of Jim Morrison, Renée's hair was stuck to her forehead. Wide-eyed, she advanced on Lola and her son, locked together in an awkward embrace.

"I heard everything! What are you trying to do, Lola? You want to sacrifice Patrick to save that bastard Maxime, is that it?"

Lola thought quickly. She cursed herself for having come alone. Her lack of skill at extracting confessions had got her into a tight spot again. If only she'd brought Barthélemy or Ingrid with her! She was a lone musketeer faced with a united mother and son, and the boy had proved tougher than expected. The video games must have honed his sense of strategy. Lola tugged Patrick round so that his mother could see the expression on his face. He was not so in control. Then she played her last card.

"It's all up for you, Patrick. There was a witness in the apartment. A little Romanian boy called Constantin. He saw everything. He's got no papers, so he only came forward to the police station this evening."

She was expecting him to laugh in her face, but instead his eyes hardened. He took on a strange, fixed look. Renée took a step towards her son, arms outstretched. Patrick quickly stepped back, his body rigid. He was trembling. Lola couldn't make out what was going on: it was all too sudden. By pure chance, she had pressed the right button.

"Vanessa wasn't afraid to open the door because she knew you. Since he wasn't supposed to be at her place, Constantin thought it was the director of the refuge centre who had come to pick him up. He hid in the wardrobe. And saw it all. How you strangled her . . ."

"Patrick could never do anything like that!"

"Shut up, Renée. Let me finish." Then, turning to Patrick: "How you mutilated her, how you fixed everything to incriminate Maxime. How you left the money from the raid so the police would think it was a crime of passion. Unfortunately, that part didn't work, because the money vanished before the police got there. Khadidja was like Constantin: it took a long while before she came to see us."

"What money, what raid is she talking about, Patrick? Don't let her gabble on! It's not possible! Say something!"

Renée threw herself at Lola. Kantor junior took advantage to pick up the computer keyboard, flip it over, and cut the wire binding his hands with a shiny object taped underneath. The cleaver! He tore it off, brandished it at the two women. Still clinging to Lola's coat, Renée started to scream and scream. Lola could not imagine how such a piercing sound could come from such a small woman. Renée let go, collapsed like a sack of potatoes, and began to sob. Patrick backed towards the half-open door.

"All this play-acting is no use, maman."

Lola started after him, cursing herself yet again for having come alone, and calculating the mass of trouble that was about to engulf them.

"PUT DOWN YOUR MACHETE AND DON'T MOVE!"

It was Barthélemy's voice. There was a metallic clang as the cleaver bounced off the wooden floor. Barthélemy was pointing his Smith & Wesson at Patrick.

"Nothing broken, boss?"

"No, lad. Everything's hunky-dory. For the two of us, at least."

Lola sank into the nearest chair. Her legs were like jelly, her lungs refused to function, the palms of her hands were clammy with sweat. She wiped them on her flannel trousers, then her eyes strayed automatically towards the framed Rinko Yamada-Duchamp illustration. Standing there in her pleated skirt, the Japanese schoolgirl peered down at Patrick with wide, innocent eyes.

37

Lola was putting one foot carefully in front of the other: patches of ice made the pavements treacherous. A snow so light it was almost invisible was falling, shrouding the street. Christmas was coming. She was shopping for her two granddaughters. She had to buy things early if she wanted their presents to arrive in Singapore in time for Christmas.

She pushed open the door of *Jouets d'hier et d'aujourd'hui.* The shop assistant was helping a client who had left her twin buggy in a corner. Lola could not help thinking of the Younis twins. Khadidja, who was trying to find success without owing anyone anything, and Farid who became an armed robber because it was easier than having to work. Farid the killer.

Well, the alleged killer. Neither Jean-Luc Cachart nor Noah Zakri had shed any light on Grégoire Marsan's murder. As for Patrick Kantor, when the officers at Rue Louis-Blanc had gone to work on him, he had soon confessed his hatred of Farid Younis, and to how it had led him to eliminate Vanessa Ringer. Kantor was absolutely convinced Younis had committed the earlier murder. So convinced that he had thrown Vanessa's diary and her hacked-off feet into the Récollets lock. An act of vengeance for his lost friend. And yet he had no proof to back up his accusation. He declared that he had discovered the truth by reading Vanessa's diary without her knowledge. But that diary was no use now, because its long sojourn in the water had rendered its secrets impenetrable. Kantor repeatedly told Grousset it was the police's turn to make an effort. He wasn't going to give them any help, because he despised them. He had not said a word about the bag stuffed with money. This was fortunate, because Lola had not mentioned it either. The five hundred thousand euros were still resting snugly in Ingrid's wardrobe. Khadidja and Maxime had well and truly split up. Jonathan, the hairdresser at *Jolie petite madame* had seen her in a small part on T.V.: she played a young Arab immigrant working at a large Parisian secondary school. A strange paradox: her role was that of a flirt who loved the only boy not attracted to her. "A T.V. film for shop-girls, but not badly done," was Jonathan's verdict.

The mother of twins chose a multicoloured troll, asked for it to be gift-wrapped, and left the shop. The assistant suggested several toys to Lola, but she chose two Bratz dolls. Two beautiful, flashy dolls with detachable feet and Star Academy looks. She paid and left with her parcels. She was proud of herself: you should never let bad memories get the better of you. Outside the Ringer affair, a doll was still a doll. Something little girls love.

She did more shopping in her neighbourhood at the same cautious pace, then went home. She laid out her purchases, and sat in front of her puzzle. The Sistine Chapel was almost complete, with only a dozen or so pieces still missing. All that was needed was the desire to fit them in. Lola looked out of the window: it was still snowing, something unheard of at this time of year in Paris. For once, the snow seemed to be settling; soon the city would be covered in a gorgeous white blanket. The morning sounds were muffled in the frozen atmosphere. Numbed passers-by were sparing of their tongues and their time, wanting above all to be home in the warm. Lola soon realised she wanted the opposite: to go out again. To leave behind this all too cosy cocoon and let the Sistine Chapel wait. She had kept her coat on.

Once she was out in Rue du Faubourg-Saint-Denis she quickened her pace. Something kept nagging at the back of her mind. Barthélemy was happy. Grousset was happy. Everyone was happy except Lola. And possibly Ingrid, who had mused out loud, "The Ringer affair isn't over yet."

The Passage du Désir was bathed in an unreal glow. An uninhabited dream-world, because Tonio had gone to find warmth in a neighbourhood shelter. The antique-seller's window had been repaired, and the little dancer was still there, pretty as a picture inside her bottle, waiting for someone to come, wind her up, bring her back to life. My, I'd completely forgotten about you, Lola said to herself, and went in. She haggled for quite a while, then bought the doll, which she slipped into her handbag. She rang Ingrid's doorbell.

No-one answered. It was too early for *Belles*, so where could she have got to? Lola paced up and down thinking about it, then set off for Rue des Petites-Écuries.

The receptionist at the Supra Gym appeared astonished that such a large lady should venture into her club, but handed her a map of the installations and explained that the tall blonde with the American accent was in the cardio-training room.

The young lady in question was wearing a tank-top and a tight-fitting pair of dark-blue leggings, spiced up by two white stripes that emphasised her long legs. She had her headphones on, and seemed to be inordinately pleased to be running on the spot. Her treadmill was going at full speed. At least so it seemed to Lola, who couldn't imagine lasting two seconds at such a pace. She watched Ingrid's profile as she ran, a happy Amazon. Lola didn't want to spoil her pleasure; she found a chair, sat down, plonked her bag on her lap.

Some minutes later, it was a beaming Ingrid who came over, bathed in sweat, glowing pink cheeks, hair in wayward strands. Lola took the gift from her bag.

"She's wonderful!"

"Yes, she looks like you, Ingrid. All you have to do is wind her up and she dances about like a mad thing for an amazingly long time. She has to be seen to be believed."

Afterwards, a showered and dressed Ingrid shared a coffee with Lola in *Le Roi Roger*, the bistro frequented by the Supra Gym regulars. The dancer was on the counter in her bottle; Ingrid had already made her perform four times. To the barman's dismay, she was about to wind her up again. The music was a pretty little ditty, but after a while it grated on your nerves.

"When I said to Patrick Kantor that Grégoire Marsan was like a father to him, it was by instinct, but I felt I'd put my finger on something."

"On a hare. Yes, I see what you mean."

"The expression is to *start* a hare, Ingrid. How often do I have to tell you that, my girl?"

"I keep forgetting. Sorry!"

"I don't know where this obsession of yours with fingering a hare comes from . . ."

"Alright, Lola, how about getting back to the meat of the matter?"

"Well, I was right. The psychiatric expert who interviewed Patrick has confirmed that Marsan was a substitute for his biological father. A certain Pierre Norton."

"That's odd. It's the name of a computer anti-virus system."

"Anti-virus or not, this fellow abandoned Renée when Patrick was just six. Norton disappeared from the scene and was never heard of again. That was twelve years ago. When Grégoire Marsan also vanished three years ago, the trauma of his father's leaving resurfaced."

"So Patrick killed Vanessa to flush Farid out. It's an interesting theory, but . . ."

"It lacks that little something to make it ring true. I agree with you, Ingrid. And I can't get it out of my head. To such an extent that I can't do my jigsaw puzzle anymore."

"That's serious."

"Go ahead, laugh. But I feel I ought to try Antoine Léger one more time. I can go on threading psychological theories the way others thread pearls, but it won't get us anywhere. It's always better to consult a professional. And above all, a professional acquainted with the people involved. Don't you agree?"

"I can see what you're plotting, Lola."

"You can?"

"Antoine Léger is a client of mine, and you want to meet him *by chance* at my place."

"You're getting very shrewd, young lady. I've done a really good job on you. When's his next appointment?"

"At two this afternoon, like every Wednesday."

"What a coincidence!"

"Lola?"

"Ingrid?"

"Don't tell me you peeked at my appointments book."

"You pronounce 'appointments' very badly in French. Repeat after me: ap-point-ments."

The snow had eased off, but it was still bitterly cold. Lola was pretending to be interested in the magazines from a floppy pile on the waiting-room table, but one after another, they fell from her hands. The fact was, it was hard to concentrate on reading when a Dalmatian would not take its eyes off you. Sigmund Léger was stretched out on the rug, muzzle on his crossed front legs, in the same pose as when he assisted his master and eavesdropped on the neighbourhood secrets. His dark eyes were beautiful, surprisingly intelligent for a quadruped, but difficult to sustain.

Lola had been waiting a quarter of an hour for his owner to emerge. Ingrid was working overtime. Nothing surprising about that: the young lady never stinted on her sessions. All at once, Sigmund raised his head and sat up on his spotted haunches. He stared at the door, then at Lola, then at the door again. Studying him over the top of her magazine, Lola told herself that dogs were sometimes stranger than human beings. The doorbell rang, and she stood up hastily, glad of this distraction. Sigmund barked briefly. Lola found herself face to face with Chloé Gardel, who had streaming eyes and a red nose. She was wearing a thick scarf swathed round her neck.

"I was hoping to borrow some anti-flu pills from Ingrid," she said in a stuffed-up voice.

Everything happened very quickly. Chloé caught sight of Sigmund. Sigmund caught sight of Chloé. The dog scuttled over to the door his master was behind. Lola was about to ask Chloé to come in, when she mumbled that in fact she thought it would be better to go home and sleep. She'd come again when she felt better. Lola commented to her disappearing back that it was precisely so as to feel better that you took medicines. She shrugged and sat down again. A few minutes later, the Dalmatian came to sit beside her.

"If you could talk, I'm sure you'd have a story to tell, wouldn't you, my boy," she whispered to the dog.

By now she had grown tired of waiting, and so she knocked on the door of the massage room. Ingrid opened it, a broad smile on her face. Behind her Lola saw Léger, fully dressed and sitting on a beanbag, drinking a mint tea. Natacha Atlas was crooning softly in the background.

"So you two are sitting here having a good time while I'm outside waiting, are you?"

"Antoine was just telling me about Pierre Norton," said a beaming Ingrid.

"Favouritism," Lola retorted. "When I ask, it's a professional secret. But he tells you everything."

"Pierre Norton was never a client of mine," Léger corrected her, a relaxed smile on his face.

It was now or never. Léger would never be as relaxed as he was now, having passed through Ingrid's hands. Tally ho!

"Ingrid agrees with me," she said. "The Ringer affair isn't over, even if her murderer has been caught."

"I know. Ingrid explained that while she was massaging me."

Lola took a sideways glance at Ingrid, who was still wearing the most innocent expression possible.

"I can't analyse the reasons that drove Patrick Kantor to commit the crime," Léger went on in his level voice. "That wouldn't be professional, because I don't know all the facts. But there's one thing I'm absolutely certain of: although Patrick's father disappeared twelve years ago, he's still very much alive. At least he was two years ago, when I ran into him in the mountains teaching a group to ski. I was waiting for a ski-lift with my wife. Pierre Norton didn't recognise me. With reason: I was wearing a ski hat and goggles. He on the other hand was bare-headed. He had on the red, white and blue outfit worn by the instructors of the French Ski School."

"Did you tell Renée?"

"And twist the knife in the wound? No."

Sigmund came into the room. They could hear the click-clack of his claws on the silvery linoleum. He headed straight for his master, and laid his head on his lap.

"I'm going to tell you what I really think, Antoine. I wonder if Rinko Yamada-Duchamp's secret lover was none other than Pierre Norton."

"Renée Kantor hasn't been my client for a long time now, so I can speak frankly. The secret lover was a woman. It was Renée."

"Is that why Pierre Norton left?"

"It was more like the excuse he had been looking for to make himself scarce. Renée and Norton were never married. He lived off part-time jobs and did comic book illustrations. Except that he didn't have Rinko Yamada's talent or courage. At least if Renée is to be believed."

38

The high-speed train was like a huge earthworm with flexible rings beneath the veil of snow. That was how Lola, who did not much like travelling, and still less by train, saw it. Snowflakes were dancing in front of their eyes. Ingrid joyfully caught them on her woollen gloves, tasted their perfect geometry. At the far end of the long white platform that muffled all sounds stood the stone façade of the small station in Savoie. Lola was wrapped in a bonnet and a scarf that covered everything but her glasses. She was pulling hard at the handle of her suitcase on wheels, sure-footed thanks to a newly acquired pair of non-slip boots. She was wearing a rather tight black ski outfit she had bought in a sale. Ingrid had pulled a very becoming, loose-fitting beige ensemble out of her wardrobe. The contrast between their two silhouettes was more striking than ever.

They found a taxi and crossed Bourg-Saint-Maurice in next to no time. The climb to Les Arcs wound steadily past tall pines weighed down with snow. It was here they had their first problem: a tourist had skidded off the road, and it took some time to pull the car out.

When they reached the hotel, they got their keys from reception, left their luggage in their rooms, and rapidly made for the ski-hire chalet. Ingrid chose platinum level; Lola opted for the bronze. They also bought ski-lift passes, then finally emerged onto the slopes. It was snowing hard, there was limited visibility, skiers riding silent, frozen, ghost-like on the chair-lift. Ingrid took a quick glance at the map she had furnished herself with, and declared that the French Ski School was in that direction. She pointed to a faint point of light in the fog. Lola nodded and watched as her companion pulled on her skis and launched herself into the whiteness. Ingrid Diesel skied as sinuously as Gabriella Tiger danced.

The descent down the red slope was too fast for Lola's liking, but she faithfully followed in her friend's tracks – a perfect parallel, to which the ex-commissaire responded with a snow-plough learned back in the 1950s.

"I love skiing!" Ingrid trumpeted as she took off her skis outside the French Ski School chalet.

"That doesn't surprise me, my girl. But if you want us to enrol for a class with Pierre Norton, perhaps you'd do better to copy my style."

Unfortunately, they drew a blank, even though Lola had perfected a story about being out of practice and on holiday with her daughter, who had been delighted with the private lessons she had been given some years earlier by an instructor by the name of Pierre Norton. The fifty-year-old installed behind the log desk assured her that there was no instructor of that name working for the school. Lola put herself down for private lessons with the first available instructor, paid, and left. Ingrid stared quizzically after her. The wind had blown away the cloud cover, revealing a dazzlingly blue sky.

"He might have changed his name," Lola said when they were outside. "It's only logical for a man who wants to burn his bridges with his family."

"He could also have moved away."

"Let's not be pessimistic. The guy left Paris twelve years ago, but Léger saw him here two winters back. We can assume he moved about a bit at first, but after a while he must have settled somewhere. Let's approach this rationally. I'm going to have a coffee to help me forget that the blizzard froze my ears off, then I'll find my instructor and go skiing. Of course, I'll ask him a thousand and one questions to see if he can put me on the trail of Patrick's father. I'm looking for a small, fair-haired man aged between forty-five and fifty, with pale blue eyes. And a small scar on his chin: Léger's description is precise."

"What about me?"

"You visit all the mountain-top restaurants. You're looking for the same man, so you ask the same questions."

"That sounds straightforward enough."

"If nothing comes of it, at least we'll have had a few days' holiday in the snow. *Ingrid and Lola Go Skiing*: don't you think that's a good title?"

"Yes, but there'll be a sequel: *Ingrid and Lola Come Back Empty-Handed*. Then it'll be *Lola Digs Her Heels In*. And so on, until we have a lifetime contract."

"Who with?"

"With the world out there. With whatever pushes people to surpass themselves."

"Yes, people like you. Mystics who don't believe in God and are searching for a substitute."

"So what do you believe in?"

"I think the bearded Karl was right about one thing: religion is the opium of the people. And it doesn't look as if things are getting any better on that score."

"You must believe in something."

"I believe in you, Ingrid. I believe you're going to visit all those snowy eating-houses one after the other without losing your spontaneity or your good humour. Amen. Ski in peace, my dear, and may the great hairy Yeti not gobble you up."

That evening, Ingrid caught up with Lola in the hotel lounge. Lola was exhausted. She was drinking a mulled wine, entranced by the flames dancing in the fireplace. Outside, night and snow were falling at their own pace. The Yank stood still until the ex-commissaire turned her head and discovered her tall silhouette enveloped in a mass of sodden beige, her ski-mask glistening with a thousand melting crystals. Ingrid was tired but exultant.

Lola invited her to sit down and try some of the mulled wine, to warm herself with its spicy aroma, cinnamon to the fore. She gave a brief account of how she had suffered in the snow trying to keep up with a far-too energetic instructor. Their conversations on the lifts had not permitted her to identify Pierre Norton.

"Well, in *Le Chamois*, the last restaurant before the summit of L'Aiguille Rouge, I talked to some Alpine hunters, and they gave me a description which fits our man," Ingrid explained proudly. "He's an instructor at a rival ski school. The Alpages. I went down there – they're based five hundred metres lower, in the resort, and identified a certain Pierre Normann. At this very moment he's accompanying a group of tourists to the Croix-Rousse pass, a trek for experienced skiers. Three days of off-piste skiing, crossing glaciers, mountain streams, and sleeping in refuges."

Ingrid flopped back in her armchair and finally took a sip of the mulled wine, screwing up her eyes and clicking her tongue. Lola stared at her speechlessly.

"What's the matter, Lola? Aren't you pleased?"

"I am, but my old body is a bit less so. Instead of staying here in the warm and waiting quietly for him to return with his band of mountain-lovers, we're going to have to find him."

"Why?"

"Because if your Normann is indeed Norton, it won't be long before he discovers that a tall blonde with an American accent is searching high and low for him."

"But you were the one who sent me out to play the detective on the mountain tops!"

"I'm not denying it. But if you've got such a good result in so short a time it's because you've given it your all. In true Diesel bulldozer fashion."

"I'll help you reach Croix-Rousse, Lola. I've already done treks like that back in Colorado. I'll be your guide, and between the two of us we'll do fine."

Lola smiled feebly. Silence descended on them. Then Lola spoke up: "What do you put in a survival-kit sleeping-bag in the high Alps? Champagne and petits-fours?"

"No, corned beef, savoury biscuits and energy drinks, among other things. Let's go shopping at the resort grocery. I also need a compass and a proper map. And we can buy two special sleeping-bags. We leave at dawn."

Lola had never demanded so much of her body. She felt like an old, furred-up boiler burning up fuel far too quickly. Her joints were sobbing in silence, her muscles were denouncing torture, her eyes were drowning in the white that was all around them. She did her best to keep up with Ingrid, but often forced her to slow down. For the first time in her life, she would have been happy to swallow some miracle doctor's potion, toss a good thirty years into the waste-paper bin, rediscover a young woman's energy. She tried to abandon herself to gliding through the snow, to silence the complaints her nerve-ends were making in the awesome beauty of the landscape. A universe of silent beauty, of straight, densely packed pines that towered above them, indifferent to their petty human gestures. A universe that in a matter of minutes could blind you with the grey blanket of its clouds, break every bone in your body on the age-old rocks of a precipice, engulf you under the weight of its avalanches.

She had been struggling along for hours behind the indefatigable Ingrid, the ice fairy, the dragonfly of the glaciers. It was true they had stopped at a refuge, where Ingrid had ordained they down a tasteless energy snack and some coffee from the thermos. Ten measly minutes' rest, their backsides parked on an icy wooden bench, exchanging the vapour from their breath and occasional remarks intended to cheer each other up. Then they set off again. It was a nightmare. A complete white-out nightmare.

39

They caught up with the group around seven the next evening at the Loup Mathieu refuge. The sky was a perfect sulphurous black, studded with a thousand diamonds. Lola was mesmerised by the density of the silence, by the unlikely journey they had made. For hours, neither of them had spoken. Ingrid waited for Lola. She smiled as she caught up, and off they went again. They were saving their strength. Lola had discovered a hidden resource deep in her veins and muscle fibres, a strange automatic pilot system that kept her on course, allowed her heart to beat, her lungs to fill and empty, her brain to remain alert.

Ten or so skiers were sheltering in the refuge. A couple on their own in a mezzanine, and eight others in a group. All of them men. Five were playing cards; the others were commenting on the game. Among these was a man of about fifty, his hair bleached by the sun, the air of a seasoned mountain dweller, and with the natural authority of a leader.

Ingrid and Lola exchanged the usual courtesies with them and spread out their sleeping-bags. They shared a few provisions, had no difficulty adopting the attitude of skiers who had earned a good night's rest, and listened in to the others' conversations. The blond man's companions called him Pierrot several times, and talked of reaching the Croix-Rousse.

Ingrid was soon fast asleep. Wrapped in her silvery sleeping-bag, with only a few tiny strands of hair poking out, she looked like an enormous glow-worm. Lola liked the idea, and did not hesitate to snuggle up against her back to benefit from her animal warmth. It took her some time to fall asleep. A thousand trains chugged slowly beneath her eyelids, and she could not run quickly enough to catch them. She tried to relax into the rhythm of Ingrid's breathing, which soon merged with the gurgling of a nearby stream. She succeeded.

In her dream, a door opened and she felt a draught on her face. She realised she was dreaming, but had no desire to wake up, to leave her sleeping-bag and confront the mountain and its icy charms. Something pushed her to swim towards the surface of reality. It was as if the refuge were about to catch fire. She opened her eyes, noted Ingrid's sleeping body beside her. There was an unpleasant smell of smoke: a cigarette. She sat up, listened to the chorus of snores around her. She prised her torch out of her pocket and shone the light on the place where Pierrot Normann, alias Pierre Norton, had been lying. Empty. She shook Ingrid, without success. To wake some people up you have to shout their name or shake them like a plum tree. Ingrid was one of those. Lola did not want to risk waking the other skiers.

Lola clambered into her ski outfit, put on her hat and gloves, and went out. The glow of her torch came up against the wall of fog, tracing a dark circle filled with huge snowflakes. Struggling to turn – the snow was up above her knees – she shone her torch on the indistinct shape of the refuge, then onto a pile of rocks she had spotted the previous evening. Then she lowered the beam to the ground, and followed Norton's tracks. She plodded twenty metres through the snow, her boots crunching in the padded silence. The tracks veered off to the left. Lola decided to seize the initiative. She would probably not get another chance to talk to Norton alone. At the same time, she knew he had deliberately enticed her out here: there was absolutely no reason for him to go outside for a smoke in seventy centimetres of fresh snow. He must have blown the smoke in her face to wake her up.

She called him by his real name several times, and said the word "police", but her voice was swallowed by the snow. So she waited, pointing her torch towards some tall grey shadows.

"What do you want with Pierre Norton?"

"To know what he did to his son that turned him into a murderer."

"Are you out of your mind?"

He was not merely inquiring; there was an edge to his voice. Lola put on her orange U.V. filter glasses, which helped her to see vaguely around her. The grey shadows must be a stand of pines, and that was where the voice was coming from. There was a roar of rushing water, so she deduced there was a ravine up beyond the trees. She instinctively took a few steps backwards.

"It was in all the papers. Patrick Kantor killed a young girl in Paris. Patrick Kantor, the boy you abandoned a dozen years ago."

"Are you here to preach morals?"

With that, there came the sound of rapid footsteps in the snow. Lola snapped her torch off, and retreated, trying desperately to find the gaping holes her boots had left. She wasn't afraid, but her body was too tired, and sent mixed signals to her nerve-endings. She started to run in a zigzag to confuse him, counting the steps she took in each direction to make sure she came back to the middle before setting off again. But he was a mountain guide. He must have seen lots of snow hares leaping about in this way – the hares Ingrid was always wanting to jab at with her finger! Why didn't she hurry up and come and do it now, for goodness' sake!

She tried to shout out "Ingrid!" but her cry stuck in her throat.

Someone had his arms round her and was crushing her. They fell onto the snow. Norton's glove was covering her mouth: the rough fabric made her feel sick. His panting breath was warm against the side of her head.

"Tell me who you're working for! You're not police, or you'd have come with gendarmes."

He pulled back his hand. She grunted: "I *did* come with gendarmes, you fool. They're on their way."

"Do you think I'm that stupid? We'll see. Come on, get up."

He pulled her to her feet, dragged her off. She wanted to hit him, to shout, but her strength was gone. She had lost all sense of direction. In her brain, a thousand confused thoughts all converged to create the same sensation. That she had reached the root of evil. That evil she had never believed in. A protean evil, the sort a father transmitted to his son. And yet she resisted the idea of such a simplistic conclusion. It was only those damned Yankees who saw the world in black and white, good against evil. A nation of G.I. Joes who only stopped to think when it was too late. The people from the south were refined; the northerners men of action. And it was the South that lost. What the hell are you up to, Ingrid, my Yankee St Bernard? Now's the time for action! Lola tried to make herself laugh, but it was no use. She could hear Norton's breathing. Nothing asthmatic about it. No, it was strong, like a well-oiled machine, like an athlete's. He was breathing hard, but still dragging her along after him. She realised they must have covered a fair distance: he with his infra-red trapper's vision, she with her immense fatigue. She could hear the swollen waters of the mountain stream roaring just below her. A terrible, cruel sound that expressed nature's magnificent, unfeeling indifference. She had made the biggest mistake of her long career by coming out of that damned refuge on her own.

She tried to make herself even heavier so that she would be impossible to drag along, but Norton was as strong as a bear, and heaved her inexorably towards the stream. She knew he was going to throw her down onto its rocky bed. That she would be smashed to pieces. After that, he would go and find Ingrid, and kill her in the same way. The snow would cover all tracks. And tomorrow, the group would leave the refuge at dawn, leaving behind two shapes asleep in their sleeping-bags. Two decoys. It would take weeks to find their frozen bodies.

"Lolaaa! Lolaaa! Lolaaa!"

Her ears could be playing tricks on her. It could be the raging waters and a sudden gust of wind, or a nocturnal bird playing a joke. But it might also be Ingrid. In a sudden burst of hope and energy, Lola tugged at Norton. They both collapsed into the snow. She felt its icy bite as she struggled to get out her pocket torch. She sent frantic signals with it as she crawled through the snow and gravel. She cried out to Ingrid: her mouth was full of snow, but she called out as loudly as she could, and Norton was up again punching and punching her, desperate, growling, nothing more than a blind ball of rage.

And then Ingrid was there. Shouting for Lola to give her the torch. There was a fierce tussle: Ingrid told her to hang on to Norton's feet while she hit him with it. Ingrid gave a cry of fury, and there was a crack as something broke. Followed by another cry, from Norton this time, not as loud, choked off in a whimper.

The two women found themselves on top of Norton's unconscious body, their muscles shredded, their lungs about to explode, their heads lolling against each other, dripping with snow, their voices a mere croak.

Ingrid waited until she got her breath back: "I've smashed the torch. We're going to have to drag him back in the dark."

"Just a . . . another minute . . . I'm too . . . worn out," Lola groaned.

"No way, Lola! Now!"

One of the skiers in the group was a doctor. He had taken care of Lola, and had made her a splint with whatever he could find – the contents of Pierre Norton's first-aid kit, and some plastic bags. The whole group was waiting for the gendarmes to arrive. They were playing cards half-heartedly, pretending they were not listening to the conversation between their guide and the two women he had almost done for. Norton was trussed up with strips torn from a blanket, and seemed resigned to his fate.

"I came to question you about Patrick, to try to understand him, to tie up a couple of loose ends here and there. Your reaction was way out of proportion."

He looked at her coldly but without great interest. His greatest fear of the past twelve years had become reality. The rest was mere routine. In a while he would be taken away by the police. But first Lola wanted to know all about him.

"To begin with, I thought you were Rinko Yamada-Duchamp's secret lover. Later on I realised just how wide of the mark I was."

"You can say that again," he grunted, with a bitter smile.

Good! He was thawing. Lola could sense Ingrid seething beside her. She found it hard to contain her anger. This guy had almost killed them, but now he was drawing out the suspense. Did he think he was in some kind of American soap opera?

"Your testimony will help him, you know. A life sentence at eighteen isn't exactly fun. You owe him that at least."

She let him stew on this for a long moment. She could sense he was delving back into a past he had tried to forget at all costs, to bury beneath a ton of snow. Suddenly, out of the blue, tears rolled down his cheeks. Lola knew that everything was resurfacing. She had seen it many times, this moment of surrender. Now she simply had to let it all come out, to avoid interrupting him: his confession would roll along like the stones in that damned stream which had so nearly been their tomb.

"I wanted to understand. I went to see the Japanese girl. To talk. But she didn't like to talk. She was closed in on herself; she mocked me with those pointed little smiles of hers. Her only wish was for me to get out of there with my ridiculous questions so that she could get back to her fucking masterpieces. I was overcome by hatred. It was my moment. The moment when fate and I collided. The bitch of a moment that changed my life forever."

The tears streamed down Pierre Norton's cheeks. The only sound in the hut was his sniffling. The card game had been abandoned. Ingrid's huffing and puffing as well.

"I put my hands round her throat, and squeezed until she was dead. I dragged her into the bedroom. I wanted to disguise her death as a crime of passion. I took her clothes off and began to tie her . . . to the bars of the bed . . ."

Lola could visualise the scene. At the same time, she superimposed on it the description Barthélemy had given her of Vanessa's death. The father's crime, and the son's. Thirteen years apart. Norton could not go on, so Lola finished for him, "The boy was there. Is that it?"

"I don't know for how long. I tied Rinko's ankles to the bed, and was about to do the same with her wrists, when I . . . I saw him. Patrick. He was there. He had followed me from the house. I had no idea what to do. As we walked along the street, his hand in mine, I was trying to think. He didn't say a word."

Lola superimposed two other scenes. One real, the other invented. Patrick watching his father tying the dead Rinko's ankles to the bed. The other devised to unsettle Patrick: Constantin witnessing Vanessa's murder. Without realising it, she had hit the bull's-eye. But this gave her no satisfaction.

"We went home. Renée was still in the bookshop. I put Patrick to bed and gave him a sleeping-pill. While he was falling asleep I whispered in his ear that he'd had a nightmare, that nothing had happened."

"Then you packed your bags and left. Just like that."

"Yes, just like that. I thought that, the next morning, Patrick would talk. That he would tell them what he had seen, but . . ."

"But Patrick never said a word."

"No, for twelve years, Patrick said nothing."

They all fell silent. Some time later they heard the sound of an engine and rotor blades. Then voices coming through a megaphone. Lola got up and walked over to the door, which she opened onto the freezing night air. As though she hadn't heard the police chopper, Ingrid said in a soft, strange voice, "Frost in the past."

40

Commandant de Gendarmerie Aurélien Passart had trouble understanding what had persuaded Lola Jost, ex-commissaire from the 10th arrondissement station in Paris, and Ingrid Diesel, masseuse by profession, domiciled at Passage du Désir in the same arrondissement, to come all this way to track down Pierre Norton, a Parisian who had made a new life for himself in Savoie under the name of Pierre Normann. He asked Lola, Lola who had her right arm in a sling and a shiner round her left eye, to repeat the whole story a second time. Ingrid was calmly drinking her coffee as she listened to her companion. She thought she was managing very well on her own. The commandant began to see things more clearly once he had spoken to Lieutenant Jérôme Barthélemy and made the link with Vanessa Ringer's murder. Talking to a real policeman in active service reassured him. The assurance that said lieutenant would arrive on the high-speed train at twenty-seven minutes past four that afternoon finally convinced him he was not dealing with a pair of dangerous lunatics. Ingrid and Lola informed him they could be reached at the *Clochettes d'argent* hotel.

Commandant Passart seemed relieved to see them go.

Jérôme Barthélemy was dying to help the boss cut up her slice of cured ham. Unable to wield the knife because of the stupid splint on her arm, she was struggling with a superb raclette. Lola allowed him to cut the ham, and concentrated on the Roussette de Savoie wine, which she judged to be "most acceptable". For her part, the Yank needed no encouragement and made short shrift of the delicious local cold meats, and the steaming-hot potatoes she dunked in the melted cheese. It was very instructive watching her eat. Barthélemy was staring at this tall, somewhat strange blonde woman with even greater interest now he had learned she had saved Lola's life. Incredible! The lieutenant had been unable to prevent himself from shaking her hand at length and thanking her again and again. In fact, it still warmed his heart to think about it. He complimented her once more: "Ah, Mademoiselle Diesel, I can never thank you enough!"

"You're growing tiresome, my lad," said the gruff-voiced Lola. "Ingrid saved my life, and that's that. We're not going to celebrate it from now until Christmas, are we?"

"I'd be happy to stay on here for Christmas," Ingrid said, helping herself to another good dollop of cheese. "It's great!"

"I'm afraid we must get back, my dear. Our work isn't quite over yet. There are a few things we still need to clear up."

Barthélemy smiled at the boss. The next day, he would escort Norton to Paris. But tonight, he was having the time of his little life. The great Lola was back. Battered, half blind, limping, but still on her feet. Standing tall. She had solved the Vanessa Ringer affair; she had solved a twelve-year-old murder. And she still had a taste for more. Just as she wanted more of the raclette and the local wine. That was a healthy appetite for you. So different to the Garden Gnome's grudging gripes. And anyway, tonight at least, it wasn't worth thinking about that miserable cretin.

"What are you talking about, Lola?"

"About Chloé Gardel and Khadidja Younis, of course. Those two kids owe me an explanation. And I'm determined to get it."

The Yank blew her cheeks out until she resembled a hamster, muttered something coarse like "Why is this so fucking important to you?", then shrugged her shoulders. She hadn't been working with the boss for long enough to understand. Fair enough, it took years of practice to get even close to the truth. And even then.

41

The brass plate declared: RING AND ENTER. So Lola rang and entered, with Ingrid and Khadidja right behind her. Khadidja had been unable to refuse, because Lola had threatened to tell Grousset about the bag stuffed with money if she didn't do as she was told. A lone man sat in the waiting room. He did not look up from his business newspaper when the three women walked in.

"Excuse me," Lola said. "Did you see a brown-haired, slightly chubby young woman go into Doctor Léger's consulting room just now?"

"Yes, madame. Why do you ask?"

"She's my granddaughter. And you don't happen by any chance to know where the dog is, do you?"

"Which dog are you talking about, madame?"

"Doctor Léger's Dalmatian. He must have taken him out of the room before my granddaughter arrived. At least I hope he did, because she's dreadfully allergic to dog hairs. I wanted to make sure he hadn't forgotten."

The man raised a suspicious eyebrow, hesitated, but eventually replied:

"I think the Dalmatian is in the kitchen."

"Perfect," Lola said.

She briefly whispered something in Ingrid's ear, then went in alone to Doctor Léger's consulting room.

The psychoanalyst looked mildly astonished. He was ensconced in his usual armchair, wearing a pair of his trademark corduroy trousers. His shirt was pink, his waistcoat a nice warm beige. Dressed in a pair of jeans and a baggy pullover, Chloé was lying on the blue couch, hands folded over her stomach. She gave a start, and turned pleadingly towards Léger.

"Is there some emergency, Madame Jost?" the psychoanalyst asked calmly.

"That all depends on how you define the term, Doctor Léger. In this case, it's an emergency that's been going on for three years now."

With that, Lola went to the heart of the matter. An affair that had begun in the yard at the Lycée Beaumarchais with a love rivalry between a class assistant and a rebellious student. So rebellious he had been expelled. And yet, although Farid Younis had given up on his studies and preferred to learn the lessons of the street, he was still seeing Vanessa. He had discovered she was making eyes at Grégoire Marsan. And he hated it. There was no way of knowing the details of what had happened between Farid Younis and Grégoire Marsan: the slow, insidious process of jealousy, a crescendo of threats and insults, even blows. There was no way of knowing, and it was not particularly important.

"We can, however, revisit Grégoire Marsan's murder. How he was stabbed to death, his body thrown in the Saint-Martin Canal, swallowed up by the Récollets lock. Chloé, what can you tell us about Grégoire Marsan's murder?"

"Nothing, madame . . . nothing."

"Lola, you're going too far. I'd never have thought you were capable of interrupting one of my sessions . . ."

"I'm not interrupting anything, Antoine. I'm jumping in feet first, which you must agree isn't the same thing at all."

The elegant psychoanalyst looked down his nose. Lola smiled and added:

"And I may possibly be helping you make progress. So, Chloé, don't you think it's high time to talk? To finally unburden yourself?"

"I don't know anything."

"Vanessa tried to make up for it by devoting herself to others. She also kept a diary. On the self-interested advice of Patrick Kantor. But it wasn't a success. Kantor discovered a dangerous secret there. A secret you also know."

"I don't!"

"Khadidja sits on her high horse. You though vomit your fear at regular intervals. You can't go on like this, my girl. You know that."

"I've no idea what you're talking about."

"O.K. Have it your own way."

Lola limped towards the door. She opened it with her good hand and called Ingrid. The Yank came in with Sigmund on a lead. Khadidja followed her, looking grim. As soon as the Dalmatian saw Chloé, it stopped short. Ingrid tugged at the lead and the dog, and closed the door behind them. Sigmund kept his muzzle down, staring fixedly at Ingrid's boots. Chloé peered at the beautiful animal as if it were a phantom hound. She had turned ashen; her lips were trembling. Léger stood up. He looked extremely annoyed. Lola raised her hand to stop him.

"Sorry to have to use methods you must think are brutal."

"That's putting it mildly, madame."

"Why can't you bear to look at Sigmund anymore, Chloé? Why is that?"

Chloé had turned to stone. She stood petrified for a long while, then turned to her shrink.

"It's your decision, Chloé," Léger said.

The young woman swallowed hard, and moved away from the couch as if doing this had a symbolic power. At least, that's what Lola was hoping. Ingrid knelt down and began stroking the dog. Lola told herself that this was a fine gesture too. An appropriate gesture that defused the situation, like a hand gently brushing a cheek or shoulder. Although her instinct told her that the last thing she should do now was touch Chloé. Keep well away from her, let her wrestle with her fear alone. Chloé spoke in a hesitant murmur.

"All the boys liked Vanessa. That night . . . for fun . . . she made a date with Greg near the lock. It was the time when we used to take the dog for a walk, so all three of us were there. Greg arrived . . . full of hope. I don't know how he found out, but Farid turned up too. He saw Vanessa. He saw Greg. He went crazy. They argued, but Farid was in a blind rage. I was . . . terrified. I . . . I held my dog against me. Vanessa and Khadidja tried to keep them apart. Farid . . . Farid pulled out a knife. There was blood. Lots of blood. He dragged Greg away, pushed him into the water. Afterwards . . . he swore he'd kill us if we said anything. After that, it was no good at school. Nothing was any good anymore. I got rid of my Dalmatian because every time he looked at me, I saw . . . reproach in those eyes that had seen everything."

Chloé flung herself into Léger's arms and began to sob. At first he stood there, arms by his sides, but eventually he wrapped them round his patient. He glanced sternly at Lola, and then Ingrid.

"Psychoanalysis is like taking the fucking bus, you spend far too much time waiting around," Ingrid declared, then left the consulting room.

Sigmund followed on her heels.

While Chloé was weeping in Doctor Léger's arms, Lola questioned Khadidja about the money. This time, she gave up her story.

"What did you intend to do with it, my girl?"

"I was going to give it to a charity for Romanian orphans," Khadidja said without hesitation. "That's what Vanessa wanted. My brother told me so. Anyway, I never intended to keep it."

"I believe you."

"Really?"

"Really. You're worth a lot more than you think, my girl."

"And you're worth a lot more than I used to think."

"O.K., now we've finished showering compliments on one another, what do you intend to do about Maxime? He doesn't know anything, does he?"

Khadidja simply shrugged. Then, trying to put a brave face on it, she went to sit on the blue couch.

"I'm afraid he'll despise me. I was silent for so long about Greg. I didn't have the guts."

"Well, now's the time to show some. Tell him the whole story. Once and for all. You can't build on rotten foundations. And I've always thought it's better to feel remorse than regret."

Khadidja and Chloé were loyal workers. They were waiting at table as usual, although Chloé avoided spending too much time anywhere near Lola. The dish of the day was a splendid roast guinea fowl cooked in sea-salt, with a chickpea purée. Lola ordered it without thinking twice. Ingrid had gone for a seared steak tartare with French fries.

"You'll need to get a move on, my girl."

"Why so?" Ingrid asked. "I intend to have a dessert as well. Saturday is chocolate mousse. Maxime always makes fabulous mousse."

"You've got an appointment at two o'clock sharp. Someone wants a Thai massage."

"First I've heard."

"It's true, I assure you."

"What've you been up to, Lola?"

"I gave our novice film director a call."

"Benjamin Noblet!"

"The same. One thing led to another, and our discussion turned to you. It wasn't hard . . . the guy seemed keen to hear about you. He even put an ad in the newspaper to find you. Something brainy along the lines of: 'Cassius Clay desperately seeking Wonderwoman . . .' But apparently you don't read the newspaper. Perhaps just the *Herald Tribune* occasionally?"

Ingrid slid back in her chair so that she could fold her arms and work on her offended expression.

"I don't need a second mother, Lola. My own was more than enough."

"So you reckon a mother would push her daughter into the arms of an aspiring film director, do you? And one specialising in gore, at that? I sincerely hope not, Ingrid. If that were the case, it would mean things today are a lot worse than yesterday, and not as good as tomorrow."

"You're blowing your irony in my face as a smokescreen, Lola, but it won't work. I can see you're trying to twist my arm."

"Twisting the arm of a masseuse is an interesting challenge."

"There you go again. I'd at least like to hear you admit you're terrible tyrant. At least that, Lola."

"You don't get it, do you? I'm worse than that. Listen carefully, and you'll understand. I'm going to catch a plane at seven-thirty this evening. It'll take me to Singapore, where for the first time in my life I hope to spend Christmas. I've got two dolls to deliver."

A brief pause, with that irritating cool stare of hers.

"So?" Ingrid snapped.

"I bought you a ticket."

"What?"

"I wanted to offer it to you as a Christmas present and as a thank you for saving my old carcass. Then I had an idea. I would let you choose your present. So now it's up to you. And if you decide against the flight, don't worry. An old friend of mine at Air France will sort it out."

Ingrid narrowed her eyes, trying to read the expression on Lola's face. She might as well have been scrutinising the grin on the Cheshire cat. A complete waste of time. She thought for a moment, rewound the conversation, and reached a conclusion that made her hold out her forearm: "Pinch me, I want to know if I'm dreaming. Your choice of presents is either Benjamin Noblet or Singapore, is that right?"

"I've no need to pinch you. Everything around you is as real as real can be, my girl."

"I could also choose to leave here and take a long walk around Paris to clear my head. You didn't think of that, did you?"

"Refusing a gift would be churlish, Ingrid. And as for that long walk of yours, I've already told you, you're just avoiding the issue. Come on, now you have to make the choice. You can do it."

Chloé arrived with her little notepad and pencil. She asked what the ladies would like for dessert.

"A calvados," Lola said.

"Nothing," Ingrid said. "My appetite has just caught a plane to Singapore."

"Well my girl, are you staying in Paris or going in search of it near the Equator?"

"I'm staying. And I need to be getting a move on if I want to be on time. You did say 'Thai', didn't you?"

"That's what I said."

"Good . . . O.K. then . . . Merry Christmas, Lola."

"Merry Christmas, Ingrid, see you next year."

Chloé Gardel was following their conversation with a bemused air. She watched as Ingrid stood up and walked to the door. Ingrid was grinning. So was Lola.

"There goes another one the robots won't get," the ex-commissaire said, turning towards Chloé. "I'm glad."

"For sure, Madame Lola. Perhaps you'd like a chocolate mousse with your calvados. Saturday is chocolate mousse . . ."

"No, young lady. I'll have another calvados with my calvados."

"For sure, Madame Lola."

"And stop saying 'for sure' every five seconds. Especially as you're not sure of anything. Because you see, what matters is to have a cast-iron belief in what you're doing, even if you're doing any old thing. You're a musician, you should know that. The same goes if you're an actor, a novelist or an amateur detective. Get it?"

"Not really . . ."

"Don't worry. You'll learn, my girl, you'll learn."

THE END

TRANSLATOR'S ACKNOWLEDGEMENTS

The translator would like to thank Lorenza Garcia for all her valuable help.

DOMINIQUE SYLVAIN worked as a journalist in Paris before relocating to Asia where she lived for spells in Japan and Singapore. She is the author of thirteen crime novels and now lives once more in Paris where she writes full-time.

NICK CAISTOR has translated more than forty books from Spanish and Portuguese, including works by Paulo Coelho, Eduardo Mendoza and Juan Marsé. He has twice been awarded the Valle-Inclán prize for Spanish translation.